Desert
REUNION

Desert
REUNION

A DANTE & JAZZ MYSTERY

MICHAEL
CRAFT

QUEST
·OVER·
PRESS

Design and typography: M.C. Johnson
Cover art: modified from images via Shutterstock and Adobe Stock
Author's photo: Aaron Jay Young

Library of Congress Cataloging-in-Publication Data

Craft, Michael, 1950–
Desert Reunion : a Dante & Jazz mystery / Michael Craft
   ISBN: 979-8-218-36507-3 (hardcover)
   ISBN: 979-8-218-37594-2 (paperback)
  BISAC: FIC011000   Fiction / LGBTQ / Gay
            FIC022100   Fiction / Mystery & Detective / Amateur Sleuth

First hardcover and paperback editions: September 2024
Questover Press
California • Since 2011

DESERT REUNION

Dante O'Donnell and Jazz Friendly might seem like a misfit pair of crime solvers. He's white and gay, a concierge at a vacation-rental outfit; she's Black and straight, an ex-cop turned private eye. With a dear old friend in trouble, though, they team up to set things right.

Zola Lorinsky, a long-retired Palm Springs decorator, has a chance to reignite her fabled career. But when she attends a family reunion hosted at one of Dante's rentals, the celebration goes horribly awry. Bad enough that one of the guests is found dead that day. Even worse, the circumstances point to murder. And the evidence points to Zola.

Dante and Jazz step in to prove that someone else—*anyone* else—was responsible for the crime. When they finally zero in on a prime suspect, though, a second tragedy strikes, throwing the investigation back to square one. And now, to save their friend, they need to name not just one killer, but two.

DESERT REUNION: Dante & Jazz Mystery #3

"Dante and Jazz shine in this quick-witted Palm Springs mystery, defying stereotypes and capturing readers' hearts ... Craft smartly balances laughs, tension, and memorable local color ... Skillful storytelling and vivid characters make it hard to resist this series." — *BookLife Reviews* (EDITOR'S PICK)

"Stellar characterization makes singling out a killer an exceedingly difficult task. Sunny California's welcoming October weather bolsters the narrative with appealing camaraderie." — *Kirkus Reviews*

"Perfectly capturing the glorious absurdity of gay Palm Springs, *Desert Reunion* sparkles with humor and the joys of found family."
— *Michael Thomas Ford, Lambda Award-winning author*

"*Desert Reunion* swept me away. With lively characters, humor in just the right places, and all of it wrapped in a juicy whodunit, Craft's novel is a delightfully satisfying mystery."
— *Sidney Karger, author of 'Best Men' and 'The Bump'*

"Michael Craft delivers deft plotting, intriguing characters, and snappy dialogue in this spirited and engaging whodunit."
— *Rob Osler, author of the Hayden & Friends mystery series*

"Readers will find *Desert Reunion* lively and thought-provoking. Its characters excel in three-dimensional depictions that reflect not only their perspectives, but their dilemmas and dreams."
— *Diane Donovan, Senior Reviewer, Midwest Book Review*

DESERT DEADLINE: Dante & Jazz Mystery #2

• IBPA Benjamin Franklin Award, Gold Winner: LGBTQ •

"Craft delivers a breezy whodunit ... and complements the impressive character development with a brain-teasing mystery. Readers will hope to hear more from Dante and Jazz soon."
— *Publishers Weekly*

"Bursts with characters as quirkily memorable as they are believably human. A delicious whodunit, as funny as it is thrilling."
— *BookLife Reviews* (EDITOR'S PICK)

"It's fun to see Craft, the author of 19 novels, plot the demise of [an] author, which he does with typical ingenuity and precision."
— *Kirkus Reviews*

DESERT GETAWAY: Dante & Jazz Mystery #1

• MWA Edgar nominee: Lilian Jackson Braun Memorial Award •

"A wild romp through Palm Springs' glittery underbelly. Fast, funny, and thoroughly enjoyable. An instant classic."
— *Tod Goldberg*, New York Times bestselling author

"Michael Craft delivers an irresistible high-camp twist to the classic detective mystery. A fast-paced and captivating new series."
— *J.D. Horn*, Wall Street Journal bestselling author

"Smart, sophisticated, and ingeniously plotted. I loved it."
— *Ellen Byron*, USA Today bestselling author

CONTENTS

PART ONE

PASS THE POSSET

CHAPTER
ONE

Generating electricity out of thin air—it sounded nuts.

"It sounds like science fiction," said Isandro, "like something Jules Verne would cook up."

It did indeed. The very notion seemed as ridiculous today as it would have been in the nineteenth century. "And yet," I told Isandro with a shrug, "Richard's 'mystery cousin' claims to know the secret to using air itself as fuel."

Richard Gibbs was the wealthy owner of an estate in Palm Springs who, several months earlier, had sold the coach house on his property to Isandro Vieira, a gay nurse who then invited me to share his new quarters, his expenses, and his bed. We had been friends (with benefits) for a year or two. Now we were lovers, perhaps even life partners—but marriage was an option we had not yet discussed.

On that late Friday afternoon, the first of October, Isandro and I preened in the upstairs loft of the coach house, dressing for a balmy evening in the California desert. We were dolling up for a casual dinner to be hosted by Richard over in the main house—on the opposite side of an expansive brick-paved terrace that surrounded a swimming pool. Inspecting each other in a full-length mirror, Isandro and I looked a bit twinsy in dark slacks and gray linen shirts.

But the similarity ended with our clothes. At thirty-four,

Isandro was younger than I was, shorter, and Brazilian. I was born in the Midwest and, after college, had traipsed out to Los Angeles, where I dabbled in acting and modeling for too many years—without much success—before landing, defeated, in Palm Springs. At fifty-three, I was "starting over" as a concierge for higher-end clients at Sunny Junket Vacation Rentals.

"Dante?" said Isandro, wrapping an arm around my waist, hooking a finger through one of my belt loops. He turned from the mirror to look into my eyes. "There's something we need to talk about, *coração*. Something about... our plans."

Uh-oh. Was he nudging us toward a more formalized commitment? He must have seen the terror in my eyes.

Then he burst into laughter—a manic, riotous laugh, laced with Portuguese—interrupted by a pause to kiss my lips. "Our plans for *tonight*. Shouldn't we bring something for our host?"

With a grin of relief, I suggested, "Wine always works."

When we walked across the terrace at five thirty, sunset was nearly an hour away, but the San Jacinto Mountains had already spread their shadow across much of the town. Lights were on in the kitchen of the main house, which had a wall of French doors, some of them open, facing the pool. Through them, I could see Richard at the stove, wearing an apron, whisking the contents of a pan with his right hand while sipping from a martini glass held in his left. He gabbed nonstop with Zola Lorinsky, pushing eighty, who perched on a barstool at the kitchen island, responding to Richard's jokes with barks of laughter. She fingered the icy remnants of a cocktail in a tall chimney glass—her usual Tom Collins, no doubt.

They turned as we entered. A spry gay man of seventy-six, Richard rushed over with profuse greetings and hugs. "You *shouldn't* have, Dante," he said, taking the bottle I handed him. When he set it aside and returned to the stove to resume whisking, Isandro and I stepped to Zola, still seated regally atop her stool, and we indulged in a round of cheek-pecking.

With the pleasantries dispatched, Isandro and I poured our own drinks and seated ourselves with Zola at the chunky granite island. Richard slid a baking dish into the oven, thumped the door closed, and raised his glass in a perfunctory toast: "Cheers, everyone."

We skoaled and drank. Zola rattled the ice in her glass, which I took. Crossing the room to mix her another, I heard Isandro tell her, "Everything is looking fabulous, Z-Doll."

Richard piped in, "'Fabulous' doesn't begin to describe it. I'd been waiting for years to finally *do* something with this place. No one was ever right for the job, and then—I still can't believe it—along came *La Decorina* herself."

Zola rolled her eyes as she took the Tom Collins, reminding me, "I was *retired*. Yet it seems there's no rest for the weary—*or* the wicked." She winked.

I laughed at her feigned long-suffering. She was a dear old friend and former neighbor at a modest six-unit courtyard complex in Palm Springs where Isandro and I had each rented tiny one-bedroom apartments (which is how he and I met). Zola had enjoyed a fabled career as an in-demand society decorator, but with the passing of time—and the passing of her aging clientele—her glory years had faded, and so had her circumstances. Her spirit and style, however, had survived intact.

She sat there tonight looking self-confident and radiant, wearing a gauzy gold tunic over a shocking-pink unitard. One of her fingers was adorned with a kebab of old wedding rings—three or four—representing past unions that I assumed were marriages of convenience, as Zola clearly had a yen for gay men. To Isandro, she was simply Z-Doll. To Richard, she was *La Decorina*. To my mind, though, she was the high priestess of pizazz.

Last spring, after Isandro and I had moved away from the apartment complex and into the coach house, it was only a matter of time before we introduced Zola to Richard, and they became instant chums. In short order, Richard convinced Zola to undertake a complete redecoration of the estate's main house—colors, fabrics, window treatments, art, custom furnishings, the works—down to accessory items, which included a stunning collection of vintage chrome cocktail shakers that adorned a service bar at the far end of the kitchen. The whole project would take nearly a year and was only half complete, but unless I was mistaken, it had the potential to reignite Zola's career.

It would have been pleasant for all of us to revel in these developments and simply enjoy each other's friendship and affection that evening. Except, company was coming. Though the house had a large formal dining room, Richard had decided to entertain more casually that night there in the great room, mere steps from the kitchen, where a table had been set not for the four of us—but for seven.

A lull drifted over our conversation as Zola set down her glass and checked her watch. "What time should they be here?"

"By now, I *thought*," said Richard, his jolly tone taking a sour turn.

Zola chortled. "Having regrets? Sorry you took that DNA test?" Her gentle razzing made it clear that her relationship with Richard had progressed beyond that of a decorator and client. Their exchange carried not only the subtext of familiarity, but sympathetic insight as well.

Quizzically, Isandro asked, "This started with a DNA test?"

Zola answered in a stage whisper, "He did it for fun."

Richard tossed his hands. "I've never known much about my extended family. From the time I was little, I was always told there'd been a feud—something to do with business, I guess— but beyond that, the details were murky. Then, in recent years, I started hearing about people piecing together a family tree through these various DNA testing services. On a lark, I signed up with one of them and sent them my saliva sample. Within a couple of months, I got an email one morning, out of the blue, from a Harold Gibkin, who'd traced me as his second cousin."

Isandro asked me, "Is that the 'mystery cousin' you were telling me about?"

"Correct. He has a business called AtmosPhuel R&D."

Richard snorted. "Must be a crackpot."

I told Isandro, "Harold Gibkin wanted to bring some family members out to the desert for an extended reunion—a *month-long* visit, if you can believe it—so Richard asked me to set them up with a rental through Sunny Junket."

Richard groaned. "What in hell was I *thinking* when I sent in that spit sample? A *month*. They must've thought I'd invite them to stay here at the house—there's plenty of room—but that would be *way* too much togetherness with a bunch of goddamn strangers." Calming himself, Richard turned to tell me, "*Thank* you, Dante. You're a peach for working this out."

I said, "They'll love the house in Rancho Mirage. It was built for a group that big—all eight of them."

Richard groaned again.

I assured him, "The house is a good twenty minutes from here, so they'll be out of your hair. Except, of course, tonight." Turning to Isandro and Zola, I explained, "In Rancho Mirage, the last group of renters didn't vacate the house till late yesterday—and left it a shambles. We deal with this a lot, and we have a crew working overtime to make things perfect by tomorrow morning. The first three members of the Gibkin party are driving out from the coast right now, and Richard will put them up for the night."

"Tonight *only*," Richard stressed.

Zola plucked the cherry from her Tom Collins and ate it. Pausing, she said, "I'm confused. This Harold Gibkin creature. What—*exactly*—is a second cousin?"

Richard said, "A month ago, I didn't know and didn't care. Since then, I've done some digging. Turns out, Harold and I had the same great-grandfather, surname Gibbs, and his two sons had a rift. One of them, my grandfather, carried on the Gibbs name, but my grandfather's brother changed his surname to Gibkin, as if to finalize the split in the family. Bottom line: my grandfather and Harold's grandfather were the feuding brothers, which means that Harold and I are second cousins."

I rattled my head. "Okay... so you and Harold must be about the same age."

"You'd think so," said Richard, "but no. Harold claims to be 'only' fifty-nine, though I've never laid eyes on any of them. His branch of the family must have been slow breeders."

"And slow drivers," said Isandro, laughing. "Where are they?"

Dingdong.

Richard sighed. "Places, everyone. Curtain going up."

Gathered in the entry hall, we stood behind Richard as he opened the front door. I had expected to see three Gibkins waiting on the stoop, but there were only two, a man and woman with a few pieces of good luggage parked at their ankles.

The man broke into a broad smile and thrust his open hand toward Richard, saying, "Mr. Gibbs, I presume?"

Richard shook hands with him and played along: "Mr. Gibkin, I presume?"

Harold Gibkin and Richard Gibbs joshed for a moment—switching to first names and clapping each other's arms in a restrained semblance of a hug.

Because I was aware of Harold's far-fetched research interests, I had conjured an image of him as the Wizard of Oz, but the man at the threshold looked nothing like that skittery old apple-cheeked charlatan. Gibkin was younger (the claimed fifty-nine seemed close enough), thinner (but far from fit), with much darker hair (shoe-polish brown). Plus... he *smoked*. Then and there, while Gibkin stepped into a home not his own, a freshly lit cigarette dangled from his lips, jerking as he spoke.

He slung an arm over Richard's shoulders and moved into the hall, nattering at his host like an old chum. Had I not intervened, he would have left the woman he'd arrived with, presumably his wife, standing outside the door.

"Uh," I said, "Mrs. Gibkin, please come in. I'm Dante O'Donnell. Welcome to Palm Springs."

She stepped inside with barely a nod to acknowledge my courtesy; she didn't introduce herself or offer her hand or even look me in the eye. She just stood there looking distant, bored, and annoyed. Though smartly dressed and nicely put together, she struck me as pale and too thin.

Isandro exchanged a discreet look with me—an apprehensive grimace—then he stepped through the doorway to bring in their luggage, setting it at the foot of the stairway that led up to the bedrooms. I closed the front door as Richard led everyone back to the great room.

After a proper round of introductions, we learned that Harold's wife was named Wendy Ames Gibkin. Richard asked, "Are we still expecting someone else tonight?"

Harold said, "Keith is on his way, got a late start from the office. He phoned from the road—won't be long."

Richard asked, "And Keith is...?"

"He's Harold's son," Wendy said flatly. These were the first words we had heard from her, and their tone made it clear she was not a doting stepmom.

Harold said, "Keith is a lawyer—he's a busy guy, has his own practice in Rancho Santa Fe. He can't stay with us the whole month, but he wanted to be here for the opening festivities, so to speak." Harold chortled, then looked about for somewhere to flick his cigarette ash.

Richard cringed—either at the reference to "festivities" or at the special needs of entertaining a smoker. Or, most likely, both. He retrieved a demitasse saucer from a nearby cabinet and handed it to Harold, saying, "Here, you can use this." Then he asked both Gibkins, "Time for a drink? What can I get you?"

Wendy replied with the slightest shake of her head, tight-lipped. It was going to be a strange party.

But Harold didn't hesitate to ask, "Don't suppose you happen to have Old Nine-Tails?"

Richard tried, unsuccessfully, to mask his horrified reaction.

Harold laughed, stubbing out his butt in the Flora Danica saucer. "Nah, I didn't think you'd have it—not very refined, of course. Lots of folks call it rotgut. But it's a hundred twenty proof, so who cares what it *tastes* like? If you have any sort of whiskey, that'll be just fine, so long as it's not Scotch."

"Then how about bourbon?" said Richard. "Maker's?"

"Sure. Neat, please."

Richard stepped over to the bar and half filled a tumbler with straight whiskey, asking Isandro, "Would you be a lamb and pass the appetizers? They're in the warming oven."

Isandro happily obliged, removing the tray from the oven and presenting it first to Wendy. "Crab puff, Mrs. Gibkin?"

She eyed the tray for a moment. "What's in it?"

Isandro grinned. "Crab."

Wendy sneered. "What else?"

Richard moved to Harold and handed him the glass of booze while speaking to Wendy, rattling off the list of ingredients in his crab puffs, "... and I like to finish them off with just a shake of chili flakes."

Wendy plucked one from Isandro's tray, sniffed it, and took a small, cautious bite—then downed the rest of it hungrily. Isandro handed her a black cocktail napkin, which she loaded up with an unseemly pile of the flaky nibbles.

When Isandro presented the tray to Zola, she took a couple of the crab puffs for herself before stepping over to Wendy, who stood away from the others. I assumed Zola intended to welcome the only other woman at the gathering by teaming up with her for some girl talk. Isandro then placed the tray on the granite island.

Richard, Harold, and I joined him there, setting down our drinks and sampling the appetizers. Harold removed the cigarette from his mouth only long enough to chew, swallow, and wash down his crab puff with a slug of bourbon. Instantly, the cigarette was back between his lips, wobbling as he spoke: "Tell me about the vacation-rental biz, Dante. Is there good money in it these days?"

I shrugged. "For some people—the property owners—there's

plenty when it's busy. But things have slowed down lately. I think the rental market is getting oversaturated in Palm Springs. I'm just the paid help, though."

Bragging on me, Isandro said, "But he's also a detective's sidekick."

Richard laughed. Harold looked skeptical. I explained to him, "I've been doing occasional side work for a local private investigator—her name is Jazz Friendly. The setup was her idea. She had a hunch I might be able to provide her with leads for new clients, based on some of the messed-up characters I've encountered through Sunny Junket. Turns out, she was right."

Mulling this, Harold blew twin streams of smoke from his nostrils. "Well"—he snorted—"hope your detective friend won't be finding any business with the Gibkins."

"I highly doubt that," I assured him. *But you never know*, I thought.

Then I turned the tables: "What about *your* work, Harold? I understand you're involved with research and development—something to do with alternative energy?"

Isandro and Richard put on their best poker faces, not daring to look at each other, having already shared some hearty yuks at Harold's expense.

Harold beamed a wide grin. "I have a vision of the future, Dante—a future freed from the curse of fossil fuels, freed from the filth and pollution and wars that result from pumping this muck from the ground and then burning it." He continued in this vein while pausing now and then to cough on the smoke of his own cigarette.

Irony aside (he was a fine one to be lecturing about pollution), I couldn't argue with his words, although they sounded rehearsed—like the opening of a stock speech he might use as a pitch to potential investors. Was that, in fact, the underlying purpose of this so-called family reunion? Had Harold Gibkin recognized in his newfound second cousin, Richard Gibbs, a likely mark? After all, Richard was an aging man of wealth—never married, no children—who just might embrace the opportunity to bet his legacy on a plan to leave a greener, cleaner planet for generations to come.

I wasn't the only one thinking these thoughts. I could tell from Richard's benign expression that he understood exactly what his distant relative was up to.

Richard listened quietly as Harold expounded on his quest to harvest electricity from nothing more than humidity in the air—a boundless resource, ripe for the picking. "*Think* of it," Harold commanded. "Think of an air-powered generator and its implications for renewable energy and climate change." He concluded with a spasm of hacking and coughing.

Harold's convulsions allowed Richard to catch my eye and wink at me, unseen, while telling his cousin, "That's an ambitious plan, Harold. Obviously, it takes big dreams to make big things happen. That said, I suppose getting there won't be cheap."

"No kidding," said Harold. "The theory is sound, and development of the needed technology has begun, with promising results. The greatest remaining obstacle is funding."

Isandro played along, asking, "How much is needed?"

"To produce a working prototype that will prove large-scale viability..." Harold paused, then stated the target in billions.

After a moment of stunned silence, Richard said, "I'm not a *billion*-aire, Harold."

"No, of course not. Me neither. So it'll take a number of investors—probably a large number of them—to pull this off. But just think of the consequences of *not* moving forward with this."

"A valid consideration," said Richard, nodding. (I was impressed by his acting skills.) He added, "But I'll need to learn much more before even considering any hard numbers."

With a sly smile, Harold reminded him, "I'll be around for a whole month—and AtmosPhuel R&D would be *delighted* to have you aboard."

A shriek from the far side of the room nipped our conversation and sent us scurrying over to Zola and Wendy, whose girl talk had evidently jumped the rails. It appeared that Wendy had hurled one of her crab puffs at Zola, but missed. Zola was telling her assailant, "This Tom Collins—what's left of it—would look charming dripping from your hair to the *ridiculous* padded shoulders of that *horrid* hip-hop Balenciaga, but I'm too much of a lady to find out."

I took the glass from her and set it aside. Not only concerned, but embarrassed, I asked, "What *happened*?"

"She started it," said one of them.

"Did not," said the other.

Richard rapped his hands like a disapproving schoolmarm. "Now, girls, girls! What in God's *name* seems to be the problem?"

Steamed, Zola told us, "Mrs. Gibkin takes issue with 'the company I keep.'"

Harold asked his wife, "Wendy? What's this about?"

Wendy went mute again. A tear rolled down her cheek. I'd learned she was fifty-five, a few years younger than her husband, but she looked shrunken and childlike, as if swallowed by her silk Balenciaga suit. And Zola was right—the shoulder pads were all wrong.

Zola explained, "Mrs. Gibkin is uneasy around gay people and questioned why I would so readily associate with them. *She* finds them abhorrent and freakish and thinks 'there ought to be a law.' I viscerally disagree, and I let her know it in no uncertain terms. She responded with a thrown crab puff. I ducked." Under her breath, she added, to Richard, "Sorry 'bout the mess."

Isandro (one of three gay men in the room) had already scraped the gooey projectile from the arm of a stuffed chair that he was now blotting with club soda. He told us, "No harm done."

To my way of thinking, though, some *serious* harm had been done—by Wendy—and it did not bode well for that evening's "festivities," let alone a visit that would inject this small-minded bigot into our midst for a full month.

Her husband appeared gaunt and crestfallen. "*Wendy*," said Harold, "how could you? Here, of all places. And now, of all times. We've discussed this again and again—it's an issue you *must* learn to deal with."

She looked up from her whimpering. Tears now streamed from both reddened eyes. Desolate, she said, "It's just ... it's just that I miss my Koo-Loo."

Zola carefully backstepped away from her. Richard and I exchanged bewildered glances. Isandro leaned close to whisper in my ear, "What the fuck?"

"My precious Koo-Loo ..."

Harold tried soothing her: "There, there now."

"Uh ...," said Richard. "Koo-Loo?"

Harold told us, "It's her pet—her pet monkey, Koo-Loo."

Zola asked anyone, "Now, *why* doesn't this surprise me?"

Harold said to me, "I was sure you wouldn't allow a monkey at your rentals. Correct?"

"Yes, absolutely." I suspected, however, that our standard contract made no mention of this.

Wendy wailed, "Koo-Loo!"

Dingdong.

Richard was still shaken, red-faced with anger over being confronted with homophobia in his own home—by a woman with a monkey fetish, no less. Trying to calm himself, he asked me quietly, "Could you see who's at the door, Dante?"

"Of course."

I was glad to escape the tensions in the great room as I made my way through the house to the front hall. When I opened the door, though, my recent vexation vanished. "*Hello,*" I said brightly.

He grinned. "Hi there. Is this the Gibbs residence?" Waiting for my reply, he looked me up and down.

"Indeed it is," I said, returning the once-over. "And I'll just bet *you're* Keith Gibkin." Extending my hand, I added, "I'm Dante O'Donnell, from the rental agency. Welcome."

He shook my hand. Since he was Harold Gibkin's son, I figured that Keith must be in his late thirties. I knew he was a lawyer and had driven from his office, which explained his business attire—a suit and tie was uncommon in the desert, even among professionals. But Keith's suit was no three-piece navy-blue pinstripe. Rather, he looked youthful and trim in matching slacks and jacket of crisp khaki gabardine, worn with a white button-down dress shirt and a repp-stripe tie of pink and gray. Sandy blond hair, neatly styled. Gray-blue eyes. Dazzling smile—untainted by tobacco. He had apparently inherited his good looks and healthy habits from his mother's side of the family, bearing little resemblance to his father. (But I was struck that he did resemble an acquaintance of mine, another lawyer.)

"Let me grab that," I said, lifting a handsome leather-and-canvas overnight bag from the stoop. "Please, come in."

Stepping over the threshold, he asked, "Is the party in high gear?"

"That's *one* way of putting it." I set his bag with the others at the foot of the stairs, then walked him into the great room.

Heads turned.

His father greeted him with a pat on the back. His stepmom avoided him and sulked. Zola and Richard sidled up to him for fawning introductions. I poured him a drink—just a glass of chardonnay, "for starters," he said. And Isandro presented him with the tray of appetizers.

Keith plucked one up. "Crab Rangoon—how fabulous!"

Isandro and I gave each other a look. No doubt about it: there were now *four* gay men in the room.

With Keith's arrival, all seven places at the table were now accounted for. His arrival also signaled a truce of sorts, with the rest of us instinctively glossing over the blowup between Zola and Wendy—as if it had never happened.

After a respectable interval for cocktails, Richard excused himself from the group, needing to put finishing touches on the meal in the kitchen. I offered to help, but Zola insisted *she* would assist Richard, assuming the role of hostess in his home. This was not altogether surprising, but it suggested that her friendship with Richard was a tad more advanced than I had realized. And the next surprise came when Harold Gibkin insisted that *he* would pitch in, assisting Zola. I had no idea what to make of that. It was impossible to tell whether Wendy, Harold's screwy wife, was fazed by this or not, as her sullen introversion effectively masked her emotions.

So, then. With three of them busy in the kitchen, and Wendy

in an isolated funk, that left Keith, Isandro, and me on our own for a while. I asked Keith, "Can we show you around?"

"Sure. I'd like that." His words were innocent enough, but his tone was open to interpretation.

We took our glasses and walked out to the pool terrace, into the twilight of a cloudless desert night. In the indigo sky, Venus was shining so intensely that it pulsed. It actually twinkled.

So mesmerizing was this spectacle, Keith took a long moment to notice another bit of eye candy. "Oh, my *God*," he blurted, clapping a hand over his mouth, sputtering with laughter, spilling some of his wine. "Where *did* you find him?"

Towering ten feet above the far end of the pool was a primitive stone sculpture of rugged masculinity—a fierce Inca warrior, nude, sporting a horizontal phallus as long as a baseball bat, with the exaggerated girth of a plump cantaloupe. A pair of spotlights beamed up at him from the surrounding foliage, giving his endowment the added bang of its reflection, which wavered lazily beneath the surface of the water.

I said, "It's just a little something Zola was able to finagle from an old client. Richard was in the mood to perk up the patio. Safe to say: *La Decorina* delivered."

Isandro added, "We call him Mr. Big."

"So did the press." I explained, "The installation was tricky, and he needed to be hoisted in from the side street with a crane—dangling him and his manhood high over the neighborhood. Predictably, this drew a crowd of gawkers, including a photographer from the *Desert Sun*. The picture wasn't worth *quite* a thousand words, but it did make a nice little feature—headlined ONLY IN PALM SPRINGS—which was picked up by more than one wire service. Our friend Mr. Big now has an official online fan page, set up by an anonymous admirer."

"He's ... amazing," said Keith, strolling around the pool for a better look.

Isandro warned, "Don't get too close—that thing'll smack you between the eyes."

Eventually, Keith's attention drifted from the giant fertility god to the more subtle details of the terrace and its surroundings. Richard's estate in the Old Las Palmas neighborhood was a magical setting, with a pair of tiered fountains that gurgled and pattered on opposite sides of the pool. Beneath a canopy of date palms, groupings of large terra-cotta pots overflowed with trailing vines and clusters of flowers—pink and white. The main house stood along the front of the property, with the coach house across from the pool, to the rear. Both buildings were in the Spanish-colonial style, with tile roofs and cream-colored stucco walls, each facing the other through a loggia and colonnade on the ground floor.

"Wow," said Keith, "what a setup. It's like Disneyland—so perfect, it doesn't seem real."

Isandro nodded. "I still have to pinch myself. Can't believe I live here."

"You *do*?"

Isandro told Keith about his recent purchase of the coach house from Richard. "As I understand it, the building was originally a stable, then later a garage, which also served as a pool house, providing a man-made view—a 'backdrop'—as seen from the main house."

I pointed out the fanciful stairway leading up to the second floor, which overhung the colonnade. "The living space is above the garage. We're still dolling it up."

Keith had listened with interest and now asked, "You *are* a couple, then?"

"Yes," I heard myself say, "we are."

Isandro grinned. I had always been careful with my words—squeamish about implications of commitment. But I was not inclined to deny that we were, at the very least, a "couple."

Keith was looking up at the front windows of our loft. "It sounds fabulous. Hate to put you on the spot—but any chance I could see it?"

Well, now. This was unexpected, but it did *not* put Isandro and me "on the spot." Both of us were compulsively neat, and our little home was always presentable—ready, in fact, to be shown off anytime. So I didn't find it odd that Keith had asked for a tour; what I did find odd was that Isandro and I hadn't already invited him up.

"Tell you what," I said. "Isandro? Take Keith up to the loft, and I'll duck back to the house to make sure there's some time before dinner. I'll catch up with you guys in a minute, okay?"

With a smile and a shrug, Isandro said, "Sure." Then he led Keith across the terrace toward the stairs.

Retracing my steps to the main house, I saw that the meal preparation was still underway, with everyone in the kitchen, no action near the table. As I entered through the French doors, Harold was telling Richard, "... so the rest of the clan is driving over tomorrow from Temecula, where my sister runs a winery. She'll have her adult daughter with her, along with a couple of hangers-on."

Richard asked, "Employees? Or 'significant others'?"

Harold hesitated. "That's a fuzzy distinction, I guess."

And then, to my surprise, screwy Wendy piped in: "Don't

forget about Rebecca. She's another fuzzy distinction, isn't she, Harold?"

Harold told Richard and Zola, "Rebecca Jiang is my personal assistant."

Wendy snorted. "Now, *there's* a euphemism."

"Stop that." Harold drank a slug of his bourbon and set the heavy glass on the granite countertop with a loud clack.

Sensing trouble, I strolled over to the group, asking Harold, "And the others will meet you at the rental in Rancho Mirage, correct?"

He nodded. "They'll arrive in the afternoon. We thought we'd have a big family meal tomorrow night—you're all invited— then maybe a Sunday brunch the next day, a pool party."

"I'll check my calendar," Zola said wryly, but I had a hunch she'd tag along if Richard was going.

"Now, *Zola*," said Harold, "you *must*—it wouldn't be much of a party without you."

When she tittered like an ingenue, I gave her a dirty look, which she returned with a wink.

Richard, I knew, was *always* up for a party. "I have a *delicious* idea," he said brightly. "Why don't I whip up a lemon posset as dessert for the brunch?"

"Sure," said Harold. "Why not?"

Wendy demanded, "What's in it?"

Richard grinned. "Lemons."

Wendy sneered. "What else?"

"It's pretty simple, really: Lemons. Cream. Sugar. Maybe some whipped cream and berries as a garnish."

This seemed to placate Wendy.

Harold explained, under his breath, "She has some food issues."

No kiddin', I thought.

From the appearance of things in the kitchen, that night's dinner was far from ready, so I told the others that Isandro and I were showing Keith around, and I returned to the patio.

Skirting the pool, I went back to the coach house, walked under the overhang of the loggia, and began climbing the wrought-iron stairs that led up to our loft. As I neared the top, I could hear laughter inside.

Opening the door, I heard Isandro ask, "Is it, like, a *chimp*?"

"*No*, thank God. Much smaller—a squirrel monkey, I think."

Keith was gabbing with Isandro at one end of the galley kitchen, which stood near the center of the large, square loft space, dividing it roughly in half. Our sleeping area and bath were behind the kitchen. In front was the main living space, which included a dining table and a corner study delineated by a partial wall of bookcases. Most of the room was devoted to a comfortably furnished conversation area at the front end of the building, with windows overlooking the pool and the main house and the mountains beyond. Front to back, the entire loft was unified by a high, gabled ceiling.

In a word, it was charming. Perfect for two. And although Isandro and I were not married, I would have a tough time faulting anyone who might describe the place as a honeymoon cottage.

Closing the door, I moved toward the kitchen, asking Isandro, "Did you have squirrel monkeys in Brazil?"

"Sure, they live there—but you can't keep native animals as pets."

Keith said, "They're not native here, of course, but all primates are illegal as pets in California." He paused before reminding us, "And, as an attorney, I'm an officer of the court."

"Aha," I said. "Might this be a source of friction between you and the stepmom?"

He blew a long, breathy sigh. "Wendy doesn't like me to begin with—she has some nasty ideas about the gay community."

"So we've heard," said Isandro.

"Plus," said Keith, "I represent 'the law,' which Wendy views as a threat to her precious Koo-Loo. The little wretch is, I concede, sorta cute—when he's not screeching, when he's not pelting you with his own shit. They really *do* that, you know."

I pictured Wendy hurling her crab puff at Zola. Had she borrowed a page from Koo-Loo's playbook?

Keith tossed his arms. "But I don't live with them, and I have better things to do than ratting out a damn monkey. I have no idea what Dad sees in Wendy—or what she sees in Koo-Loo—but it doesn't matter what I think, so long as they're happy."

"*Are* they happy?" I asked.

Keith smirked. "I can't speak for Koo-Loo, but yes, Dad and Wendy seem to click. Hope so. I mean, he *married* her, in spite of her awful views."

Isandro handed us fresh drinks, telling me, "Let's sit down. Keith was asking me something that you might find of interest."

Intrigued, I followed Isandro as he led us to the front of the room, where we arranged ourselves on a pair of love seats that faced each other near the windows. Isandro and I sat next to each other, with Keith facing us from the other side of a cocktail table. We set down our glasses.

Isandro turned in his seat, saying to me, "I was telling Keith about your sideline with Jazz."

Keith said, "And *I* was wondering if your detective friend might be able to help me with something."

I felt my brows arch. "Help... with what?"

"Can I speak to both of you in confidence?"

We both gave Keith a ready nod. Isandro mimed zipping his lips.

Keith said, "This regards my father's secretary, who's arriving tomorrow. Her name is Rebecca."

I recalled, "Rebecca Jiang. Her name came up about three minutes ago when I was in the kitchen. Harold said she was his 'personal assistant,' but Wendy implied that Rebecca might be a romantic interest."

"Wendy's not stupid—wacky, for sure, but not stupid. To be honest, I don't think Dad sees Rebecca as anything other than a helpful employee. But I agree with Wendy that Rebecca may have other ideas. I think she might be an opportunist—romantically, financially, or both."

"Forgive an indelicate question," I said, "but can I assume there's significant money in the family?"

Keith paused. "There was. And to a degree, there still is. Dad's always been a visionary, but he's made some bad investments. I'm sure he's been a drain on the Gibkin legacy; how much, I don't know. Meanwhile, Wendy came into the marriage with family money of her own—and a prenup. They have separate finances."

Isandro said, "Then along came Rebecca. How old is she?"

"I believe she's forty-five. Not a kid, certainly, but that's fourteen years younger than Dad. She's worked for him for six or seven years. She's smart, competent, and professional. But I can't help wondering if she's also a schemer."

"So," I said, "you're in the market for a private investigator."

Keith thought it over. "Yeah. I guess I am. I've been reluctant to hire someone at home—it'd raise a shitstorm if word ever got out. But since the bunch of them will be *here* for a month, it might be the right time to bring in your friend for a background check. Her name is Jazz?"

I pulled out my wallet, where I always carried a few of her cards, and handed one to Keith, telling him, "Jazz Friendly. Maybe I could bring her tomorrow night. Your dad's planning a big bash at the rental house."

"Sounds good. Hope she's available—I'd like to meet her."

With that bit of business out of the way, I said, "Your dad also mentioned that his sister is arriving tomorrow. She runs a vineyard?"

"Yes, that's my aunt, Heather Ferris. Her husband, Jason Ferris, died a few years ago. They started up the Trot-n-Tipple Equestrian Winery in Temecula and turned it into quite the thriving enterprise. With Jason gone, Heather now runs it by herself—that is, by herself with *lots* of help. Dad still calls her his 'kid sister.' She's fifty-two."

I asked, "And Heather's daughter is also arriving tomorrow?"

"I wasn't much involved in making these plans," said Keith, "but yes, that's what I hear. Heather's daughter is my cousin, Brooke Ferris. She's around twenty-eight, single, and a nurse."

Isandro and I glanced at each other, sharing a grin. I told Keith, "Isandro is a nurse."

"Really? What sort of nursing?"

Isandro explained, "I worked emergency-room shifts for a few years, and it was rewarding because it truly made a difference— you deal with *everything* in that setting. But the crazy shifts were burning me out, so now I work for a gastroenterologist. Not too exciting, but it's regular office hours." Then he asked, "What does your cousin do?"

"Brooke used to work in a physician's practice, but more recently, she's been providing hospice and palliative services as a live-in caregiver to terminal patients at home. One of them just died, so she's looking forward to getting away for a while. This visit will be good for her."

"Well," I said, "the rental property in Rancho Mirage is a great place to relax and recharge—it's spectacular. I'm sure you'll all enjoy it."

"If it's anything like *that*," said Keith, gesturing through the windows toward the house across the terrace, "how could anyone *not* enjoy it?"

"Actually, the rental doesn't look much like Richard's house—it's sleek and contemporary."

"Good. That's more my style, anyway."

I added, "Aside from styling, though, they're about the same size. Meaning, huge. The rental has six bedrooms, including two in a separate guesthouse, more than enough for the eight of you staying there. You can work out who-sleeps-where when everyone arrives tomorrow."

With a sly look, Keith asked, "And tonight?"

"Richard has a nice guest suite ready for you on the second floor. And another for your dad and Wendy."

"That's... uh, not what I meant," he said coyly, eyeing a sizable daybed we had there in the living room.

Piled with a colorful assortment of scatter pillows and a faux-fur throw, it served as extra seating while entertaining or as a place to lounge while watching television. Also, once, it had accommodated an overnight guest. Was I reading this wrong, or was Keith angling for a slumber party? And where might *that* lead?

Though totally unexpected, this was an intriguing prospect, and I could tell from Isandro's grin that he was weighing this possibility as well. Long seconds passed in silence, as no one seemed ready to speak the next words.

The tension was nipped when Isandro's phone buzzed with an arriving text. He looked at it, laughed softly, and passed it to me. It was a message from Richard, in the main house: DINNER IS SERVED. COME AND GET IT. OR HAVE YOU BOYS GOTTEN "INVOLVED" IN SOMETHING?

While I was holding the phone in my hand, it buzzed again, and Richard sent a big yellow winky-face with its pink tongue hanging out.

CHAPTER
TWO

Saturday morning, I would need to put in a few hours at Sunny Junket's offices in downtown Palm Springs. Cruising along the main drag, Palm Canyon Drive, in my vintage Karmann Ghia convertible—graphite silver, with oxblood leather seats—I never failed to catch a few admiring glances. The car was meant for a warm autumn day in the desert, and its classic styling fit right in with the town's retro-modern vibe.

After parking behind our office, I walked along the side of the building to its front corner and entered through the glass doors from the street. October was barely the start of tourist season, so we were lightly staffed that day, with only one of the slots at the reception desk occupied.

Gianna couldn't be bothered looking up from whatever game she was playing on her phone. "What's a five-letter word for 'milquetoast'?"

"Not a clue, girlfriend."

"Bite me." With her middle finger, she nudged her harlequin glasses higher on her nose.

My desk was littered with piles of paper that needed pushing, but that could wait. I sat down and phoned Jazz. She didn't answer with a conventional "hello" or "good morning," but pounced on the business at hand:

"Got your text last night. What's up, Dante?"

"I think I've snagged another client for you. Interested?"

"That depends. I'll have to check my calendar. Let me just…" Her voice trailed off as she supposedly scrolled through her work schedule.

She was having a bit of fun, and I played along, waiting patiently. I'd known her for about two years, when she resigned under pressure from the Palm Springs police force, her career derailed by a racist colleague. Black, in her mid-thirties, Jazz had been struggling with anger and booze issues that had also scuttled her marriage. So she'd found herself starting over, hustling to establish her own practice as a private investigator—at the very time when I was rebuilding my own life. Our first couple of encounters had been nothing short of toxic, but then we ended up collaborating on an investigation that taught us some mutual respect, which led not only to friendship, but to more side work from me on her behalf.

Business was now, in fact, picking up nicely for her, but I doubted if it was booming to the extent that she needed to check whether she could squeeze in a new client.

I laughed. "Cut the act."

She laughed. "Just messin' with ya."

I filled her in. She was already well acquainted with Richard Gibbs's estate and with Zola's redecorating project there, so I told Jazz about Richard's DNA discovery of the Gibkin branch of his family, now arriving for an extended reunion. "Richard's second cousin, Harold Gibkin, arrived last night with his wife—and his gay son from a prior marriage. The son is a lawyer. Five others are arriving today, and all eight of them will take up residence at a rental in Rancho Mirage. They're having a big dinner party tonight—more like a casual supper, I'm guessing—and I'm invited. So are you. Can you be there?"

Jazz paused before answering, "I ought to play hard to get—Saturday night, late notice, *blah-blah-blah*—but the truth is, I was looking for something to do. Christopher has Emma this weekend, and Blade is in LA, gettin' wined and dined by some hoity-toity gallery there."

She was talking about local attorney Christopher Friendly, her white, closeted ex-husband, and their biracial daughter, Emma, a delightfully precocious five-year-old who had just started kindergarten. Meanwhile, Jazz had been keeping company (and getting serious, it seemed) with Blade Wade, a Black painter of growing renown with his home and studio in Palm Springs.

"So," she said, "count me in. But what's this about?"

"First, some background." I told Jazz about Harold's long-shot research with AtmosPhuel R&D and my suspicion that the purpose of his visit had nothing to do with reconnecting lost family—and everything to do with sniffing out potential investments in his venture. I added, "His wife, Wendy, has some family wealth of her own, but it seems she has no interest in funding Harold's project."

"Can't say I blame her," said Jazz. "Sounds like Wendy must be the levelheaded one."

"Not ... *exactly*. She's openly, brazenly homophobic—in spite of having a well-adjusted gay stepson—and when Zola stood up to her bigotry, Wendy responded by throwing food at her. Later, at dinner, Wendy pouted and picked over everything that was served, demanding to know 'what's in it' again and again. She looked gaunt and sickly, but then stuffed herself with everything in sight, frequently rushing to the powder room, leaving the rest of the table to sit there listening to the sound of her retching. She's obviously bulimic, but Harold dismissed her behavior as merely 'food issues,' including a severe allergy to honey—which was in nothing we ate last night. Plus—"

Jazz interrupted, "There's *more?*"

"In fact, there is. Wendy, you see, has a pet monkey. The little scamp is named Koo-Loo. Harold wouldn't let Wendy bring it along on their visit, thank God, which has left her bereft and oh-so-lonely. All evening long, when Wendy wasn't spouting her hate speech or puking her guts out in the powder room, she was wailing and moaning about that damn monkey."

"She sounds fuckin' *nuts.*" Jazz had a way with words—and a street mouth when it suited a need for extra swagger.

"The rest of us," I explained, "could barely finish a complete sentence without Wendy upstaging us with her antics. It was, in a word, dreadful. However: Wendy did display a moment of rational clarity when she voiced her suspicion that hubby Harold might not have an entirely 'professional' relationship with his personal assistant, Rebecca Jiang, who will arrive with the others today."

"Aha," said Jazz. "So Wendy wants to hire me to dig some dirt?"

"No. Her stepson—Keith, the lawyer—wants to hire you. Last night, he told Isandro and me in confidence that he thinks Wendy's suspicions, while plausible, are backwards. He thinks that Rebecca, not his father, is the one who's looking for romance."

"Got it," said Jazz. "Glad I won't be involved with that Wendy chick. And I've always sorta liked working with lawyers—I *lived* with one long enough."

I didn't want to tell Jazz that Keith strongly reminded me of Christopher, her ex. I also didn't want to tell her that Keith had expressed interest—if only jokingly—in spending the night with Isandro and me in the coach house. And I certainly didn't want to tell her that Isandro and I had been—not so jokingly—interested.

But Keith, Isandro, and I didn't go through with it. By the time we'd finished dinner last night, enduring several hours of Wendy's hysterics, any playful pipe dreams of hanky-panky were simply shot to hell.

Because I wanted to be on hand to welcome everyone to the rental property, I needed to be at the house in Rancho Mirage by one o'clock. I would remain for as long as necessary to help everyone get settled, which might take all afternoon, so it made little sense for me to return to Palm Springs before that evening's dinner party. Jazz, therefore, planned to arrive on her own, joining me around five.

By twelve thirty, I had hopped into my car and was heading east on Highway 111, which would land me at the rental house well before one. Strapped into the passenger seat of the open convertible was a lavish welcome basket—a fitting gift for monthlong guests at one of our more expensive properties.

Passing through Cathedral City and into Rancho Mirage always felt like "arriving." The glitz and the billboards disappeared. The road opened up, and the landscape was instantly less touristy, more manicured. Plus, it was a pristine October afternoon under a cloudless, endless sapphire sky.

The house rented by the Gibkin party was not one of our mountainside properties, which better suited an elite class of guests seeking privacy and serenity. Instead, the Gibkins had chosen a sizable estate on the valley floor, adjacent to a country club's golf course. It could accommodate up to a dozen overnight guests, and with its large pool and outdoor entertainment area, it appealed to those with a taste for celebrating, rather than relaxing.

Except, city ordinances took a dim view of rowdiness at vacation rentals, with strict limits on decibels, parking, and un-registered visitors. When our clients got out of line, the city got involved and, sometimes, the police as well. In an effort to avert that entirely, I had recommended that Sunny Junket should put Jazz on retainer for occasional duty as our private code-enforce-ment officer. She could look damn fierce when she wanted to—I'd listen up fast if she rang *my* doorbell.

I felt confident, though, that she would not be needed in that capacity during the Gibkins' stay. They had their quirks (What family doesn't?), but they didn't strike me as immature party an-imals.

Parking at the curb along the quiet side street, I saw that the gate to the house's motor court had been opened by the pool service, which I had scheduled to do an extra cleaning that day. Their truck was parked on the street, ahead of my own car.

I lifted the welcome basket and my file of paperwork out of the convertible, then walked through the courtyard to the front door of the house. I paused to take it all in.

The architecture was clean and minimal—all white in the style of the day—a composition of sleek interlocking boxes, with their surfaces modulated by rectangular slabs of darkly tinted window glass. It could have been a tony art gallery, a discreet clinic, or a pricey steak joint, but no. This had been built specifically as a sprawling, rentable vacation house, both impressive and imper-sonal, intended for anyone who could afford it. Was I really so jaded that I saw this house as serviceable but unremarkable? Our guests were routinely blown away by it.

Opening the front door with the keypad, I stepped inside. Acres, it seemed, of shiny white quartz flooring spread out be-neath my feet as I made my way into the main space—a "great room" that lived up to the term, a *huge* open room that was half kitchen, everything gleaming white and stainless steel. To either side of this living area were bedroom wings with spa-size bathrooms. The back wall of the great room was all glass, all of which disappeared into wall pockets as I stepped outside. Beyond was the limestone terrace of the pool, with a separate two-bedroom guest cube off to one side, which also contained a kitchen and lounge. White. White. White.

This eyeball-searing monochrome was finally relieved at the edge of the property, where a vast green fairway led off to the ruddy mountains and the sky above.

"Hey, *Dante*. How's it goin'?"

I'd forgotten I wasn't alone. Max Hazer, the pool guy, had stepped out from behind a service wall—white, of course—which concealed the filter equipment. He always reminded me of an aging hippie, though I had no idea how old he was. He looked like any one of the hundreds, maybe thousands, of guys who made their living by cleaning pools in the valley, many of them Latino, but not all of them, not Max. He wore a battered white pith helmet, white canvas shoes, khaki shorts, wire-rim glasses with yellow lenses, and a vividly patterned tropical shirt that had long ago faded to pastels beneath the searing sun. He asked me, "Everything pass inspection?"

"Looks great, Max. Thanks for taking care of it."

"Anytime, anytime," he said while squirting something into the water with a squeeze bottle. "We're here to serve." He laughed, but then broke into a cough—a smoker's cough. The stub of a cigarette, little more than a butt, still hung from the corner of his mouth. Clearing his throat, he took the cigarette from his lips, pinched it out, then tossed it into the sand behind the service wall.

Naturally, this reminded me that Harold Gibkin was also

a smoker, and he'd had no qualms about lighting up in Richard Gibbs's house. So I assumed he would do the same here in the rental house—which was forbidden. Sunny Junket had a no-smoking policy inside *all* of its properties, with stiff fines for infractions. It was spelled out in the contract he had signed, but I would need to make sure he was aware of it.

"Know what?" said Max, laughing again—without coughing this time. "There's a lady on the next block, and she's got this thing for peach yogurt, I guess, cuz she's always out on the patio when I get there on Tuesday mornings, early, about seven thirty, and she's sitting there in this silk kimono or whatever—it's gold, real fancy—and her legs are stickin' out while she's eatin' the peach yogurt..."

Why, I wondered, *is he telling me this?*

"... and sure enough, when I get there last week, she's got this *second* bowl of the stuff sittin' there, and she says, all ladylike, 'Would you care to taste it, Mr. Hazer?' And I'm like, *I dunno.* And she tells me, 'I have muesli, too. It's like trail mix. It adds crunch.' And me, I'm thinkin'—"

"What in *God's* name," I said, "are you getting at, Max? Did she try to lay you?"

He paused in thought. "Now, *that* never occurred to me."

I refrained from thumping my forehead. I thought he might be high, but I was *sure* he was a gossip—and a lousy one at that. He began to gather his chemicals, brushes, and skimmer, preparing to leave.

"Point is," he said, "I liked the trail mix, but not the peach yogurt. Yech."

A voice called from inside the house, "Anybody home?"

Grateful for the interruption, I told Max, "Gotta run," then trotted from the pool back into the great room.

"Is that *your* car?" said Keith Gibbs. "The Karmann Ghia?"

My eyes widened. He was a looker, all right, and clearly no stranger to the gym. He'd ditched the gabardine suit and was wearing shorts today with a knit shirt and that big bright smile. My smile aped his as I approached him to shake hands, but he went for a quick hug instead.

I said, "That's my baby," then clarified, "the car."

"What model year *is* that?"

"It's a 1958, fully restored. Believe it or not, it was a gift from a grateful client. He even had it air-conditioned."

"Wow. You must have provided *exceptional* service."

I knew a double entendre when I heard it, so I volleyed one back: "I certainly did."

"Hmmm." His eyes had a hungry look (but that might have been my imagination).

I asked, "Are the others on their way?"

"Dad and Wendy were almost ready to leave, so they should be here soon. As for the rest, Dad sent them texts—anytime after one—so who knows?" He paused to glance about. "This place looks *great*, by the way. Thanks for setting it up."

I shrugged. "It's my job."

Keith grinned. "And Isandro? Is he here yet? Coming later?"

"Uh, no, actually. He's running his Saturday errands today. And tonight, Dr. Gastro—as he's known behind his back—is throwing an 'office appreciation' dinner in Palm Springs, so Isandro needs to be there. But he's looking forward to the brunch here tomorrow."

"Nice."

I found Keith's comment—*Nice*—to be ambiguous. Was he pleased that Isandro would be with us tomorrow, or was he pleased that Isandro was *not* with us now, in this otherwise empty house? Evading that question, I told Keith, "But I will, in fact, have another date tonight."

He gave me a curious look, a bit bewildered.

I laughed. "It's Jazz. She'll be happy to meet you regarding that background check on your father's secretary. And tonight's gathering will be a good opportunity to observe everyone's interactions. She'll join me around five, if that's okay."

"Sounds like a plan."

"So, then. Luggage. Can I help bring things in?"

"I don't have much, since I'll be staying only a few days at a time. But the others—brace yourself."

Turned out, Keith and I had the place to ourselves longer than anticipated—all the others seemed to be taking their time that day. When it became clear that I could be of no immediate service to the remaining guests, I gave Keith a full tour of the house and acquainted him with some of the tech features: lock codes, security system, Wi-Fi, audio-video, and on and on.

I said, "No matter how often I explain this stuff, no two houses are alike, and a day later, most guests have questions." Handing Keith one of my cards, I added, "Don't hesitate to call me."

"I won't," he assured me, pocketing the card. Then he handed me one of his own.

After walking through the sleeping accommodations, ending up in the detached guesthouse, I said, "In total, you have six bedrooms, each with its own bath, which I figure is one more than you need. Don't get me wrong—everyone's free to sleep wherever they wish—but I just want to make sure the setup is adequate."

Keith nodded. "We'll be fine. But let's think this out: One bedroom for Dad and Wendy, although I think they sometimes sleep in separate rooms, since Dad tends to be a night owl. Then, another bedroom for Dad's assistant, Rebecca Jiang. And another for me."

I suggested, "That could account for the four bedrooms in the two wings of the main house. Which would leave the two bedrooms here in the guesthouse. Will that work for the Temecula gang?"

"I *think* so." Keith considered this for a moment, adding, "My aunt Heather and her daughter, Brooke—they're each 'bringing someone,' two guys I've never met. But I assume their purpose is to warm the ladies' beds."

"Great," I said. "If that's the case, we're all set."

We walked back to the main house together, and I led Keith to the massive center island in the kitchen, where I'd set out the gift basket and several stacks of paperwork. "Do you mind if we go over a few particulars?"

He grinned. "I'm a lawyer. It's what I do."

"Excellent. Your father's signed rental contract is here, which takes effect when he arrives today, minus the prorated portion of the rental charge for last night, since Sunny Junket needed an extra day to have the house ready. But once he checks in, he's on the hook for the rest of the month."

"Got it. Sounds reasonable."

"Also, Rancho Mirage has city ordinances governing vacation rentals—regarding noise, parking, and such—which are detailed here." I tapped the file. Tapping another file, I said, "And Sunny Junket, as agent to all of our represented property owners, has its own list of 'house rules,' covering, among other things, the strict prohibition of smoking indoors."

Keith asked wryly, "Are there fines for noncompliance, damage, cleanup?"

"Yes, and we'll charge them to your father's credit card on file."

With a soft chuckle, Keith told me, "That'll do the trick. I'll mention this to him."

Dingdong.

As Keith and I headed to the entry hall, I called, "C'mon in. Door's open."

And when it opened, there stood Harold and Wendy.

Keith checked his watch and laughed. "It's two thirty. I thought you were right behind me. *Where* have you been?"

Harold led his wife through the door. "Oh, we just decided to stop for a nice lunch somewhere. There was a shady patio. But it was crowded." As he spoke, a cigarette bobbed between his lips.

"Better late than never," said Keith as he stepped up to his father and, without comment, snatched the cigarette. He then took it to the kitchen, where he extinguished it with water at the sink before tossing it into the trash.

"Welcome," I told the Gibkins. "I hope you'll enjoy your new home for the next month. If you find that anything's not to your liking, please, just give me a call at Sunny Junket." I handed my card to Harold.

"Thanks, Dante." He patted my back. "This place looks fantastic."

"One of our finest," I assured him, but my smile sagged. "Wendy," I said, "you're looking rather pale. Is there anything I can get you?"

With a stiff, microscopic shake of her head, she replied, "No. But where might I find the powder room?"

Uh-oh. Lamely, I pointed the way.

Keith returned from the kitchen. "Can I show you around, Dad?"

"You bet. Let's have a look-see."

I suggested, "If you'd like to give the tour, Keith, I can bring in their luggage."

They looked at each other, nodding their agreement. Harold handed me his keys, then headed out to the patio with his son.

In the stillness of the house, I could hear Wendy doing her thing in the powder room as I went out the front door to the parking court.

The smart little Mercedes presumably belonged to Keith. The other vehicle had to be Harold's. What it may have lacked in Mercedes elegance was compensated for by its sheer, staggering scale. A behemoth of an SUV, this sparkling white Chevy Suburban looked oddly at home with the boxy white architecture surrounding it; even the tinted windows of its cargo area mimicked those of the house. It was the sort of vehicle that people use to haul stuff—*lots* of stuff.

Walking behind it, I tapped the key fob, and the liftgate rose. Oh. My. God.

The back seat had been folded down, and the entire area behind the front seats was crammed to the roof with luggage, boxes, garment bags, golf bags, and various totes, plus a slapdash array of loose items that had been wedged in wherever space allowed—hair dryer, bar blender, a thick three-ring binder, a bed pillow—and that was just the crap I could see from the rear opening.

Granted: Harold and Wendy would be here a month, but it looked more as if they were planning to move in for good. It took me nearly half an hour just to get everything out of the SUV and to stage it on the pavers of the parking court.

"Holy Christ," said Keith, emerging from the house to check on me. "I had *no* idea—sorry." He trotted out to give me a hand.

As we brought the first few items into the house, I saw that Harold and Wendy had made themselves comfortable out on the patio, drinking wine from the welcome basket, which they had already torn into. They lounged on chaises near the edge of the pool, shaded by big white umbrellas.

Pausing with a heavy armload of their crap, I asked Keith, "Where to?"

"They haven't decided on bedrooms. Let's leave it here."

So we began stacking piles of their things in the middle of the great room, in an open space between the kitchen and the conversation area. By the time we had trekked everything inside and attempted to get it reasonably organized, it was pushing four o'clock.

Dingdong.

Keith and I glanced at each other with weary smiles and headed to the front hall. He opened the door to an explosion of greetings. The ruckus roused Harold and Wendy, who came in from the pool and joined the crowd.

Of the four new arrivals from Temecula, Keith knew only the two women—Heather Ferris and her daughter, Brooke—while I, of course, knew none of them, requiring introductions.

Heather, who ran the equestrian winery that she had founded with her late husband, had a wholesome, outdoorsy look about her, wearing her long blond hair in a thick ponytail, gathered with a tanned leather cinch. She was still pretty, looking youthful in her early fifties, and I could detect some family resemblance to her handsome nephew, Keith. She wore a white shirt unbuttoned like a jacket over a simple gray halter top, along with tight, stretchy brown pants that could have been riding togs. No boots, though—she wore suede Gucci loafers with delicate horsey-themed buckles.

She said, "Pleased to meet you, Dante." Leaning near, she added in a loud whisper, "You'll have your hands full with *this* crew."

Her daughter, Brooke Ferris, who I knew was a nurse, had none of Heather's natural sense of style and ease. Still in her late twenties, though earnest and intent, Brooke struck me as a work in progress. She had an indoor, "sheltered" look. Her hair was more brownish than her mother's, worn in a shorter, serviceable pageboy bob. Her attire was ... well, *unimaginative*. She wore a casual, lightweight baby-blue pantsuit, rumpled from travel, which forced me to blink away the image of hospital scrubs, as if she were unable to project herself beyond her job.

She said, "Hello, Dante. Thanks for looking after us. Hope we won't be too much trouble."

From the little I'd already heard about Brooke and her mother, they largely matched my expectations. But I was surprised—and intrigued—by the two men they'd brought along.

The younger woman's companion, a Black guy named Tyler Evans, looked slightly older, maybe thirty. He was an inch or so shorter than Brooke, with a *very* nice body and a clean-shaven face that was more "cute" than handsome. Tortoiseshell glasses complemented Tyler's caramel complexion and gave him an attractive, bookish air. Carrying a slim case that probably contained a laptop, he wore cargo shorts, a green silk camp shirt, and flip-flops.

He said, "Hey, Dante—good to know you." His look and manner exuded a puppy-dog quality.

By contrast, the *other* escort in the entourage struck me as decidedly feline.

Näzh Hoyle, Heather's companion, was a good ten years younger than she was, around forty. They both wore ponytails. While she was blond, he had long black hair and a trim black beard flecked with silver. Her build was almost rugged compared to his, which was lithe and sinewy. He seemed odd at many levels, but the corker was his attire: a white linen jumpsuit worn with silver lamé sandals on his feet and a rhinestone choker around his neck.

When he spoke, his voice was soft, colored with an effete tone of tedium. "Dearest Dante, such a pleasure. Have you discovered the powers of manifestation?"

Was he joking? With an uncertain laugh, I pivoted to Keith, telling him, "I'll bring in their things. Feel free to spend some time with your family."

"Nonsense. I'll give you a hand." He asked Heather, "Do we need keys? Two vehicles, I presume?"

She handed him one set of keys. "We all came together."

At least *that* was promising.

But when Keith and I headed out through the front door, we both stopped in our tracks, exchanging a look of wide-eyed dismay. Yes, there was only one vehicle, a sturdy pickup with a four-door cab, but hitched behind it was a gleaming stainless-steel horse trailer.

Decorative signage ran along its side: TROT-N-TIPPLE EQUESTRIAN WINERY. Actual horseshoes and painted bunches of grapes embellished the lettering. I was certain, however, that the trailer contained neither horses nor grapes.

"Jesus *Christ*," muttered Keith as we opened the rear doors.

We had just finished hauling another mountain of baggage and boxes into the great room, which by now looked like a hotel lobby that was backed up with check-ins for a mob of conventioneers. The Gibkins and the Ferrises and their boy toys had yet to show any interest in laying claim to bedrooms and putting things away. Instead, Näzh wandered about with his phone, snapping pictures like a tourist, while the others were gabbing and catching up and rummaging through their piles of stuff to retrieve this and that. Harold had found the blender, which now whined and screeched as he played bartender.

Dingdong.

I didn't see Keith around, and no one else seemed to have heard the chimes, so I went to answer the door myself.

When I opened it, an attractive middle-aged woman with Asian features stood there in the entryway holding an iPad, which she scrolled as if checking a list. She wore smart business attire—matching jacket and skirt of nubby rust-colored silk, with kitten-heel pumps.

I guessed, "Rebecca Jiang? I'm Dante O'Donnell, from the rental agency. We've been expecting you. Welcome."

She reached to shake hands. "Sorry I'm late, Mr. O'Donnell. Traffic. And last-minute requests from Harold."

"Nothing to apologize for," I assured her. "And please, call me Dante. If you'd care to come in and join the others, I'll get your things."

She breezed past me, saying with a chortle, "Good luck, Dante."

By now, I knew what to expect.

Sure enough, her silver Lexus SUV was packed tight with not only a month's worth of clothes (and *lots* of shoe bags), but mostly consumables—groceries, more groceries, cases of wine, several boxes of assorted liquor bottles, and a flimsy plastic shopping bag containing cartons of cigarettes. At some point, Keith came looking for me and helped me haul everything inside.

It was now past four thirty, with all eight of Sunny Junket's guests accounted for. The great room, to my eye, was a mess—with piles of luggage *still* not assigned to bedrooms, and heaps of food parked randomly on the kitchen counters amid a profusion of booze bottles. It was a scene worthy of a frat house.

This was not my idea of fun. This was not how I would entertain. But the laid-back, carefree chaos seemed to suit the Gibkins and Ferrises just fine. The exception was Keith, who huddled with me from time to time, exchanging comments of dismay while watching the others in action. They made their way to and fro, grazing in the kitchen, drinking on the patio, digging through their jumbled belongings, having a jolly time—but not Wendy, of course, who wandered about, pouting, missing her beloved Koo-Loo, gorging herself on chips and dips and junk, then slipping off to the powder room for another gag and flush.

I also noticed an odd dynamic between Harold Gibkin and Rebecca Jiang. Harold's wife had expressed her suspicion that he harbored a romantic interest in Rebecca. Harold's son believed the opposite—that Rebecca was the one who was scheming, with either romance or money on her mind. Harold himself had maintained that he simply thought of Rebecca as an able and efficient personal assistant.

While I stood there watching them, however, it seemed to me that none of them had it right. It struck me that Harold's attitude toward Rebecca was neither professional nor personal. Rather, he treated her like a servant. Though the image she projected was all business, what I saw her *do* was simply tending to Harold's needs and wishes. She ran his errands, delivered his drinks, bought his cigarettes. He barely looked at her when they spoke.

Dingdong.

It was past five now, and by my estimation, the only people still missing from this promised "dinner party" were Richard Gibbs, Zola Lorinsky, and Jazz Friendly—none of whom, thank God, would arrive with more baggage.

When I answered the door, Jazz leaned in, asking me, "A fuckin' *horse* trailer?"

She was there that evening to meet Keith as a potential client, so she'd dressed for business, wearing a dark, mannish suit. Her only jewelry was a single large pearl that served to button the band collar of a silvery blouse under her jacket. As always, she wore a short no-nonsense Afro, conveying a take-charge attitude that she projected with style.

Keith was the first to spot her enter the great room with me, and he rushed over so I could introduce them. They seemed to click instantly, and I wondered if it was because Keith reminded Jazz of her ex-husband. Had she noticed this yet?

"Tell you what," Keith said to her. "Let's go to the guesthouse. It's quiet there, and we can discuss things privately."

She shrugged. "Lead the way."

He offered, "Can I get you a drink first?"

"Thanks, but I'm fine." Jazz had sworn off alcohol nearly two years ago, with only one slip that I knew of, early on.

As they moved through the room, heads turned. None of the others had seen Jazz before, and she was hard to miss. She and Keith stepped out to the pool terrace and went over to the guesthouse, which they entered, closing the door behind them.

Dingdong.

I moved to the front hall and, as expected, found that Richard had arrived, along with Zola, whom he'd brought as his date. "Hope you're not hungry," I told them through the open doorway. "Things are a tad disorganized here."

Warily, Zola asked, "Is the bar open?"

"Definitely."

With a croak of a laugh, she said, "First things first." And she stepped ahead of us, into the fray, presumably in search of a Tom Collins. Unless I was mistaken, she was in the same outfit she'd worn last night at Richard's. This was … unusual. Plus, she was carrying an oversize purse, a flamboyant brocade satchel with a long shoulder strap, which I couldn't recall having seen before. But I reminded myself that Zola's collection of clothing and accessories was vast, and she *loved* to make a sartorial splash with her unpredictability. Still, I couldn't help wondering what the hell was *in* there. Swimwear? A makeup kit, curlers, and hair dryer?

Before moving forward from the hall, Richard placed a hand on my arm; with his other hand, he carried a liquor bottle by its neck as it dangled at his side with a droopy ribbon attached. "Dante, love. Are they *horrid*? My extended family—is this a *total* disaster?"

I grinned. "Keith's not too bad."

"Mm-*hmm*"—Richard purred—"not bad at all. But his father is a philistine, Wendy's a whack job, and I haven't even *met* the rest."

"Then let's get you introduced."

"Ughh," he muttered. "God help me."

We had made our way only a few feet into the room when Richard was spotted by Harold, who darted toward us from between two mounds of luggage. With a toothy yellow smile, Harold told Richard, "Welcome to my second home! Hope ya like it!"

Uneasily, Richard presented the bottle, which I could now identify as Old Nine-Tails.

"*Zowie*," said Harold, who'd clearly had a few from the open bottle he was carrying. Taking the gift, he suggested, "Let's go out back, where I can smoke—and we can talk some business and have a little drink together. You gotta try this." He waggled both bottles.

With a halfhearted smile, Richard told Harold, "I cracked it open this morning after I bought it. Had a nip—just curious to taste it. But it's not 'me.' I'm more of a martini guy."

"Richard," said Harold, setting down the gift bottle and wrapping an arm over his cousin's shoulder, "a martini can easily be arranged." Then he snapped his fingers at Rebecca Jiang as they moved out toward the pool.

The martini must have improved Richard's humor. When he came in from the patio, he asked me brightly, "Where's Zola? I need to get hopping with that posset."

I rattled my head. "Huh?"

"My *lemon* posset." He reminded me, "I offered to make it for dessert for tomorrow's brunch. It'll need to set in the refrigerator, preferably overnight, so I thought I'd whip it up fresh, here. Might as well get at it before things get busy with *tonight's* meal."

Okay, I thought, that sounded reasonable. "But what does Zola have to do with it?"

"She has the *ingredients*—packed in her bag."

"Aha." I pointed across the room. "She's gabbing with Heather."

Richard looked confused. "Heather?"

"Your *other* second cousin. The wine-making horsewoman."

"Oh, of course. She seemed quite nice."

I caught Zola's attention and waved her over.

Moments later, she joined us—with her big purse, as well as Heather, in tow.

"Zola, love," said Richard, "I ought to work on my posset while I'm still sober enough to remember the recipe—though I admit, it's baby simple."

With a soft laugh, Heather said, "Posset? Isn't that the concoction Lady Macbeth used to poison the king's guards?"

"Very *good*," said Richard. "That's exactly what it is. But I promise: the results of my own culinary efforts won't be nearly so odious."

On an expanse of countertop that Richard had cleared for his preparations, Zola began unpacking her purse. First came the lemons and a zester, a whisk, several cartons of heavy cream, boxed sugar, and a small container of raspberries and blueberries that would be used as a garnish. Then she unloaded more than a dozen ceramic ramekins that looked like miniature soufflé dishes, which would be used as custard cups. And finally, she pulled out a folded white chef's apron and handed it to Richard, saying, "Work your magic, maestro."

As Zola set her satchel on the floor, Richard fussed with donning and tying his apron, then began opening and closing kitchen cabinets, searching out saucepans, large spoons, and a paring knife. With everything assembled, he went to work, squeezing and zesting lemons while the rest of us gabbed.

Wendy, the crazy monkey-lady who'd attacked Zola with a crab puff the night before, now cruised through the kitchen, keeping an eye on every ingredient that went into Richard's posset. She exchanged a few words with him, and with me, but said nothing to Zola, which came as no surprise. But I found it intriguing that Wendy also avoided her husband's sister, Heather. Though the two women stood just a few feet apart, neither of them allowed their eyes to meet.

Others popped in and out of the action, including Rebecca, who said, "I suppose that's my cue to get dinner started," and she literally rolled up the sleeves of her nubby silk jacket before clearing a different expanse of countertop, allowing her to work back-to-back with Richard. Her kitten heels pecked the slick quartz flooring as she bustled about.

Jazz returned from the guesthouse with Keith, who came over to the kitchen, curious about tomorrow's posset. His father, Harold, breezed in to check on Rebecca and her early progress with tonight's dinner—she was his personal assistant, his servant, and also, it seemed, his cook.

I mentioned to Keith, "It's starting to get dark. Maybe you could nudge everyone to pick their bedrooms—and move their things."

He laughed. "It'll be like herding cats, but I'll give it a try."

And he did a good job of it. His good-natured prodding, coupled with the kitchen smells and the waning sunlight, seemed to signal that it was time for everyone to settle in. He successfully proposed the logistics that he and I had floated earlier: The Temecula gang would take the two bedrooms in the guesthouse. His father and Wendy would take the two bedrooms in one wing of the main house. And that left the two bedrooms in the other wing, one for Rebecca and the other for Keith himself.

Then began the arduous task of sorting and distributing all the baggage and whatnot that had been dumped in the great room. There was endless confusion regarding what belonged where, but thanks to another round of drinks, the process took on the tone of merry pandemonium as bags got shuttled back and forth among the rooms.

We all pitched in. Richard's posset was at the stage where the

MICHAEL CRAFT

entire mixture had ended up in a large Dutch oven, pressed into service as an oversize saucepan, where it needed to be slowly but constantly whisked over low heat. Richard gladly deputized anyone willing to take over this duty, and it seemed everyone helped out, finding it preferable to toting heavily packed bags and boxes. What's more, the posset's tangy-sweet aroma now filled the room, tempting anyone on whisk duty to grab a spoon and take a taste. I certainly did.

Eventually, the messy stacks of luggage in the middle of the room dwindled and disappeared. Richard was back in the kitchen, spooning his posset mixture into the ramekins, which needed to cool before going into the refrigerator. Rebecca had dinner under control, with something broiling in the oven. Harold, at the bar, was playing sommelier, uncorking bottles of wine to let them breathe.

He poured two short glasses, swirled them, and walked over to his niece, Brooke, the nurse. They talked quietly awhile, and Brooke's boyfriend, Tyler, came over to join them. Harold offered his glass to Tyler, then returned to his bar duties.

Keith and I had hauled a *ton* of stuff that day and had not yet had a cocktail, so it was time. We helped ourselves, then joined Richard in the kitchen, who was gabbing with Zola and Heather. Harold finished decanting a few bottles of red wine, then moved over from the bar to join our circle of conversation. Screwy Wendy lurked a few feet away, watching Harold. Not far from her, Näzh Hoyle, in his white linen jumpsuit, sipped something green from a snifter while keeping an eye on Heather.

Richard had filled the last of the ramekins and was enjoying a few licks of still-warm posset from his spoon while Zola prattled wistfully about getting older ... and fresh starts ... and unexpected turns. She then paused to look Richard in the eye, placing her hand on his. "I'm not sure how to describe it, but something seems to be budding—a 'platonic romance,' maybe?"

I expected Richard to drop his spoon, bug-eyed.

Instead, he leaned to Zola and kissed her forehead.

Whoa.

CHAPTER
THREE

As a gay man in my early fifties, I had spent most of my life as an outsider looking in. I had been viewed—variously—as an outcast, an outlaw, an outlier, an outlandish excuse for a corn-fed American male, engaging in outrageous proclivities and relationships. But in spite of all that, I was still proudly, unapologetically "out."

So I recognized a hint of hypocrisy—or at least inconsistency—in my uneasy reaction to Zola and Richard's budding "platonic romance." I, of all people, should have applauded them as they weighed the possibility of an unconventional coupling. Not that I was aghast, not exactly, but I was confused and skeptical.

This was not uncharted territory for Zola. I easily understood her prior couplings with gay men, since chaste marriages of convenience were common during their generation, when many gay men desperately felt the need to hide, or to at least have a cover, a beard.

But times had changed, and Richard had no pressure to hide who he was; *au contraire*, he was a flaming old queen who'd weathered the worst and loved to flaunt it. What, then, drew him to this apparent attachment to Zola? What was in it for either of them?

Friendship, I guess—a deepening friendship that involved

sharing and affection and trust. In *that* light, my cynicism seemed peevish, and I now felt more supportive.

That night in the kitchen, however, others had grown quiet, as if assessing this development. The Gibkins and the Ferrises exchanged furtive, quizzical glances. Did it *matter* to them that Richard, their newfound relative—an aging, single, childless, wealthy man—was now, at the moment of their arrival, in the process of forging new bonds?

Dinner was awkward. Food was good, wine great. But the conversation was stilted, at best. The tight-lipped lethargy could have been the result of nerves, anxiety, or simple fatigue.

Jazz must have sensed the need for an icebreaker. During an especially long lull at the table, she asked everyone, "Did Dante ever tell you how we met?"

Most shook their heads. Others shrugged.

"*Well,*" she said, "I was a cop back then, responding to a bloody crime scene in Palm Springs."

I picked up the narrative: "And she arrested me for murdering my husband." When they gasped, I added, "It didn't stick."

Jazz laughed heartily. "But that's a *whole* nother story."

Sunday morning, I lingered in bed with Isandro, who was still asleep. His "office appreciation" dinner with Dr. Gastro and the staff had run late. He and the doctor were the only men involved, with the others consuming as much liquor and making as much noise as a bachelorette party run amok. The restaurant manager finally had to throw them out, making a show of locking the door and turning off the lights.

So I let him sleep. I kissed his shoulder (nothing else was accessible in the jumble of sheets), then slipped out of bed and padded out to the kitchen to make coffee.

I was at the table, starting my second cup while checking news on my iPad, when I heard him walk up behind me.

He mumbled, "Good morning, *coração*."

I turned. He was naked, dragging his robe behind him in one hand. He clearly needed some attention.

So I brightened his day and helped wake him up.

We didn't bother with breakfast (not really, just toast), since he was going to the brunch with me in Rancho Mirage. I felt I'd already seen enough of those people, but keeping them happy was my job. Isandro looked forward to seeing Keith again (I couldn't quibble with that notion). And Jazz was now "working" for Keith (they'd made it official), so she wanted to be there to observe Rebecca again as part of the background check. Since the three of us would be coming from Palm Springs, Jazz volunteered to drive and would pick us up.

Richard and Zola would also attend the brunch. I assumed they would arrive together, as yesterday, as a couple. Which forced me to wonder if Zola was *staying* at Richard's house, if she was *living* with him on the other side of the pool from our coach house. Were they possibly sharing a bed (as opposed to "sleeping together")? All of this, of course, was none of my business. Still, I was struggling to parse out the boundaries of a "platonic romance," whatever *that* meant.

While Isandro and I waited for Jazz at the curb along one of the side streets bordering Richard's estate, I glanced over the ficus hedge toward the tile-roofed gables of the main house, wondering what, if anything, was happening in those second-story rooms. Would I find the answer in a flutter of the curtains?

"Here she is," said Isandro.

I followed his glance down the street and saw Jazz approaching, fast—she was always an impatient driver, as if practicing a chase scene in the next big blockbuster crime caper. Her monster SUV fit the role—black, with tinted windows and fat tires, like something from a Secret Service motorcade. Stripped of all badging, it had one of those pugnacious crash bumpers bolted to the front.

She screeched to a halt at the curb just long enough for Isandro and me to hop in—him in back, me in front. We barely had the doors closed when she hit the gas and barreled away.

"Morning, boys! Sleep tight?" she asked over the thump of a rap station.

I noted, "It seems *you've* had your coffee."

"Yeah, got a lot done already. Drew up a contract for Keith. Also did a quick background search of Rebecca Jiang online— hardly anything there, though."

Isandro said, "So I guess you didn't learn much."

"Actually"—the vehicle swerved as Jazz turned her head to Isandro—"that tells me plenty. When someone leaves barely a footprint out in cyberspace, you can bet there's a reason."

"Hmm," I said, "maybe Keith's suspicions are justified."

Within fifteen minutes, shortly before noon, Jazz pulled up to the entry gate of the rental house in Rancho Mirage and braked to a gentle stop without burning rubber. I told her the keypad code, and she punched it in.

As we rolled into the parking court, I noted the four vehicles that accounted for all eight out-of-towners, but not Richard and Zola.

Jazz paused after getting out of her SUV, checking messages on her phone. Isandro and I walked up to the front door. Previously, I had always let myself in, but now that Sunny Junket's guests were settled in, I rang the bell.

"Dante!" said Keith, swinging the door open. "I was *hoping* it was you."

"Really?" Did I blush? Isandro jabbed me with his elbow.

"Yeah." Keith's smile drooped. "We're having some problems with the Wi-Fi."

(I should have guessed.)

As we entered, Isandro got a hug from Keith, who told him, "Missed you yesterday." I might have gotten one too, but I had already moved in the direction of the closet where most of the electronics were hidden. Jazz traipsed in after us, pocketing her phone and closing the door behind her.

The house looked much better than it had the night before, now that all the luggage was where it belonged. There was bacon in the air. The kitchen had been tidied up and organized, doubtless due to Rebecca Jiang's efforts, who now seemed to be in charge of putting brunch together. She was more appropriately dressed for these duties than she had been yesterday, now wearing comfortable slacks and a breezy blouse—no silk business suit—but she still wore heels.

Harold greeted me from the bar, where he was already fussing with drinks. Furtively snuffing out a cigarette, he asked, "Getcha something?"

"Maybe later, thanks—need to work on your Wi-Fi."

"That, I admit, is priority one. Have at it, Dante."

The electronics were in a hallway leading to one of the bedroom wings. The closet was next to a window that gave me a clear view of the pool area. I noticed that a long outdoor table had been set for brunch, shaded by the rear overhang of the house.

On the patio near the guesthouse, Harold's sister, Heather, lounged with her companion, Näzh, under one of the big white umbrellas. Both wore dark sunglasses. She was reading a thick hardcover book; he scrolled his phone.

In the pool, Heather's daughter, Brooke, frolicked with her boyfriend. Light-skinned Brooke wore olive-tinted glasses and a floppy straw hat; dark-skinned Tyler did not.

After restoring the Wi-Fi connection, I returned to the great room, where Rebecca was setting out a few serving dishes, empty, on a long table to be used as a self-serve buffet, just indoors from the patio. Harold stepped over from the bar, sipping something brown in a highball glass and checking Rebecca's progress in the kitchen.

Jazz sat with Keith on a sofa near the fireplace, out of earshot from the rest of us, presumably discussing details of her contract and services.

Dingdong.

Feeling adrift in the middle of the great room, I made myself useful and went to answer the door. As expected, Richard and Zola had arrived—together.

"Good *morning*, dah-ling," said Zola, leaning to kiss my cheek.

I checked my watch. "Afternoon, actually. Sleep well?"

She shook a finger at me.

Richard said, "Seems we're the last to arrive. Hope we're not late." He carried a wine caddy with four bottles in it as he moved to the kitchen island. I noticed that he had a curious spring in his step, but I refused to consider that it might be due to... *afterglow.* A far more plausible theory was that he simply enjoyed Zola's company.

"Howdy, cousin!" said Harold, joining Richard and inspecting the wine.

Zola took me aside, asking *sotto voce*, "How's the harridan today?"

"If you're asking about Wendy, I haven't seen her yet."

"Good," said Zola, setting down her purse, the same brocade satchel she'd brought yesterday. "That bigoted bitch made the last two gatherings unbearable—and I am *not* up for a third."

"Now, now. You're a guest in her home, remember."

Zola glanced about, assessing her surroundings. With a wry smile, she said, "Nice place—but anyone can *rent* it."

The smell of bacon was joined by other aromas—roasting chicken, baking bread, scrambled eggs, cheesy sauces, hot maple syrup, fruity glazes, cinnamon, fennel, thyme—as the brunch preparations neared completion. Harold was pouring wine at the table as Brooke and Tyler got out of the pool and took turns toweling each other dry. Heather and Näzh got up from their lounge chairs and spritzed each other's faces with Evian water.

When Harold stepped inside with an empty wine bottle and fetched a full one, Keith asked him, "Hey, Dad. Where's Wendy?"

Unconcerned, Harold said, "She couldn't get to sleep last night, so she's probably zonked out. Could one of you gals let her know it's chow time?" And he left with the wine.

The gals in the room were Zola, Rebecca, and Jazz. Since Zola and Rebecca would surely have preferred to let Wendy sleep all day, Jazz said, "I'll rouse her." Then she asked me, "Where's her room?"

"C'mon." And I led Jazz down the hall to the bedroom wing assigned to Wendy and Harold. One of the doors was open, with sunlight pouring into the room from curtains drawn wide; the bed was mussed, but unoccupied, with a carton of cigarettes on the nightstand. Out in the hall, the other bedroom door was closed.

I rapped on it. "Mrs. Gibkin?"

We waited, then Jazz knocked. "Wendy? Time to eat." After a few seconds, she called, "The others are waiting."

Jazz and I glanced at each other. I gave her a nod.

She rapped on the door again, then opened it slowly and took a step in.

From where I stood, just outside the doorway, I could see that the room was still darkened for sleep, with the blackout drapes drawn. The only light came from the dim glow of a small lamp on the bedside table. In the rumple of sheets, Wendy hadn't been roused by our knocking.

I reached inside for the light switch and turned on a bright ceiling fixture.

Jazz exhaled a low, deflating whistle. "Oops," she said quietly.

We approached the bed with slow, solemn steps.

There lay Wendy Gibkin's lifeless body, sprawled in the mess of her own vomit. On the nightstand, a toiletries kit, zipped open, had come to rest on its side, with its contents strewn wildly about. And next to the empty bag sat a small ceramic ramekin that resembled a soufflé dish.

It, too, was empty.

PART TWO
CLOSED CIRCLE

CHAPTER
FOUR

Plans for that lazy Sunday brunch took a sudden turn when Jazz reported the suspicious death, phoning Detective Arcie Madera, of the Riverside County sheriff's department, on her private number. Arcie was not on duty that day, but she summoned a response team from the sheriff's substation in nearby Palm Desert and told Jazz that she'd catch up with them at the rental house in Rancho Mirage—"as soon as I can get *dressed*," I heard her say over Jazz's phone.

We were still in Wendy's bedroom when Jazz finished her call. I heaved a sigh before saying, "Time to alert the others, I guess." She nodded, and we left the room as we'd found it, closing the door behind us.

When we emerged from the hallway and into the great room, activity was at a festive pitch. Rebecca arranged an assortment of steaming platters on the buffet table. Some of the guests were already circling the table, sampling what they could with their fingers. Some topped up their drinks at the bar, while others mingled and gabbed—all of this against a background of tropical-themed party music and the happy rhythm of steel drums. You could practically smell the coconut oil.

Zola stood near the kitchen island, checking her makeup in a little mirror from her big purse. On the opposite side of the island, Richard turned to open one of the doors of the extra-wide

Sub-Zero. I noticed that he had a spoon in one hand as he reached with the other to remove one of the ceramic ramekins from the refrigerator. Jazz, wide-eyed, also saw it.

I yelled, "*No*, Richard—don't eat it!"

All heads turned. Conversation stopped. The plunking of the steel drums now seemed to mock the deadness of the room.

"But, but"—Richard stammered—"whyever *not*?"

Jazz asked anyone, "Where's Mr. Gibkin?"

Keith said, "I think Dad's out back—for a smoke. Why?"

I said, "He needs to hear this. Could you get him, please?"

Looking confused and concerned, Keith trotted out to the patio.

Richard told me, "I just wanted to make sure the posset had set properly."

"I know. But there might be a... a problem with it."

Richard held the ramekin near his eyes, scrutinizing it. He sniffed it. Then he set it aside, on the counter, taking a cautious step backward.

Keith appeared from the patio with his father in tow. Stepping into the room, Harold blustered, "What the devil's going on?" A half-smoked cigarette jiggled between his lips.

Keith pulled it from his mouth and took it over to the kitchen sink, dropping it in the disposal.

"Harold," I said somberly, "something's happened to Wendy."

After a wary pause, he asked, "Whataya mean—'happened'?"

Jazz said, "Your wife is dead, sir." She added, "I'm so sorry."

Someone turned off the steel drums.

Harold didn't believe it. He wanted to see Wendy, but Jazz wouldn't let him: "You'll be asked to identify her soon enough."

Struggling for words, he asked, "But what *happened*?"

I said, "It appears she ate a cup of the lemon posset last night."

Richard stepped over to Harold, fretting, "They seem to think my posset was *poisoned.*"

Harold told everyone, "It wasn't *poisoned,*" as if we were dense. "Not possible—because I had some myself. This morning. And I've never felt better."

Then we heard the approaching sirens.

Jazz took over, leading the medical and forensics teams through the hushed crowd in the great room, then down the hall to Wendy's bedroom.

I remained with the others, waiting for Detective Madera to arrive. The party was over before it began, but some of the guests tried to pick at the food.

Zola sidled over to us. "I don't suppose we can leave, can we?"

"Nope," I said, shaking my head. "I'm sure there'll be questions for Richard, since he made the posset. But *you're* not off the hook, either—they'll want to take statements from everyone."

She rolled her eyes.

Isandro said, "Sorry, Z-Doll."

She muttered something.

I couldn't help asking, "Penny for your thoughts?"

Zola didn't mince words: "That *dreadful* woman. Wendy—even in death, she's a pain in the ass."

My dear old friend's reaction to that afternoon's tragic development might have struck me as callous, but I sensed she was not alone in her harsh judgment of Wendy.

Certainly, many of the guests appeared stunned, or at least rattled, by Wendy's unexpected demise. Her husband was mournful and soppy as a result of his loss. Richard was agitated and fearful due to the role his dessert had apparently played in the death. And the younger men—Keith, Näzh, and Tyler—displayed a fitting measure of sympathy for the deceased as well as respect for the gravity of the situation.

The same could not be said, however, for the women. Zola, of course, had not hesitated to voice her feelings. No one else *said* it—at least not to me—but as I watched Rebecca Jiang, Heather Ferris, and her daughter, Brooke, they signaled not the slightest sign of grief. Quite the opposite. Their faces, their manner, their glances, the inflections of their speech—these were all easily decoded as satisfaction and relief that Wendy was gone.

Engrossed in these thoughts, I hadn't noticed the arrival of Arcie Madera. When the first responders arrived, we had left the front door wide open, and now the sheriff's detective approached Isandro and me in the great room.

I set down a sausage link I'd been nibbling, wiped my fingers, and extended my hand. "Hello, Arcie. Thanks for coming over—on a Sunday, no less."

Offering a little hug as well as a shake, she reminded me with a grin, "The law never rests."

"You're right," I said. "It seems we've been through this before." She had worked with Jazz and me on a few prior cases, and I had come to admire her—and like her. She was a consummate professional, a credit to her department. What's more, as a Latina in her mid-fifties, she had struggled more than most to prove herself and to rise through the male-dominated ranks of law enforcement. That background had equally impressed Jazz, who had come to view Arcie as a role model.

She turned to Isandro. "Mind if I borrow your boyfriend? I need someone to show me to the scene of the incident."

Isandro replied with a thumbs-up.

In the brightly lit bedroom, a photographer snapped every

possible detail of the scene, including each item that had been scattered from the toiletries kit. The ramekin and the spoon had been bagged as evidence, as had a sample of vomit from the bed. The medical examiner hunkered near the edge of the bed, peering at the body and making notes.

He told Arcie, "The victim exhibits a lingering skin rash on the upper parts of her body, as well as swollen eyes and lips. Examination of the upper airway revealed that the throat and tongue were also swollen—and obstructed by vomit. My initial diagnosis is that she died by asphyxiation as the result of choking."

I said, "She was known to have lots of 'food issues,' including allergies and bulimia."

Jazz said, "The allergies—could that have caused anaphylactic shock?"

The medical examiner stood, nodding. "That was my first guess, and it remains my best theory. We'll know more after analysis of the vomit and stomach contents."

Arcie asked, "Time of death?"

"Temperature, rigor, and lividity of the body—coupled with the fact that the room had been closed and held at a steady seventy degrees—the totality of that puts her death between ten and twelve hours ago."

Arcie looked up from the notes she was taking. "That means she died after midnight—sometime between one and three o'clock."

"Sounds about right," said the medical examiner. "I'll be able to narrow that down after getting the body back to the lab."

Arcie asked Jazz and me, "When you entered the room earlier, did you leave everything exactly as you found it?"

Jazz said, "Of course."

I added, "Only the bedside night-light was turned on. We

turned on the ceiling light to get a better look at what happened. The door was closed but unlocked before we entered, and that's how we left it afterward."

Arcie turned to the medical examiner, asking, "Just to be clear: There were no external wounds on the body? No signs of a struggle?"

"None at all. By all appearances, whatever did this to her, it was something she ate."

I thought aloud, "And she was *very* careful about what she ate—annoying as hell, in fact."

Jazz reminded me, "She treated it as a matter of life or death."

"And if that was the case," said Arcie, "if she knew she had life-threatening allergies, and if she was always careful—wouldn't she have carried an EpiPen?" Arcie was referring to a gadget used to self-inject epinephrine, which counteracts allergic reactions in an emergency, making it easier to breathe.

The medical examiner said, "Under those circumstances, *I'd* certainly carry one. She'd be nuts if she didn't."

Arcie followed up: "So, did she try using an EpiPen when this happened? Did she even *have* one?"

He crossed his arms, shook his head. "It's the first thing we looked for. If she had one, she probably kept it in that Dopp kit—there were other meds in it, along with everything else that got scattered around, but no EpiPen. We've checked everywhere: floor, drawers, bedding, bathroom, the works. If she had one with her, she couldn't find it, and neither could we."

Arcie, Jazz, and I let this sink in for a moment.

"Which means," said Arcie, tapping her pen on her pad, "Mrs. Gibkin could have been the victim of an accident—consuming an unknown ingredient and then losing, or forgetting to bring, her EpiPen."

"Or," said Jazz, continuing with Arcie's logic, "Mrs. Gibkin could have been the victim of murder—consuming posset that had been deliberately tampered with by someone, who also snatched her EpiPen."

Arcie scrunched her brow. "What's 'posset'?"

I told her, "It's like a custard. Richard Gibbs made a batch yesterday, here, and then let it refrigerate overnight, to be served as dessert today. But it couldn't have been 'poisoned,' not in the classic sense, because Wendy's husband said he tried some this morning, and he's fine."

"Meaning," said Jazz, "if the recipe was spiked with something, it was lethal only to Wendy—which would prove the intent to kill."

I recalled, "There were endless opportunities to spike the recipe. The situation in the kitchen was chaotic while Richard was working on it. People were hauling luggage through the great room, deciding on bedrooms. Lots of back-and-forth. And Richard let others take over the stirring as the mixture cooked. Everyone pitched in—with both the luggage and the stirring—so if the posset was spiked, *anyone* could have done it."

Arcie told the forensics techs, "Be sure to take a sample of this posset stuff and order an analysis of what's in it."

I said, "Probably the first thing to check for is honey. During dinner on Friday night, while Wendy was making one of her many visits to the powder room, her husband mentioned that she was severely allergic to it. I gathered she had many allergens, but he wasn't specific about any of the others."

The forensics team began collecting their gear. The medical examiner asked Arcie, "Okay if we move the body from the bed, Detective?"

"Sure. Let's get her on a gurney."

Jazz said, "The husband asked to see her. I told him you'd probably want a formal ID."

Arcie turned to the medical team, "Clean her up."

Jazz left the room to summon Harold.

The full impact of what had happened finally hit Harold, now a widower, when he entered the bedroom and saw the obscured form of Wendy's body laid out on a gurney, covered with a sheet. As the medical examiner folded it back to reveal her face, Harold vented his grief with a loud moan. Sobbing, he managed to tell us, "Yes, that's her. That's Wendy Ames Gibkin. She was my wife."

The scene out in the great room was no less somber as the medical team wheeled the gurney through the house and out the front door, followed by the forensics team—and the gaping stares of all the guests. Arcie Madera remained at the house with two deputies.

We waited for her to speak. The Gibkin-Ferris party now numbered seven, rather than eight, joined by Zola, Richard, Isandro, Jazz, and me. So there were twelve of us—an even dozen—wondering what was next. No one made a sound, except Harold, who still wept. Fumbling, he lit a cigarette. I let it go.

Arcie said, "Hello, everyone. I'm Detective Madera from the Riverside County sheriff's department, which provides police services to the city of Rancho Mirage. First, let me extend my condolences. The sudden loss of your friend and loved one must surely come as a shock. Unfortunately, because of the suspicious circumstances surrounding Mrs. Gibkin's death, I'll need to intrude on your grief and spend some time this afternoon questioning you as a group—and some of you individually. In addition, my deputies will take turns with each of you, taking statements and exclusionary fingerprints, but also asking questions that will help establish a timeline of what happened. Your cooperation will be appreciated."

"How long will this take?" asked Heather the horsewoman, sister-in-law of the deceased.

"Maybe an hour. Maybe two," said Arcie. "If you'd care to get comfortable—have something to drink or find a seat—you can take care of that now."

Everyone began to mill about, engaging in quiet conversation, which seemed to dispel the immediate tension. Richard and Zola claimed a settee for themselves near the fireplace. As Zola sat down, Richard said, "I think I'll get a glass of water. Something for you?"

"No, thank you, dah-ling. But could you bring me my purse?"

"With pleasure."

During this pause, Arcie summoned Jazz and me with a finger-wag.

When we joined her, standing at the end of the front hall where it opened into the great room, she gestured toward the assembly, asking, "Is this everyone? Meaning, has anyone *else* been inside the house this weekend?"

I said, "I wasn't here overnight, but otherwise, I've been here since everyone arrived yesterday—and they're all here now." Needlessly, I added, "Except Wendy."

Arcie said, "I noticed security cameras outside. Any *inside*?"

"No. But if anyone 'dropped by' last night while I wasn't here, the perimeter cameras would catch it. I'll have the security service call you." I gave Arcie the name of my contact.

"Perfect," she said. "Thanks."

"So," said Jazz, mulling all this, "if no one else came to the house last night, and if Wendy was murdered, her killer is in this room."

With a nod—and a trace of a wry grin—Arcie said, "Logically, yes, that seems to be the case. A neat and tidy case, at that."

I noted, "How *very* Agatha Christie."

Jazz suppressed a smile while giving me a dirty look.

Richard had poured himself a glass of water and returned to join Zola on the settee, placing her purse on the end table next to him. Others had fetched cocktails; a few had made up small plates of food before finding a seat, then picking at brunch items from their laps. Harold had found a saucer, which he used as an ashtray as he sat and smoked and used the side of his hand to wipe snot from his upper lip.

Arcie cleared her throat. "It seems everyone is settled, so let's get started. I have a few basic questions for all of you, as a group. First, is it true that you were all here, on the premises, from the time you arrived yesterday until now? Just nod or speak up, as you wish."

The seven members of the Gibkin-Ferris party all nodded, some making affirmative comments. Zola, Richard, Isandro, Jazz, and I—who had not spent the night at the rental property—gave details of our arrivals and departures.

"Second," said Arcie, "all of you who slept here, can you vouch for each other? In other words, did any of you ever notice another guest's conspicuous absence?"

They weren't so quick to respond this time. I explained to Arcie, "Four of the guests slept in the detached guesthouse, and the other four, including Wendy, slept here in the main house, so they can't conclusively account for each other during the night." All of them nodded, in agreement with my explanation.

Harold raised his hand.

Arcie said, "Yes, Mr. Gibkin?"

"Detective," he said, "it sounds sorta like you're asking us to provide *alibis* for each other, as if we're all *suspects*. But that's nuts."

Keith told him, "No, Dad, it's not. By any objective measure, the investigation needs to treat *all* of us as potential suspects at this early stage. If Wendy's death was anything but accidental, the police need to start by figuring out which of us can be crossed off the list."

"He's right," said Arcie. She then asked Keith, "And you are…?"

"My name is Keith Gibkin. Wendy was my stepmother. And I'm an attorney."

"Ah," said Arcie, taking notes. "Perhaps each of you in the visiting party could introduce yourselves with a bit of background. That'll help move things along."

I already knew all of their names, but I did not know the occupations of either Näzh Hoyle or Tyler Evans, the "companions" brought along by Heather Ferris and her daughter, Brooke.

So I listened with interest as Näzh described himself as Heather's "spiritual adviser." He explained, "I'm a manifester. The practice of manifestation affects the pathways of our brains. It's a mental exercise that helps achieve desired real-world outcomes. Journals, mantras, 'scripting,' and vision boards are tools that help motivate us to reach our goals. In short, you might say that I'm Heather's manifestation guru." He twitched his eyebrows and broke into an odd grin—like a Cheshire Cat wearing a bejeweled collar and an exotic white tunic.

Heather listened to all this with a straight face, making me wonder if she considered it mumbo jumbo. Or did she actually buy into it?

I noted that Keith had also been listening to Näzh. Intently.

The last of the group to introduce himself was Brooke's boyfriend, Tyler—the short, bookish Black guy with tortoiseshell glasses. I learned that he was a graphic designer and digital illustrator, working freelance jobs. "So this visit isn't really a vacation for me. Wherever I've got my laptop, I'm busy."

I leaned to ask Jazz quietly, "Cute, huh? Like a puppy dog. Totally cuddle-worthy."

Under her breath, she replied, "Down, boy. That dog is *straight*."

Arcie told Tyler, as well as the others, "Thank you. This is helpful. But before we continue, I need to mention that this investigation has barely begun, and it'll go on for some time. I'm sure we'll need to talk to each of you again, probably more than once, so it's important that all of you remain here for a while."

Harold said, "We planned to be here for a month, Detective, and I sure as hell want to get to the bottom of this. So we're here if you need us."

Keith raised a finger, catching Arcie's attention.

"Yes, Mr. Gibkin?"

He approached her with his business card and handed it to her. "As I mentioned, I'm an attorney. I have cases pending and court dates. I never planned to be here the entire month, but I can easily stay for the next few days. My intention was to drive back and forth when I can."

Arcie nodded. "Since you're a sworn officer of the court, I think you can be trusted, Mr. Gibkin. But if I'm wrong, I'll know how to find you." She cracked a smile while pocketing his card.

The two deputies conferred with her briefly, then she told everyone, "We still need to take statements from each of you, as well as your fingerprints, and to expedite that, the deputies and I will set up three conference areas in opposite corners of the room, with perhaps one of us out on the patio, to provide some privacy for the interviews. That way, we'll each process four of you, and then we can wrap this up for today."

Isandro and Keith joined me as we pitched in to help move a few tables and chairs about. When everything was arranged, Arcie began interviewing Harold at the far end of the room. One of the deputies sat down with Keith at the island in the kitchen, and the other sat with Rebecca on the patio. That left nine of us gathered in the conversation area of the great room, awaiting our turns.

Zola and Richard were still on the settee near the fireplace, gabbing quietly. Not far from them, I sat with Isandro and Jazz, scrolling our phones, killing time. I could hear Zola offering Richard words of reassurance that he could not possibly be responsible for Wendy's death, even if the posset had been involved. I was sure she was right—if Wendy had died as the result of foul play, the killer had to be one of the guests staying at the rental house.

During a pause in her conversation with Richard, Zola discreetly cupped a hand over her mouth and sniffed her own breath. With a grimace, she asked him, "Could you hand me my purse?" Like most men, I have always been mystified by the secret contents of ladies' purses, but I deduced that Zola's big brocade satchel must have contained mints or breath spray among its personal sundries and frilly whatnot. It was sufficiently spacious to have also carried a complete change of clothes, plus shoes.

With a chuckle, Richard patted Zola's knee, telling her, "I am here but to serve, *mia decorina*." He turned to reach for the purse over the high, rolled arm the settee, but his grasp was uncertain, jerking the strap, which not only knocked a small lamp off the end table, but also sent the purse itself tumbling to the floor, where the wide mouth of the open bag disgorged its *many* contents, which—frankly—looked like a trash heap.

We gasped in unison, averting our eyes, sympathizing with the humiliation of having milady's stash so unceremoniously bared. Richard stood, horrified, stammering lame words of apology.

But Zola laughed, also standing. "Good excuse to get organized—this was *long* overdue."

I considered offering to help, but I knew instinctively that this, if anything, was *women's* work. Jazz leapt to the rescue of her sister in distress, helping Zola remove the purse and its contents from the floor, placing everything on the cushion of the settee for sorting. They huddled over it like surgeons working on a hit-and-run.

I picked up the lamp (a survivor of the accident), set it back on the table, and moved out of the way, nattering with Richard and Isandro, trying not to watch—but hell, who could resist?

Jazz and Zola gabbed amiably while tending to the task at hand, but then their conversation abruptly stopped. In a decidedly different tone, Jazz asked, "What the *fuck*?" She handed something to Zola, who turned to give the rest of us a look.

"How odd," she said. It was a clear plastic squeeze bottle in the shape of a teddy bear, almost empty. "It's... honey."

On the other side of the room, Detective Madera dropped her questioning of Harold and turned in her seat to face Zola with a hard, blank stare.

Richard stepped in for a closer look and scrutinized the label. "Raw, natural, unpasteurized, pure premium honey—it's the *good* stuff, all right. When I tasted the posset mixture yesterday, before setting the ramekins in the fridge, I thought it had a certain *je ne sais quoi*—a pleasant but unexpected earthiness."

I reminded him, "Wendy Gibkin had a severe honey allergy. We heard about it Friday night."

"Oh," he mumbled, "good heavens."

Jazz turned from the settee, handing something else to Zola. "There's also this."

Zola showed it to us, bewildered. It looked like a chubby cigar tube, covered with yellow and orange warning labels. She asked, "What the devil *is* it?"

Striding over to us, Detective Madera answered Zola's question: "That's an EpiPen."

Caught with the goods, Zola found that her chances of being quickly scratched from the list of potential suspects ... evaporated. I *knew* in my heart that she didn't kill Wendy. Obviously, the killer had planted the incriminating evidence in Zola's purse, a lame attempt to frame her for the crime. Ridiculous. And Detective Madera knew Zola well enough to reach that same conclusion.

Objectively, though, Arcie couldn't simply dismiss what had just happened. She would need to follow up, and when she did, she would learn from multiple witnesses about Friday night's food fight and screaming match between Zola and Wendy. What's more, Zola had subsequently made no effort to mask her disdain for the deceased, telling me that Wendy was a "bigoted bitch" and a "pain in the ass." God only knows what she might have said to the others.

There on the spot, Arcie questioned Zola about the honey and the EpiPen while a deputy bagged those items as evidence. Zola, of course, denied any knowledge of how they had ended up in her purse, pointing out that she hadn't even recognized what the EpiPen *was*. Her denial was both credible and plausible—but the same denial could easily be made by the actual killer.

Arcie didn't grill Zola, didn't cuff her and recite her rights, didn't haul her away. But it was clear enough that, for now, Zola was not only a suspect, but she sat at the top of the list. As this new reality set in, Richard tried to comfort Zola, whose usual wisecracks and smart-mouthing now failed her—this was *no* laughing matter.

Isandro, Jazz, and I stood a few feet away, mumbling our concerns to each other, none of us doubting that Zola had been set up. Keith Gibkin joined us, sharing our concern but suggesting, from his perspective as a lawyer, that the case against Zola could probably not be made to stick. He repeated, "*Probably.*" But it was clear that his sympathies rested solidly with our friend, not with his late stepmother. I was grateful for his support, but not surprised by it, as he'd been on the receiving end of Wendy's brazen homophobia.

What did surprise me, though, was the support of Keith's father, Harold—the murdered woman's husband—who stepped over to our huddle and joined us. The tobacco on his breath was overwhelming at close range, but at least, at the moment, there was no lit cigarette involved. Wedging himself between his son and me, he yoked our shoulders with his arms and swung his head, saying, "It's a rotten shame. Whoever did this to Zola—what a raw deal."

Jazz caught my eye with a weird expression. She, too, had noticed that Harold had made a remarkable recovery from his earlier weeping and grief, and now, only a few hours since the discovery of his wife's death, he didn't even mention her name. Instead, he was lamenting Zola's predicament.

I recalled a fleeting incident on Friday evening at Richard's estate, when I ducked into the kitchen to see how dinner preparations were going. Harold had been talking about plans for entertaining at the rental house over the next few days and insisted that Zola *must* attend—because it "wouldn't be much of a party without you." In response, she had tittered like an ingenue, telling him coyly, "I'll check my calendar."

At the time, I couldn't help interpreting this as a come-on from Harold, but I doubted that he'd found Zola attractive *that* way. Though a stylish woman with sparkle and pizazz, she was nearly eighty—old enough to be his mother. Which made me wonder if Harold had concluded, mistakenly, that Zola was a woman of means who might be an easy mark for investment in his Atmos-Phuel venture. If he had yet to be disillusioned of this, was he still trying to wheedle himself into her affections?

"Keith," he said, turning to face his son, inches away, practically nose to nose, "it looks like Zola might need our help. Can I put you on retainer to represent her?"

Keith appeared no less gobsmacked than I felt. "*Dad*," he said, "that might create a conflict of interest—for me. There's no telling what turns this investigation could take, and at some point, *you* might need a lawyer. Or I could end up defending *myself*. Point is, I shouldn't represent more than one person in this case, and if I take on Zola, that closes other options."

"Hmmm," said Harold, scrunching his face, grinding his gears. Then he brightened. "How about *you*, Jazz?"

"*Me?* I'm not a lawyer."

"I know that. But you're a private eye. And right now, it seems to me that the surest way to get Zola off the hook is to prove who really *did* kill Wendy."

Jazz told him, "Detective Madera is already working on that."

"Yeah, yeah, yeah. But *her* interests in this case aren't necessarily *our* interests."

Jazz was firm. "The *sole* interest we have in this case is: the truth. Only your wife's killer wants an 'alternate truth.'"

Harold nodded. "Understood. Even so, two heads are better than one, and I'd like to put you to work on Zola's behalf. I mean, we *know* she didn't do it. Right?"

Jazz paused. "I don't come cheap."

"I'm sure you don't. Whataya say?"

He'd made a good pitch, but I wondered if Jazz saw her own conflict of interest—she'd already agreed to work for Harold's son, digging for dirt on Harold's personal assistant, Rebecca Jiang (who, just then, was carrying platters from the buffet table to the kitchen, dumping picked-over brunch items into an enormous black trash bag).

If Jazz had reservations about any of this, she didn't let on. "Tell you what," she said to Harold. "Let's discuss this tomorrow morning at my office in downtown Palm Springs." She gave him her card. "Ten thirty?"

He took the card. Winked at her. "We're on."

Meanwhile, that Sunday afternoon, Detective Madera and the deputies left the rental house shortly after three o'clock. Soon after that, Zola left with Richard, both of them exhausted, returning to his home in Palm Springs. Jazz had asked if I could join her on "an important errand" and then dinner that evening. With a smooch, Isandro agreed to drive my car back to the coach house. "No worries," he told me. "I'm a big boy—I can fend for myself tonight."

Riding with Jazz as she pulled her SUV out of the parking court, I said, "This was unexpected. What's on the agenda?"

"I need to pick up Emma at her father's house; she'll be with me this week. But as long as we're there, I thought we could talk to Christopher about Zola's situation."

Jazz's ex-husband owned a prominent law firm in Palm Springs.

"Good idea," I told her. "Hope we won't need him—but you never know."

"And then," said Jazz, "we'll take Emma over to Blade's place." She was referring to her artist friend, Blade Wade.

I said, "I thought he was in LA."

"He was, but he texted this afternoon while he was driving back. Sounded happy about something. Said he'd pick up some steaks and fix dinner."

"And that involves *me*?"

"Well, brunch was a fizzle. I figured we both need a good meal. He said to bring you."

"Nice." I enjoyed the company of both of the men in Jazz's life—her ex, as well as her current love interest.

Within twenty minutes, we were cruising into a north-side neighborhood in Palm Springs near the historic Movie Colony, where Christopher Friendly lived. We parked near the low wall surrounding the house, which Jazz had once shared with Christopher.

The gate along the sidewalk was open, so we didn't bother buzzing. As we walked up the path toward the house, the front door swung open, and Emma skipped out to the stoop. "Hi, Mommy. Hi, Dante." Having just turned five, starting kindergarten, she wore a pretty pink frock on that Sunday afternoon—perhaps her father had taken her somewhere dressy for a nice lunch. Her butterscotch complexion and dark, wondering eyes reflected her biracial parentage. Black hair, worn in an asymmetrical burst of tight braids, flopped over one shoulder.

Jazz hunkered down to kiss her daughter, pulling her into a hug. I leaned to hug her as well. Then Jazz and I each took one of Emma's hands as we entered the house together.

"Dante!" said Christopher, who apparently hadn't known I was coming. He gave Jazz a dutiful peck, but said to me, "Great to see you again."

"Good to see you, too, Christopher." And it *was* good to see him. He wore light, tailored slacks and smart Italian loafers with a crisp dress shirt—collar open, cuffs turned up a few inches. Seeing him now, I doubled down on my earlier impression that he strongly resembled Keith Gibkin. Not only were they both lawyers, about the same age, but they also had similar features and the same sense of style. *And*, although Christopher had not openly acknowledged it, I was fairly certain they were both gay.

Had Jazz not yet noticed how *alike* the two men were? I found it hard to miss.

Christopher walked us through the large comfortable house to the kitchen, which opened to a casual entertaining area, with a mammoth TV on the far wall. It was not turned on, but music played in the background. Emma scampered off to her bedroom, presumably to put her things together for the routine shuttling between households. Christopher asked Jazz and me, "Can I get you something?"

Just water for Jazz, but I followed Christopher's suggestion to try the bottle of French rosé he had opened. "Nothing special," he said, "but it's dry and drinkable." Tasting it, I found it far better than he had led me to expect.

As we settled in chairs around a low table, Jazz asked Christopher, "Good weekend with Emma?"

He beamed. "As always. It never fails to amaze me—she keeps herself so busy and *engaged*. Painting, dance lessons, and now school. I know it's 'just kindergarten,' but Emma, somehow, manages to *apply* herself to it." He laughed. "Where did she get *that*?"

He and Jazz looked at each other, shrugged, and said in unison, "Not *me*."

Chuckling about this, Christopher asked her, "You've heard the latest about the fundraiser, haven't you?"

She nodded. "Got the e-blast from school." She turned and explained to me, "Gilded Palms is planning an addition to their creative-arts building, so it's time for the 'school family' to pony up. There's an ongoing pledge drive—it'll take a few years, I guess—but the kickoff event is next weekend with a *big* la-di-da dinner and auction, hosted by a student's parents at Wasi'chu Hills." She was referring to one of the oldest, toniest country clubs in the valley, located in Rancho Mirage.

Christopher said, "The usual dinner, drinks, dancing, and auction. But in keeping with the purpose of the funding drive, there'll be a program that includes a *ballet* performance."

Under her breath, Jazz asked me, "Can you guess where this is headed?"

I laughed. "Don't tell me—little Emma will make her stage debut."

"*Yes*," said Christopher, the doting dad. "Don't get me wrong. I know how *dreadful* these things can be. But unless I'm mistaken, this should be *fab*-ulous."

"Well, of *course*," I said. "Emma's in it."

"Not just that. Guess who's going to *direct* it."

I looked to Jazz for help, but she replied with an empty shrug. I told Christopher, "Sorry, I'm clueless."

"Well, here's a clue, and a mighty big one." With a tantalizing wink, he said, "Directing it will be none other than Servando Ureña himself."

Jazz gave me another empty shrug.

Christopher groaned. "Ughh. The two of you—how could

you *not* know this? Servando Ureña is the visiting dance master at Gilded Palms School for the Gifted. He's semiretired from a long, storied career, and now he's doing his bit to nurture the next generation of ballet artists. Emma adores him—and frankly, who wouldn't?"

"Oh?" I asked. Christopher had caught my interest.

He flapped his hands, fanning his face. "Oh, *mama*. Servando has strutted his stuff on the greatest stages of the world, performing encore after encore to standing ovations from sold-out audiences left weeping by not only his artistry, but his sheer athleticism. And now, he's right here at Gilded Palms." Christopher lowered his voice, telling us in a confidential tone, "Word is, he *might* indulge us with a solo at next weekend's festivities."

"Sounds wonderful," I said.

Jazz turned to Christopher. "We have room, don't we?"

He quickly counted on his fingers. "Why, yes!" Turning to me, he said, "I popped for a table, Dante. Why don't you join us on Saturday night? Isandro, too."

Jazz gave me a discreet, eager nod, telegraphing that she'd appreciate my company. Were the other guests hopelessly stodgy?

I tossed my hands. "How could I possibly decline such a delightful offer? And I'll extend your invitation to Isandro as well—he'll love it."

"*Fab*-ulous," said Christopher.

"Will it be ... formal attire?"

"That's not *strictly* required. But I'll dig out my tux."

I nodded. Message received.

Emma popped out from her bedroom. "Ready, Mommy."

"Just a few minutes, honey. I need to talk to Daddy about something."

"Okay," she chirped, then disappeared into her room, where a trove of amusements surely awaited her.

Christopher gave Jazz a curious look. "What's up?"

"Do you remember Zola Lorinsky, Dante's decorator friend?"

With a soft laugh, he said, "She's hard to *forget*. Quite a character. She made the curtains for your office, right?"

"Correct. She's not only a character, but an absolute sweetheart."

I interjected, "And she may be in trouble."

Christopher looked skeptical. "Zola? In trouble? How?"

Jazz and I took turns explaining what had happened. I then wrapped up the story, telling Christopher, "With the evidence found in Zola's bag—essentially proving that Wendy Gibkin was murdered—the prime suspect is suddenly Zola herself, even though we're convinced that someone tried to frame her."

Jazz added, "I'm sure Arcie Madera understands this, but she has to follow procedure—so the investigation begins."

Christopher asked, "Did you discuss it with Detective Madera?"

"No, not directly, not yet. It wasn't the time or the place."

He nodded. "Well, naturally, I agree—Zola is clearly the innocent victim of a setup, not a scheming killer. But I'm glad you've brought this to me."

"If needed," said Jazz, "could you help her out?"

"Of course. Say no more."

"Keep track of your time, and we'll figure out the rest later."

"Stop that," said Christopher. "If I'm needed, I'll be happy to pitch in—and chalk it off as *pro bono*."

He and Jazz shared an affectionate smile. It seemed to transcend the years of their breakup, stretching back to the time that had drawn them together.

And then he turned to me—with the very same smile.

Emma was ensconced in her child seat behind Jazz and me in the ferocious black SUV as we pulled away from Christopher's house and began the short crosstown trek to Blade Wade's studio. The vehicle swerved as Jazz turned her head, telling her daughter, "Put your headphones on, honey."

I knew from experience: this meant that Jazz intended to unload a few choice words not meant for tender ears. She waited as Emma got into her pink plastic headphones and began humming along to some childish tune. Sitting in the passenger seat, I braced myself for a flurry of boisterous expletives.

But I was wrong. Her tone was soft and earnest, almost secretive, as she glanced over, asking, "Did you *notice*?"

With an uncertain laugh, I asked, "Could you be more specific?"

"Christopher. And Keith Gibkin. Did you notice the *resemblance*?"

"Uh, now that you mention it—"

She elaborated, "Not just the *physical* similarities. The same *vibe*."

"Actually," I said, "I noticed that the first time I saw Keith, on Friday night. I wondered if it was just my imagination, but now *you've* picked up on it. Strange, huh?"

She considered this for a moment. "Yeah, but not 'bad-strange.' It's just unusual, unexpected. Sorta 'cool-strange,' if you think about it."

It was time to stop dancing around what was really on our minds. I said, "Keith is gay. He's open and comfortable with it. On the other hand..."

"On the other hand"—Jazz nodded—"Christopher was always a mystery to me."

Jazz and I had already discussed this more than once. She had sensed something in Christopher even when he married her and later fathered their child. I had presumed she was just masking her own insecurities—until I finally met Christopher, who instantly tripped my gaydar. His behavior slipped into and out of being queeny, or even flirtatious, but he consistently seemed to have no self-awareness of what he was doing or why he was doing it. To describe him as merely "closeted" didn't begin to cover it. He was apparently in such deep denial that he didn't even understand there was something to deny.

Though they were no longer married, I knew that Christopher loved Jazz. I also knew, deep down, that he needed something else. I had confided to Jazz that I thought he was "bisexual," a term that usually struck me as a cop-out (like an atheist claiming to be agnostic). During that same conversation about Christopher, Jazz had told me, in a moment of supreme honesty, "He deserves to be happy."

Now, as we pondered this in the SUV, the silence was broken only by the thrum of the tires on the asphalt—and by Emma's humming in the back seat.

When Jazz gently cleared her throat, I turned to look at her.

She spoke while watching the road ahead: "They say opposites attract. But I think the same can be true for two people who are so much alike that they might be meant for each other."

"Good point," I said slyly. "But Christopher and Keith haven't even met—yet."

Blade Wade's home and studio shared a large space above the ground floor of a strip mall consisting of galleries and arty shops. The neighborhood, only partially paved, was located near the outskirts of Palm Springs, a block or two behind a row of luxury car dealers, where the ruddy granite foothills of the San Jacinto mountains ended abruptly at the edge of town.

We turned from Highway 111, the main thoroughfare running through the resort cities of the Coachella Valley, and made our way back to the parking lot of the mall, which was a popular destination for browsing on a Sunday afternoon. But it was now past four o'clock, with the cool shadow of the mountains beginning to spread—a nap before dinner, perhaps—and we had no trouble parking in the row closest to the shops.

Jazz lifted Emma free of her safety seat, and as soon as the girl's feet reached the ground, she charged ahead, leading us to a darkened glass door between two of the shops, identified only with the address letter H. She knew the way well by now. When we passed through the outer door, Jazz lifted Emma so she could press the buzzer at the door.

"Yes?" said a low, husky voice over the intercom.

"It's *Emma*, Mr. Wade."

Buzzing the lock, he said with a hearty laugh, "Then you'd better come up, darlin'. And bring your friends, too."

I swung the door open, and Emma dashed ahead through a winding hall, then up a long flight of stairs. As we climbed the steps behind her, the subtle but distinctive smells of linseed oil and turpentine drifted from above. Nearing the top, I heard music: laid-back rock, played low.

"*Hey*, you," said Blade as Jazz stepped into his arms. They kissed.

"Glad you're home," she said. "Emma's been hot to get back to her new painting."

"She's already at it." Blade jerked his head in the direction of his studio, separated from the living quarters by the stairway. He was a big-hearted Black man with a football build and a baritone voice that sounded sexy even when he wasn't trying. Not quite my age, fifty at most, Blade was twelve or thirteen years older than Jazz. Despite that difference, they were a great match. And they'd both had the wisdom to approach their relationship slowly, letting it evolve.

I reached to shake his hand. "Thanks for including me, Blade. Sorry I didn't bring anything—it was sorta short notice."

He abandoned the handshake and gave me a quick hug (he could have crushed me—literally squeezed me to death—if he were so inclined). "Nonsense," he said. "You never need to 'bring anything,' not here, Dante. Glad you can join us."

And he led us from the top of the stairs into the main room of his loft. This was no starving artist's garret. It was jaw-dropping, a melding of industrial chic with designer furnishings and significant art. The living room itself had a two-story ceiling, under which a high ribbon of windows framed the interplay of light and shadows on a ruddy expanse of nearby mountainside. A spiral metal staircase at the far end of the room led up to an open bedroom, where more windows looked out toward the snowy peak of Mount San Jacinto.

Blade said to me, "I hear you've had a rough afternoon. Wine? Something stronger?"

"Uh, wine's fine—whatever's open."

Walking over to the sleek, open kitchen, he didn't need to ask Jazz about drinks. Fully supportive of her commitment to swear off booze, he would, as always, pop her a bottle of Perrier and serve it in a gleaming stemmed balloon glass. I noticed that he had set out a few things on one of the kitchen counters, getting organized before preparing dinner. Conspicuously, one of these items was a hefty package of fresh meat, still wrapped in waxy brown butcher paper.

Jazz and I moved to the conversation area and seated ourselves on two of the big square leather ottomans that surrounded a hefty stone cocktail table. She called over to Blade, "You sounded mighty chipper on the phone earlier."

He laughed but didn't speak as he brought three wineglasses to us, handing the one containing water to Jazz. He set the other two on the low table, then sat on the ottoman with Jazz, facing me. I took my glass, he lifted his, and the three of us skoaled.

"Now," said Jazz, setting her glass aside, "what happened in LA?"

"What *happened*?" said Blade. "What happened was: I signed on with a new rep—a 'gallerist,' as they say—who happens to be *the* top dog on the entire West Coast. *That's* what happened."

"Congratulations!" I said.

Jazz leaned to kiss his cheek, "That's wonderful, sweetie. Anyone I've heard of?"

He shook his head. "These people are strictly behind the scenes. But 'those in the know' have definitely heard of Marc Albré."

Jazz and I shared a glance. Shrugged.

I asked, "What about your relationship with the Heimlich Gallery in Palm Desert?"

"They've been *great*, and they'll continue to represent me locally, but trust me—Marc Albré will open doors I never dreamed of, starting with a solo exhibition in New York." Curiously, Blade's expression then soured. "Albré will finally be doing exactly what Noreen *could* have done, but didn't."

He'd raised a touchy topic. Noreen Penley Wade, Blade's former wife, now deceased, had been executive director of a specialized art museum in Los Angeles, with extensive contacts throughout the art world. Blade had grown to resent her indifference to his career, to the extent that their marriage was crumbling. But then, she died—victim of a suspicious drowning.

"But you know what?" said Blade, brightening. "All's well that ends well."

Jazz grinned. "Now *that's* worth celebrating—and I understand why you picked up some steaks for tonight. But: a year or two down the road, when all those big dreams are coming true, you're not gonna run off to *Paris* or wherever, are you?"

He wrapped an arm around her. "Well, I might go there on business, but not to *live* there. I mean, you're *here*."

With a satisfied smirk, she bought his answer.

He added, "And Emma. She's here, too."

If I'd wondered how things were progressing with Jazz and Blade, this seemed to confirm that they, as a couple, were moving along nicely. And I wasn't surprised that Blade had brought little Emma into the discussion. His long marriage to Noreen had produced no children. Because of her job, they had split their time between her apartment in Los Angeles and his studio in Palm Springs, but as the years wore on, they increasingly kept to their own turf, with shared time on weekends. But then, even those visits petered out. And although Blade would have welcomed kids, Noreen wouldn't hear of it—bad for her career.

I've never been one to consider children a necessary or even expected component of marriage—to each their own. But it was clear that Blade would have enjoyed being a parent. It was equally clear that Emma had begun to fill this void for him, especially because she had demonstrated such an interest in, and strong aptitude for, painting. Blade had relished the opportunity to teach and mentor her, with remarkable results even before she had turned five years old. And now, at that very moment, she was busy on the other side of the loft, in Blade's studio, brush in hand, experimenting with yet another precocious new direction in her work.

Jazz told Blade, "You're right: I'm here, not in Paris or New York. And Emma's here, too." Meaning, Jazz and Emma were a package deal. And judging from a glint in Blade's eyes, that seemed to suit him just fine.

I asked him, "Have you heard about the ballet program?"

"Nonstop." He laughed. "I don't know where she gets the energy."

Jazz told me, "Blade's coming to the fundraiser next Saturday."

"I'll be there," he confirmed. "Of course."

Of course, I thought.

Jazz said, "Not only will Blade *be* there, but he's donating a painting to the auction."

I asked, "Big one?" He was known for his large-scale, energetic abstractions, predominantly red. Large-scale pricing as well.

"Nah," he said modestly. "This is just a little bitty one—six by six." He was talking feet, not inches.

Jazz told him, "Dante and Isandro are coming, too. So things are looking up—there won't be *quite* as many gasbags at our table."

Later, while Jazz and I helped Blade in the kitchen, Emma strolled out from her session in the studio, still in her smock. "What smells?"

With a sputter of a laugh, Jazz asked, "Is it a *good* smell, I hope?"

"Yeah!"

"That's meat," said Blade. "New York strips. We're having steak."

Warily, she asked, "Is it a cow?"

Jazz flashed Blade a look, a warning to tread carefully.

"Well," he said, "yes, darlin', it's sorta like a cow. More like hamburger. But better. You like burgers, don't you?"

She nodded. "Cows are nice. Did they have to *kill* the cow?"

Jazz jumped in: "No, honey. The cow died, and they found it."

"Oh." Emma unbuttoned her smock, which must have been one of Blade's old shirts with its sleeves rolled up.

Jazz took it from her, asking, "Potty? Need help?" When Emma shook her head, Jazz added, "Wash your hands." And Emma bustled away, down a hall.

Blade and I waited for Jazz to say something.

"All right, all right," she said. "I *know* this is sensitive, and I *don't* know exactly how to handle it, but for now, this is how we're playing it. She'll have plenty of time—later—to make her own decisions."

Within two minutes, Emma returned. "Mommy? Where did they find the cow?"

"In a farmer's field, honey. She was out late one night, making milk. And the next morning, they found her there, like she was asleep in the grass—with wildflowers all around."

Emma smiled.

Kids. Gotta love 'em. They're so easily deceived.

CHAPTER
SIX

Another matter of childish innocence: Who sleeps with whom, where, and under what circumstances?

Emma surely understood that Blade and her mother had a warm, special friendship. She'd seen them kiss and could hear the tone of how they spoke to each other. But she knew nothing about sex yet, so the implications of sleeping arrangements were still a mystery. Jazz wasn't ready to answer the questions Emma might ask about her mommy sleeping with Blade, so the little girl had never stayed overnight at his home. When Jazz had custody of her, they always returned to Jazz's apartment at night, where Emma could wake up in her own bedroom before going to school.

So. That Sunday night, after dinner at Blade's and helping him clean up, we congratulated him again for landing a new agent, then said our goodbyes. Emma and I left with Jazz in her SUV.

While riding through the dark, quiet streets, Emma quickly nodded off. I said to Jazz, "What a pleasant evening."

She nodded, smiling. "It felt *right*, didn't it?" She paused, enjoying the moment, then reminded me, "Meanwhile, we've got a murder on our hands."

When she dropped me off at the curb behind Richard's estate in the Old Las Palmas neighborhood, where a back gate led to the coach house I shared with Isandro, Jazz said, "Tomorrow morning? My office?"

I confirmed, "Ten thirty."

Nine o'clock the next morning, I stepped through the street door into Sunny Junket's offices, where Gianna, goddess of snark, looked up at me from the reception desk, setting aside a half-eaten jelly roll, frosted pink. Between licks of her fingers, she said, "If you'd ... check in more often ... you might've already ... heard the news."

I hesitated to ask, "What news?"

"Can't say." She nudged the bridge of her catty rhinestone-framed glasses with her middle finger. "Talk to Ben."

"Is he in?" I noticed that the door to my supervisor's office was closed.

"No. He came and went. Out dealing with something."

With crossed arms, I eyed her for a moment. "My, you're just a gushing *font* of useless information this morning, aren't you?"

She returned my stare. "It's what I do." Strawberry jam smeared her teeth.

I went to my desk and busied myself for a while.

Ben had not returned by ten o'clock, so I decided to leave early for my meeting with Jazz. Her office was only a block away, on Palm Canyon Drive, so I walked.

On the ground floor of her building was a popular coffeehouse called Huggamug. Sometimes Jazz liked to hang out down there, working from her laptop at a quiet back table. I checked through the windows, but didn't see her.

So I followed the narrow walkway leading back alongside the building to a single glass door in the white stucco wall. Inside was a bleak little cubby of a lobby with a rickety elevator, which I *never* used, and a stairway leading up. I took the steps by twos and arrived at the door to her outer office: JAZZ FRIENDLY, PRIVATE INVESTIGATOR.

Stepping inside, I called, "Just me, Jazz."

"Back here."

Closing the door behind me, I paused. When I'd first set foot in this room, about a year and a half earlier, I was appalled by the squalor and found it laughable that Jazz intended to establish herself as a professional in such surroundings. The outer office, intended as a reception area, with a desk for an assistant, had needed a serious dolling up, and it was Zola Lorinsky who came to the rescue, contributing a drop-dead set of floor-to-ceiling curtains for the window that looked out to the street. Back then, she had never even met Jazz, but she used a treasured old bolt of fabric she had saved, adorned with a wild, oversize pattern of banana leaves, figuring it was exactly right to perk up a dreary room. And, in a way, this act of generosity seemed to coincide with Jazz's first big break in launching her new private-eye biz.

Now, of course, it was Zola, not Jazz, in need of help. And although I regretted that Zola found herself in such a predicament, there was a serendipity in knowing that Jazz and I were in a position to repay her earlier kindness.

At the rear of this reception room, a little stub of a hallway separated two other rooms. To the right, a windowless conference room had more recently undergone a transformation, now looking stylish and urban. To the left, the remaining room served as Jazz's office, with a window to the street below. Although the room was well organized and efficient, it still needed some work.

When I entered it, Jazz was sitting at her desk, writing notes on her computer. She looked up, saying while she typed, "Guess who's free for dinner tonight."

I gave her a confused look.

She stopped typing and sat back in her chair. "Yesterday, we were talking about Keith Gibkin and Christopher—how they have so much in common, but haven't met. So I gave Christopher a call this morning."

"I hope you didn't tell him we were scheming to hook him up. You didn't—did you?"

"No, Dante. I was doing some 'background research,' camouflaged as small talk. So here's the deal. Obviously, since I have Emma this week, he won't be busy with *her* tonight. I idly asked if he had any meetings or client appointments this evening, and he said, 'Are you kidding—it's Monday.' Bottom line: he's got nothin' tonight. If *someone* offered a spur-of-the-moment invite, I'll bet he'd snap it up."

"Interesting...," I said. "Isandro and I have no plans. Maybe we could ask Christopher and Keith—separately—over to the coach house for dinner tonight, and they would just happen to 'meet.' I'll have to run it past Isandro, but I bet he'd love to do it. So the unknown variable is Keith. I'm not even sure if he'll be in town tonight."

"Well," said Jazz, "he'll be here in a few minutes with his father. When I called Harold this morning to confirm our meeting, he mentioned that he wanted to bring Keith—maybe it's sinking in that he *does* need a lawyer."

A voice from the front office called, "Jazz? Harold Gibkin."

Under her breath, Jazz told me, "Speak of the devil." Rising, she called, "Coming, Harold."

When we walked out from her office, Harold and Keith were

standing in the reception area, looking out the window. Harold said, "Nice view."

Keith said, "Fabulous curtains!"

"Thank you," said Jazz. "In fact, they were designed—and made—by Zola."

"Well, how 'bout that." Harold chuckled. "And sorry we're early. Didn't know how long the drive would take, and I didn't want to bring the big Suburban. So Keith drove."

The smart little Mercedes, I recalled.

"No problem," said Jazz. "Better early than late. Follow me, then?"

As Jazz strolled Harold into the conference room, Keith and I held back a few paces. He leaned near, telling me, "Didn't realize you'd be here. Good to see you."

"Likewise." It was indeed good to see him. Despite all of yesterday's commotion and stress, he looked as put-together and charming as ever. I asked, "Will you, uh, still be in town tonight?"

He shrugged. "Sure. Why?" (God, that smile.)

"I'll just need to check something first."

In the conference room, Jazz had already arranged four chairs at the slick black Parsons table, and each place at the table was set with bottled water, notepad, and a folder containing her proposed services and fees.

As we settled in, Keith said, "Wow—that is one *striking* painting."

"So glad you like it," said Jazz. "I'll let the artist know—he's a friend."

The artist, of course, was Blade. The painting, predominantly red, was eight feet square and would have looked at home in a much larger space, but it made a remarkably energizing statement in the confines of the windowless room. Jazz eyed it with such pride, it seemed to empower her.

She said, "Let's get started. And once again, Harold, my sympathies for your loss. Now then, you're here today because you want to hire me to investigate the circumstances of your wife's death, correct?"

"Yes"—he nodded—"but the point of finding Wendy's killer is to clear Zola. Someone did a half-assed job of framing her, but the police detective took it seriously, and it's just not *right*."

I found it odd that he expressed no interest in finding Wendy's killer out of a sense of simple justice or, less nobly, retribution. Instead, it was all about Zola.

"And why is that?" asked Jazz. "Why do you want my services on Zola's behalf?"

He shrugged. "Simple justice. For Zola."

Was he really that dense? Maybe he *didn't* care that his wife was gone, but in voicing this obsession with Zola, he drew a highly unflattering picture of himself. Fidgeting for something in his jacket, he pulled a pack of cigarettes from a pocket. He asked Jazz, "Do you mind?"

"Actually, I do mind. Please don't."

Chastened, he put away his smokes with a sigh. Ah, the long-suffering miseries of an addict.

His son, Keith, had been quiet, and when I glanced at him several times, trying to read his reaction to Harold's words, I learned nothing. Keith had slumped back in his chair with the tented fingers of both hands touching his chin as he looked vacantly at the floor.

From where I sat, I didn't see Jazz glance at Keith even once. While she wasn't the type to avoid eye contact—on the contrary, she was an in-your-face sorta gal—she was now acting as if Keith wasn't even present. I understood that she wanted to hold in confidence that Keith had already hired her to investigate Rebecca

Jiang (which would come as astonishing, disagreeable news to Harold), but just the same, the wall of silence between Jazz and Keith created a heightened sense of tension in the room.

Jazz said to Harold, "Yesterday's tragedy would be a shock to anyone, and I understand your desire to focus on the living and on the future. But it serves no purpose to slip into denial. For my investigation, as well as Detective Madera's, everything hinges on what happened to Wendy, and why. So I'll need to ask a few probing questions, which you might find uncomfortable. Are you okay with that?"

Harold nodded, offering a weak smile. "Sure, Jazz. Fire away."

She opened her notes and clicked a ballpoint pen. "How long were you and Wendy married?"

"Twelve years. My first wife, Marla, died four years earlier, just a few days before Keith graduated from college, at Berkeley. It was a rough time. She was only forty-three. Way too young. Cancer." Harold turned to look at Keith, who had straightened up in his chair and now shared a wan smile with his father as they recalled their shared loss.

Jazz prompted: "Then along came Wendy…"

"Right," said Harold. "She was a member of our country club in Rancho Santa Fe, and I'd seen her around—but I didn't realize *who* she was."

I had to ask, "Who *was* she?"

"She was the older child of the Ames family, Southern California blue bloods in a league of their own, not to be confused with the East Coast clan. Her father was a pork baron—nothing prestigious in the usual sense, but *plenty* profitable."

Jazz asked, "How did you finally figure this out?"

"At the club. Dinner one night. A golf buddy introduced us, and the pieces of her story fell together. She was… a bit weird, I confess. But she was beautiful and trim—*unusually* trim—and in spite of her quirks, she was good with numbers and a worthy steward of the family fortune."

In other words, I thought, *he married her for her money.*

Jazz was more tactful: "Did you love her?"

"Yes, very much. When we met, we filled deep but different needs in each other's lives."

I recalled that, on Friday night, Keith had told Isandro and me that his father and Wendy maintained separate finances. Leaving Keith out of this, I asked Harold, "Given the wealth handed down in both families, did you and Wendy have any arrangements or 'understandings' regarding money?"

"We did, in fact. She wanted a prenuptial agreement, and I readily signed on. Other than the typical shared expenses, we didn't mix funds, and we filed our own taxes. That's one of the reasons I'm hunting for investors in AtmosPhuel. I wouldn't want anyone thinking that my *wife* bankrolled me. How degrading would *that* be?"

Keith caught my eye and held it for a moment, confirming my assumption that Wendy had *refused* to bankroll Harold—again.

"So," said Jazz, "there were no financial disputes between you?"

"Heavens, no." He laughed at the very thought of it.

Keith's eyes bugged for an instant before he blinked away his apparent disbelief.

Jazz said, "This is a particularly difficult question, Harold, but I need to know: Can you think of anyone who might have wished Wendy harm?"

"Well"—he gathered his thoughts—"it's no secret that she could be abrasive. That's gotten much worse in recent years. Plus, she held some *terrible* beliefs that, frankly, I find reprehensible. I don't know if she always felt that way, or if the rancid state of tribal politics has 'permitted' her to nurture these views, but she has deeply offended—and *hurt*—many people, including members of my own family. When it came to all that craziness, I could no longer defend her. And yes, now that she's gone, I'm relieved of that vexation." He paused and leaned forward, fixing Jazz in his stare while telling her, "But: despite what Wendy had become, I could *never* have been driven to kill her. That's an option that never once crossed my mind. She was my wife, and I still loved her."

Jazz wrote something in her notes, then told Harold, "I believe you when you say you loved her, but it's safe to say there are others who did *not* love her and possibly hated her. Fact is, somebody wanted her dead. Any theories who that might be?"

He shook his head. "I really can't imagine that anyone could've sunk to that—especially anyone here for the reunion. We're a family. We have our problems, sure. But we don't fuckin' kill each other."

I reminded him, "Zola's not family. You seem certain she had nothing to do with this, and I absolutely agree with you. But *someone* did it, and so far, we have *nothing* to go on. Where do we even start, Harold?"

He sat back, tossing his hands. "I'm afraid I don't know." He looked over to his son with a questioning shrug, as if to ask, *Any ideas?*

Keith blew a long, breathy sigh. Then he looked at Harold with a squint. "What do we know about Wendy's brother? There was some trouble with him."

"*Oh.*" Harold's eyes widened at this suggestion. "There was trouble, all right." Turning to Jazz and me, he explained, "Cecil Ames is Wendy's brother, about eight years younger than she was. Because of that age difference, they didn't really 'grow up' together, and Wendy would tell anyone who'd listen: 'Cecil robbed me of the pleasure of being an only child.'"

"Christ," said Jazz, "what a charmer—no disrespect intended for the dead."

Harold rolled his eyes, "Doesn't matter. Both Wendy *and* Cecil were raised in a privileged but dysfunctional family—Daddy was in pork, Mummy was a lush. Of the two kids, Wendy was the older and smarter, so she ended up holding the purse strings when the folks were gone. Cecil's legacy was held in trust, with an allowance doled out by Wendy, which he resented. Who wouldn't? Even so, he never needed to work, so he lapsed into the lifestyle of a playboy, bitterly estranged from his older sister. He spends his time traveling the world and taking up residence from time to time in faraway places, waiting for those monthly deposits to show up in his account. I haven't actually *seen* him since Wendy and I got married—he was at the wedding, high on something, and during the cutting of the cake, he gave a spiteful harangue of a toast. She wanted to kill him, and I'm *sure* the feeling was mutual."

"Sounds like a motive," said Jazz. "Where *is* Cecil?"

"Not a clue."

I asked, "Did he know about the reunion?"

"He didn't hear about it from me. And I can't imagine that Wendy would tell him—I think they gave up all communication long ago. She wanted nothing to do with him."

"Hmmm." Jazz looked up, tapping her pen on her notepad. "So Cecil had a strong *motive*, but no apparent *opportunity* to kill Wendy. The other relevant factor is whether a suspect had the *means* to commit the crime. In Wendy's case, the suspect would need to know that she was allergic to honey and that she carried an EpiPen."

Harold said, "Cecil probably knew that."

Jazz made a check mark on her pad. "Then he's one step closer to being an active suspect."

"But how?" asked Harold. "As far as we know, he's off sipping mai tais somewhere."

She reminded him, "Just hop on a plane, anywhere in the world, and you can be here in a day—two max."

I asked Harold, "Closer to home, there were eight of you staying at the rental house. Who knew about Wendy's condition?"

He thought it out: "Everyone in the *family* knew about it— me, Keith, my sister Heather, her daughter Brooke. And Rebecca, of course. She worked in our home and often cooked for us, so she was well aware of Wendy's food issues."

I said, "That leaves Näzh Hoyle and Tyler Evans, staying in the guesthouse with Heather and Brooke. Did they know about the allergies and the EpiPen?"

"Tyler did. On the Fourth of July, he came with Brooke to a barbecue we had at our place in Rancho Santa Fe. Wendy was there, with all her usual fussing and griping about food, so Tyler had to get the picture—or enough of it to ask Brooke what was going on."

Jazz said, "And what about Näzh?"

With a harrumph, Harold said, "*That* one—weird as fuck, right? Honest to God, I have no idea what Heather sees in him. But I learned long ago that, when it comes to men, there's no reasoning with my kid sister. Different strokes, I guess. Anyway: Heather had other plans for the Fourth, so she wasn't at the barbecue, and Näzh didn't meet Wendy till this past weekend. I can't say if he knew anything about her food issues. Heather might've told him the story—but *I'd* have just told him to roll up his yoga mat and get the hell *out*."

Keith laughed. "Well, Dad, I guess we know how you feel about Näzh dating your sister. But how do you feel about Tyler dating your niece?"

"Nice guy. Tyler seems like a hard worker. Focused. Brooke has always been levelheaded—she wouldn't hook up with a flake. I probably shouldn't say it, now that Wendy's gone, but it pleased me no end that Brooke arrived on the Fourth with a Black boyfriend. I got a kick out of Wendy's reaction—ruined her holiday, and it served her right."

While I shared Harold's sentiments on this matter, I was nonetheless perplexed by his willingness to trash his dead wife on the day after her murder.

Jazz told Harold, "Let's return to Wendy's playboy brother, Cecil. Is it safe to assume he stands to gain from Wendy's death? Will there be a windfall inheritance?"

Harold seemed unsure. He turned to his son with a questioning look.

Keith said, "Don't ask *me*. I've never been privy to Wendy's estate planning. I don't even know if she had a will."

Harold nodded. "She did, of course—not a will, but a full-blown revocable trust, not unlike her parents' trust, which named her as trustee."

Keith asked, "Did Wendy name you as trustee of *her* revocable trust?"

"Uh"—he shrugged—"she never said."

Keith's brow pinched. "Trustees usually *consent* to be named in a trust. So you don't know what's *in* it, right?"

Harold answered lamely, "Guess not."

Jazz said to him, "Pardon an indelicate question, but do you have reason to believe that you yourself will be a beneficiary?"

Harold gave her an odd look. "I have reason to believe I will *not* be a beneficiary. That seemed to be the whole point of the prenup. Maybe she left me *something*, but it wouldn't be much."

"As you can imagine," said Jazz, "anyone with a lot to gain from Wendy's trust will naturally be considered a strong suspect in her murder case. If she wasn't planning to pass her wealth along to *you*, then who?"

"The only one that I'm *sure* will be taken care of is Koo-Loo." With a laugh, he added, "But how much does it take to keep a monkey in bananas for a few years?"

"Jesus *Christ*." Jazz slapped her pen on the table. "Wendy *said* that? She said the fuckin' monkey's in the goddamn will?"

Harold nodded slowly, with certainty.

Keith was no less surprised to learn this than Jazz was, but he allowed himself to see the bright side. "Well, Dad, if that's the case, you're probably off the hook for the murder."

"I never knew I was *on* the hook."

Jazz told him, "Spouses and 'significant others' are always at— or near—the top of the list."

"But unless I'm mistaken," said Harold, "*Zola* now bears that dubious distinction. And that's why I'm here today. I want you to figure this out."

Jazz paused in thought. "Okay, Harold. But before we make it official, just two more questions."

"Anything. Just ask."

"To help me understand all of the possible reasons why some-one might wish Wendy harm, can you tell me, did she have any 'vices'?"

Harold gave Jazz a weird look. "Vices? Like what?"

"Was there anything going on in her life that could have got-ten her into trouble with … 'the wrong people'? For instance, did she gamble or do hard drugs?"

Harold and Keith shot each other a glance. Harold said, "No, she didn't gamble."

I asked, "Now, *why* do I think you're leaving something out?"

Keith nudged his dad: "If you don't tell them, I will."

Harold sat back in his chair, hands folded on the table. Looking at none of us, he said, "Wendy did, in fact, have a drug habit—she dismissed it as 'just coke,' but I think there was meth involved, too. She had plenty of money, so getting the stuff was no problem, but I'm sure it brought her into contact with some 'wrong people.' She was in and out of rehab a couple times, maybe three, but it never stuck. I didn't like it, but I had no leverage to fix it, so Wendy's little 'vice' was just part of the package, part of who she was. Eventually, it might've killed her, but I doubt if it had anything to do with the poisoned posset."

Jazz said, "I'm inclined to agree. Still, I appreciate having this background. Which brings me to one final question, Harold. You've already said that you loved your wife—but were you *happy* together?"

He had to think about that one. "What we had, the way it evolved—it was no fairy-tale romance. But I can safely say that we were happy *enough*. We were reasonably content together, reasonably satisfied. Like most people, after a certain point, what more can you expect? In any event, that's what Wendy and I had—and it worked for us. Now it's gone."

Grim, I thought. Was Harold's reasoning coldly realistic? Or was he—I hoped—simply beyond the point of caring?

Jazz told him, "Thank you for your candor. If you'd like to move forward with this, please open your folder, and I'll walk you through a schedule of my proposed services and fees."

As Harold and Keith began studying the proposal, I got up from my chair, telling Jazz, "I'll be in front if you need me. Need to take care of something."

Out in the reception room, I pulled out my phone and punched in a number. While the line rang, I sat in the chair at the unused desk and blew a thin layer of dust from its surface. Then I tidied up a messy stack of mail, mostly junk, that had been tossed there.

A young woman answered the phone at Dr. Gastro's office. I said, "Could I speak to Isandro if he's not busy? This is Dante... his other half."

He happened to be seated at the next computer, crunching a patient's data. "*Coração!*" he said. "What's up?"

"This'll have to be quick—I'm taking a break from a meeting. How do you like the idea of inviting Christopher Friendly and Keith Gibkin to dinner at the coach house tonight? Just the four of us—but they won't know to expect each other."

"They've never met, right?"

I laughed. "That's the point."

"Sounds *nice*. But I can't get out of here till five."

"No problem. I can ditch the office by four, do the shopping, and get things started in the kitchen. You just need to show up and be beautiful. Thought I'd ask them to come at seven."

"Perfect. Gotta go now. *Mwah!*"

I disconnected—one down, one to go—then I placed the other call.

"Friendly Law Offices, Professional Corporation," said the receptionist, sounding very self-important.

I told her, "I'm wondering if by any chance Christopher is available for a brief call. This is Dante O'Donnell, a friend of his wife—I mean his ex-wife—Jazz."

"Hold on, please."

I heard the call transfer two or three times. Then Christopher connected: "*Hello*, Dante. You caught me in the car. Is every-thing... all right?"

"Absolutely. Didn't mean to alarm you."

"So this is a... *social* call?" Whether he intended it or not, his tone had turned flirtatious.

"Correct. Isandro and I were just talking. You've never seen the coach house where we live now, and we thought you might like to come over for dinner tonight, around seven. Any chance you're free?"

He laughed. "Your timing is *fab*-ulous. I hardly *ever* have an open evening, but this is one of them. What can I bring?"

"Just yourself," I assured him.

After we rang off, I dug out Keith's card, and although he was sitting in the next room, I sent him a text: DINNER TONIGHT? COACH HOUSE AT SEVEN.

Then I pocketed my phone and stepped back to the confer-ence room, where Harold was signing a few forms, wrapping up his agreement with Jazz. As I returned to my chair and sat at the table, Keith set down his phone.

Catching my eye, he gave me a wink.

Back at the Sunny Junket offices that afternoon, things seemed *very* slow—I spent more time planning dinner and making a shopping list than I did on actual work.

Around two, I saw Ben enter through the street door. He ex-changed a few words with Gianna, then waddled toward my desk. As managing director of the company, he was my boss. He wore his dad jeans and bright yellow polo—the company uni-form—with pride.

Two years earlier, it was Ben who had hired me, and although I was a few years his senior, he treated me in a manner that seemed almost fatherly. He was plump. He was nice. And because I frequently interacted with the company's top-tier clients, he had allowed me to ditch the dreadful uniform and to dress as I saw fit. In short, I could tell he liked me.

"Howdy, Dante," he said with a smile—he always wore a smile, but that afternoon, it looked forced.

Warily, I asked, "What's up, Ben?"

He rocked on his heels, still smiling, hooking his thumbs in the pockets of his jeans. "Have a minute?"

I surveyed the empty, quiet room. "I think I can squeeze you in."

He smirked. "My office—okay?" And he led the way.

When I followed him inside and closed the door behind us, he said, "Have a seat."

This was serious. I sat in one of the chairs facing his desk while he settled on the other side, woke his computer, and scrolled through messages.

I said, "Gianna was vague, but she told me there was 'news.'"

Ben turned from his computer, sat back in his chair, and breathed a heavy sigh. Looking me in the eye, he said, "It's Alex."

Alejandro was our top agent. He was invisible to our guests, but he secured properties for our rental listings and negotiated terms with the owners. He was part of the background machinery that kept Sunny Junket humming.

I asked, "Is it my imagination, or has he seemed rather 'scarce' lately?"

Ben nodded. "We talked this morning. He made it official. He's jumping ship—going to West Valley Rentals."

"Christ," I said. Our top agent was moving to our top competitor.

"Ready for the rest of it?" said Ben. "Alex has been planning this for quite a while, and he's arranged with most of his property owners to make the move with him."

"Christ," I repeated. Alejandro was responsible for over a third of our rental inventory, including most of our higher-end listings.

"The timing couldn't be worse," said Ben. "The market is already oversaturated here, and every outfit in town is feeling the pinch. Now this. It's like a one-two punch. *Darn* him." (Ben didn't curse much.)

"Ummm... so what does this *mean*?"

Ben tossed his arms. "I don't know yet—still trying to get my head around it. But it's obviously a major blow. In the long run, I think Sunny Junket will survive this, but we'll need to make some changes, fast."

I asked him bluntly, "Is my *job* on the line?"

He waggled his hands. "*No*, no—of course not." He paused, a thought wrinkling his brow. "At least I hope not."

"What can I do? I'll help any way I can." My mind was spinning.

Ben sat forward in his chair, elbows on the desk, leaning toward me. Quietly, he said, "You're the best guy I've got, Dante. Just keep on making us so lucky and proud to have you. I'll need to let a few people go right away—at least until our feet are back on the ground. You're fine, though. Don't worry. But depending on our bookings, I might have to ask you to take some reduced hours."

I didn't like hearing this, but it could have been worse—for me—and I knew that Ben, at that moment, was struggling with far more than I was.

I said, "You've always been thoroughly decent to me, Ben. Whatever works best for you, just let me know. After yesterday's 'trouble' in Rancho Mirage, I'll have some more side work for

Jazz coming up, so that'll help me out if you need to cut hours."

Ben allowed himself a chuckle. "Forgot about that—seems another guest of ours had an unintended check-out."

With a cringe, I agreed, "That's *one* way of putting it."

Cutting out of the office early was no problem—the phones had rung only twice that afternoon, and one of the calls was a wrong number. I had hoped to get out at four, and I ended up leaving by three thirty.

Zipping around town in my open convertible, I felt my mood brighten as I ran errands to prepare for that evening's impromptu dinner party. I had my list, so groceries would be easy—a simple salad, as well as the ingredients for a hearty chicken casserole that seemed right for an October night. The flowers in the supermarket looked past their prime, so I swung over to a florist shop, where a clerk and I put together a small white arrangement of roses, carnations, and baby's breath for the table. Didn't need to stop anywhere for wine—we always had plenty stashed away at home.

By four thirty, I had parked the Karmann Ghia in the garage space beneath our loft. There were more shopping bags than I could carry at once, so I left two at the foot of the stairs and trotted up with the others. After putting a few things in the refrigerator, I went back down the stairs to fetch the remainder.

"Yoo-hoo. Dante." It was Richard, stepping out from the main house, carrying a frosty martini glass, filled to the brim. As I strolled across the pool terrace to greet him, he checked his watch and hoisted the glass. "Twenty to five. Close enough." And he took his first sip.

"Cheers," I told him.

"Would you like one?"

"No, thanks. I'm putting groceries away. But if you'd like some company, we could sit and gab for a few minutes." This was fortuitous, as I'd been hoping to catch him alone.

"Delightful," he said, sashaying past me to a chaise longue, where he sat, then pulled his feet up to the cushion. Patting the seat of the chair next to him, he commanded gently, "Sit."

The tranquility of this space was surreal—an oasis in an elegant garden with mountain views and fanciful architecture all around. Birds rustled and chirped as the low slant of late-afternoon sun sliced through the palms, streaking everything with alternating slashes of gold light and black shadow.

I asked, "Where's Zola?"

"She has her... outings. Lady friends, I suppose. She's still settling in, and I wouldn't want to spook her by coming off as possessive. I try not to pry."

I felt as if I was the one prying when I asked, "But she *is* settling in? She lives here now?"

"She's transitioning, so to speak. Hasn't let go of her apartment yet, but she *sleeps* here." He must have read something in my face when he asked, "Too much information?"

"Uh... *no*, not at all. It's wonderful that you're both working this out."

He laughed. "It's all a bit unexpected, I admit."

"I imagine so"—a supreme understatement.

Confidentially, he told me, "She's worried, you know."

"About... transitioning?"

He gave me a get-real stare. "*No*. About being framed for murder."

"Oh. *That*. I'm plenty worried about that myself. Thank God we all heard Zola's reaction when the EpiPen was found in her purse: she didn't even know what it was."

"Well"—his head wobbled—"even if she were guilty, she'd *say* that, wouldn't she? I mean, anyone can play dumb."

I thought, *You're not helping, Richard.*

"But," he continued, "we *know* she wasn't involved. Trouble is, it can be damn hard to prove you *didn't* do something."

"Exactly. So you'll be happy to know that your cousin Harold has now signed on with Jazz—to prove who *did* do it. Plus, Jazz asked Christopher Friendly, her ex-husband, if he'd help Zola with legal problems—if it goes that far—and he quickly agreed. Bottom line: Zola has plenty of the right people on her side."

"Well, now," said Richard, "that *is* heartening." He paused to savor a long sip of his martini. "Then again," he added, "this whole investigation has the eerie feel of a demonic roulette game. Here we all stand, a closed circle of suspects—any one of whom could have poisoned the posset—waiting for the wheel to stop spinning. And when it does, the ball could land on any one of us. Even *me*. Have I lost any sleep over this? You bet."

In the canopy of trees, the cheery twitter of birdsong suddenly hushed. Richard's eyes bugged as he looked past me, over my shoulder. Waving his arms, he yelled, "Shoo! Get *out* of here!"

I turned, and there, a few feet away, perched on the stone phallus of the Inca warrior, a huge raven—sleek and inky black—let out a piercing, painful *caw* as a hearty gob of his droppings splatted on the bricks of the terrace.

I've never had the slightest belief in omens or superstitions.

But *that* did not look promising.

Isandro told me, "It was *just* a raven. They're everywhere here."

He was right. In Palm Springs and throughout the Coachella

Valley—as well as the surrounding desert—ravens were as common as crows in Kansas. I said, "But *this* one was different. He was no birdbrain. He meant trouble."

Isandro laughed. "Get over it. Company's coming."

It was well past six now, nearly seven. Isandro had gotten home from Dr. Gastro's office in plenty of time to shower, make himself beautiful, and help me with the last of the dinner preparations. The table was set, the bar cart was stocked, and night had fallen. We were ready for our guests.

He asked, "Any bets on who arrives first?"

"Well...when I invited them, separately, they each accepted at once, *eagerly*. So I suspect they'll both be prompt."

"But which will get here *first*?"

Crossing my arms, I asked, "What is this—a game?"

He grinned. "Just a friendly wager."

Arbitrarily, I said, "Okay, I bet Christopher will arrive first."

"So I'll bet on Keith. Deal?"

"Sure," I said. "It's a deal." I wasn't sure what I was agreeing to, but this sort of meaningless bet often led to payback demands at bedtime. (Either way, I'd win.)

Dingdong.

Isandro said, "It's showtime." Then he and I moved to the door together.

When I swung it open, there stood Keith Gibkin—under the porch light, on the landing at the top of our stairs. (Isandro gave me a smug glance. Having won the bet, he must have been mulling his payback.)

"Come *in*," we told Keith. "You *shouldn't* have," we said as he handed us a bottle of wine.

Stepping into the room, he said, "I couldn't show up empty-handed, could I? And I appreciate being invited." Glancing about, he added, "Wow, you guys really fussed. Everything's gorgeous."

Isandro said, "That's Dante's doing. He sets a table fit for a queen, so to speak."

I told Keith, "Don't get your expectations up—dinner's a chicken casserole."

"Sounds perfect. Smells great, too."

I added, "And in case you didn't notice, it's dinner for four."

"I did notice. Who's coming?"

I'd already moved over to the bar cart. "Just a friend. What can I get you?"

Checking the cart, he said, "A martini would be great—on the rocks, no vermouth."

"In other words"—I laughed—"a glass of gin. Olive?"

"Sure." While I fixed his drink, he said, "So tell me about this friend."

Isandro was pouring himself a glass of wine. He told Keith, "Our mystery guest is Christopher Friendly—he was married to Jazz. They're divorced, but things are amicable now. They have an amazing little girl."

"*And*," I said, "Christopher has never seen the coach house. *And* he happens to be a lawyer. So I thought, Why not include him? Hope you don't mind."

"Of course not. If he's a friend of yours, I'll enjoy meeting him."

We raised our glasses in a casual toast, then sipped.

Keith said, "Just so I've got the whole picture: If Christopher was married to Jazz, he's straight, right?"

Isandro and I glanced at each other. I told Keith, "The jury's still out on that, counselor."

But Isandro was more blunt: "Oh, *Mary*. No way he's straight."

I explained, "Christopher shows some ... *signs* of being gay, but to my knowledge, he doesn't follow through. I wouldn't call him closeted, though, because his manner suggests that he's *way* out there."

Keith said, "He sounds like a bit of a tease."

"He can come across that way, but I don't think it's intentional. For instance, a few months ago, Christopher and I had a heart-to-heart one night, and I was sure he was finally ready to come out to me. But I was wrong. He still loves Jazz, and he's an adoring father to their daughter. I do get the impression that Jazz has been the only woman in his life. What still puzzles me is whether he's had any experience with men. He might be 'bi.' He might be a so-called metrosexual. *Or*, he might be waiting for the right moment to take the plunge."

Keith asked, "Bottom line, then?"

I shrugged. "Speculation abounds."

Dingdong.

"Judge for yourself," I told Keith as I walked to the door.

"Dante!" said Christopher as I opened it. Another bottle was thrust at me, this one in a gift bag. Stepping inside, he continued, "What a *fab*-ulous surprise, getting your call today. I've been dying to see the new place—and my *gawd*—it looks just marvelous. You boys have certainly got 'the touch.'"

Isandro came over to greet him, which included a quick hug (I hadn't gotten one).

"I want the *complete* tour," said Christopher, glancing around, "and I can't wait to be introduced to your *friend*. Who's this?"

Keith joined us, extending a hand, which Christopher shook, holding on for just a beat longer than customary.

I made the introductions, concluding, "... and I thought you might enjoy knowing each other, since you both happen to be lawyers."

"Oh?" said Christopher, pleasantly surprised. "What sort of practice are you in?"

Keith told him, "I have a one-man office in Rancho Santa Fe, keeping busy with a bit of everything—mostly business and family law, with some trial work thrown in for good measure."

I watched as they compared notes. It had *not* been my imagination—these two had reminded me of each other because, now that I saw them together, they were practically clones. Same height: within an inch of six feet. About the same age: Keith thirty-eight, Christopher forty. Same body: fit, gym-toned, but not muscle boys. Same hair: sandy brown, professionally styled, short, businesslike. Same style of dress: both looking nicely turned-out in sweaters, slacks, and fine leather loafers, with an overall vibe of prosperous preppy-casual. Plus, of course: they were both attorneys, Stanford Law for Christopher, and Berkeley Law for Keith. Totally top-shelf.

They exchanged business cards, which I interpreted as more than a professional courtesy, as it left open the possibility of future communication—for any reason.

I asked Christopher, "What would you like to drink?"

He asked Keith, "What are you having?"

Keith rattled the ice in his glass. "It *was* a martini."

Christopher told me, "Same. But 'up,' please."

While I went to work fixing both drinks, Isandro said to Christopher, "There isn't much more to see, but you asked for the 'complete tour,' so follow me."

Keith had visited the loft on Friday night, so he hung back with me while Isandro and Christopher wandered back toward the kitchen and the sleeping area beyond.

I had to ask: "Well, Keith, what'd you think?"

He struggled for *le mot juste*. "Interesting," he declared.

"Care to be more specific?"

With a little sigh that verged on dreamy, Keith said, "Not sure what he's into, but he's plenty hot."

"Agreed," I said with a grin.

Keith's expression turned quizzical. "It was sorta weird—I thought Christopher looked a bit like *me*. Just a little. Don't you think?"

"Well"—I tried to look pensive while sizing him up—"a little, maybe. Yes, now that you mention it, you're *both* plenty hot."

Keith's features sank. "Oh, gosh, *sorry*. I wasn't fishing, honest."

I chortled. "Trust me. I didn't think you were fishing—because you don't need to."

"Thank you. I'll take that as a high compliment."

Isandro wandered back with Christopher, telling me, "Someone's getting thirsty."

I gave the cocktail shaker a few more vigorous rattles, then poured Christopher's martini and handed him the stemmed glass. I'd already refreshed Keith's glass, which he now had in hand. Isandro and I lifted ours, and we all chorused, "Cheers!"

Dinner conversation was lively, at times turning campy. It provided me with a much-needed escape from the anxiety caused by yesterday's murder and today's reversal of fortune at the office. In fact, none of that even came up—because all of our gabbing focused on Keith and Christopher while they tiptoed through the niceties of getting to know each other, as if they were on a first date in the company of mutual friends.

Which wasn't far from the truth. Before they had arrived, Isandro and I discussed the seating arrangement at our small round dining table, deciding to put Keith and Christopher next to each other, facing us, "couple to couple," rather than alternating partners. Our pretext for this was allowing them to have the view through the window, but they never questioned it—and certainly never protested it—as they happily settled in together.

(I also figured that this setup would allow them to play kneesies or steal a grope, if they were inclined, under the tablecloth. Just sayin'.)

Their "discovery process"—as lawyers might call it—covered such topics as music, films, books, pets (none), sports (not much), clothing brands (plenty), restaurants (endless). On the other hand, their chitchat scrupulously avoided any mention of past relationships or future hopes in that realm. They did, however, make a point of establishing that they were both "currently single."

Keith and Christopher were so focused on each other, it was not until dessert was served—a fail-safe concoction of ice cream, berries, and Grand Marnier—that their attention drifted back to Isandro and me. Keith turned to ask me, "How's Zola doing? Have you talked to her today?"

"No, but I talked to Richard, and he says she's worried."

Christopher interrupted: "Excuse me. I guess I'm confused. Keith? You know *Zola*?"

Keith shrugged. "Well, *sure*."

I jumped in: "I am *so* sorry, Christopher. Things have moved so fast the last couple of days, I must've neglected to fill you in. Keith is with the party staying at the rental house in Rancho Mirage, where Richard's extended family is having that reunion."

Half-enlightened, half-concerned, Christopher thumped his forehead. He told Keith, "I was *wondering* why you happened to be here tonight, and then we got involved in our own conversation, but I never did get around to asking you about it. So: it seems you were *there* yesterday when Zola got framed for the murder."

Keith nodded. "It was awful."

Christopher touched his hand. "Will you accept my apologies? I've been so glib and flighty all evening—you must've thought I was *terribly* insensitive."

Keith put his other hand atop Christopher's (their hands were starting to stack up, resembling a club sandwich). "Nonsense," he assured Christopher, "nothing to apologize for. You simply didn't *know*, and that's that. Besides, it's not as if I'm grief-stricken. Wendy was my *step*-mom, and we were anything but close."

Piecing it together, Christopher asked, "Wendy was the victim?"

"Right. Dad's having a hard time with it—he has his moments—but frankly, no one *else* is bothered that she's gone. Sure, the circumstances are tragic. She shouldn't have died that way, and the killer needs to be brought to justice. But even so, it's no stretch to believe that Wendy has reaped what she's sown."

And things went downhill from there.

As Christopher sat back, his hand slipped away from Keith's. After an awkward silence, he said, "Everyone at Saturday's dinner and Sunday's brunch is a suspect in Wendy's murder, correct?"

Keith nodded. "Until we're cleared, one by one—yes, everyone's on the list."

"Meaning," said Christopher, "your father is a suspect."

"Certainly. The spouse of the victim ... well, you know the process."

Christopher asked, "Are you *representing* him?"

Keith shrugged. "Not yet. Not if I don't need to. If things get dicey, I'll step in." Trying to lighten the conversation, he added, "Unless things get dicey for *me*. Then I might need to represent *myself*."

Christopher responded with a blank expression.

Keith grinned. "I'll let you in on a little secret: I didn't do it." His tone was cheery and facetious.

But Christopher looked—for lack of a better word—appalled.

"What's wrong?" said Keith.

"I, uh... I'll need to think this through. I've already agreed to work on Zola's behalf, if it comes to that, which could put me in a compromised position with you and your father." He paused before adding, quietly, "And things were going so well. What a shame."

The remainder of the evening, what was left of it, was strained. Agonizingly strained.

CHAPTER
SEVEN

When my phone rang early the next morning, the caller ID informed me that it was Jazz on the line, and I knew what she wanted.

Picking up, I wasn't allowed time to say hello. She instantly asked, breathless, "How'd it go? Tell me about it. Did they click? Any chemistry?"

"Oh, there was chemistry, all right."

"Yes? And...?"

"Unfortunately," I told her, "the chemistry turned a tad explosive when Christopher's inner lawyer kicked in. I think he felt ambushed, and he's probably right. We meant well, but it *was* deceptive, and it backfired."

Sounding pouty, Jazz muttered, "Well, fuck."

It was just past seven o'clock on Tuesday, and I was still at the coach house, having helped Isandro tidy up after the prior night's "festivities." Now sitting at the same table where things had gone awry, staring out the window as Richard's pool cleaner arrived for his duties, I felt tired and demoralized. The first cup of coffee hadn't helped, so I poured another.

I could hear the hiss of the shower at the back of the loft—Isandro was already putting himself together to report for work at Dr. Gastro's office. When we'd gone to bed the night before, neither one of us had been inclined to discuss payback options for our silly bet.

Interrupting these thoughts, Jazz asked me on the phone, "Busy day ahead?"

I gave her the glum news: "We've got big problems at Sunny Junket. Business is bad, and it's about to get worse. Ben needs to lay off a few people—not me—but I'll be working reduced hours. The office will be a *very* unhappy place today, so I'm not going in. Which is a long way of telling you: my day is wide open."

Her tone, it seemed, was intended to buck me up: "Then let's get *busy*. We need to do some interviews. I'm scheduled to see Heather Ferris, the victim's sister-in-law, at the rental house in Rancho Mirage—this morning at ten. Then, at noon, I'm meeting Rebecca Jiang for lunch—at Huggamug. Join me?"

"You bet," I said at once. "I'll drive my own car, so I'll meet you in Rancho Mirage."

When we rang off, I was feeling more focused and purposeful—and since there was no rush, I could enjoy another leisurely jolt of coffee.

By the time I was ready to leave for my appointments with Jazz, Isandro was long gone. Before leaving, however, he had noticed the change in my attitude. Nestling up behind me as I stood at the kitchen sink, cleaning the coffeemaker, he said, "Did I hear you...*singing*?"

"I'm sure you're mistaken."

"I'm sure I'm not, *coração*. But I thought you were dreading work today."

"Change of plans—I'll be doing some side work for Jazz instead."

"Aha." He nuzzled closer. "Sidekicking seems to agree with you."

He was purring now, but unfortunately, there was no time to repay my gambling debt. And off he went.

But he'd made a valid point—sidekicking did indeed seem to agree with me—and an hour later, I was looking forward to the day ahead when I pulled the Karmann Ghia out of the garage and headed east, toward Rancho Mirage.

Arriving at the rental property some twenty minutes later, I parked at the curb, even though the gate to the courtyard was open. Walking through the courtyard, I noticed that the Trot-n-Tipple horse trailer from Heather's winery had been unhitched from the big four-door pickup, which was gone. This led me to wonder if Heather had left with it. Keith's smart little Mercedes was gone, which came as something of a relief, as I didn't feel prepared to rehash the prior night. Harold's Suburban and Rebecca's Lexus were still parked where I'd last seen them.

I heard the sturdy thud of a vehicle's door out on the street, so I waited, and sure enough, Jazz had arrived and was now walking through the open gate, into the courtyard. When she noticed that the pickup was missing, she told me, "Let's see what's going on."

We stepped up to the front door, rang the bell, and waited. I didn't want to use the entry code without another try of the doorbell, so I rang again. And this time, the door swung open.

"Oh," said Harold. "Hi, Dante. Hi, Jazz. Didn't realize you were coming over." He was bedraggled and ungroomed, wearing a bathrobe that was sloppily cinched beneath his pregnant-looking belly. At ten in the morning (five minutes past, to be precise), I found this unseemly, but I reminded myself that Sunny Junket's guests weren't here to punch timecards.

I said, "Sorry, Harold. Hope we didn't wake you."

"Nah." He yawned, pulled a pack of cigarettes from his robe, and began tapping one out—but tucked them away when I gave him a steely look. "Oops."

Jazz said, "Heather is expecting me, but I noticed her truck is gone. Do you know if your sister is here?"

He tossed his hands. "Beats me. Have a look." And he wandered back to his bedroom, passing the bottle of Old Nine-Tails that stood next to an empty glass on the kitchen island. No wonder he was bleary-eyed.

I closed the front door, then Jazz and I walked through the great room and made our way out to the patio, where we crossed over to the guesthouse. It did not have a formal entryway or doorbell, as it had been designed as more of a pool house than a casita. Access was provided by sliding glass doors that formed the outer wall of a central lounge area and its adjacent kitchen. I rapped on one of the sliders.

Within a minute, Heather emerged from one of the bedrooms and let us in. "Hi there, Jazz. Sorry to keep you waiting—just wrapping up my daily check-in call with the vineyard manager."

"No problem at all."

Heather turned to me. "Welcome to you as well, Dante— didn't realize you were coming, but glad you're here."

I asked wryly, "Trouble with the Wi-Fi?"

"Nope. Just good to see you." She smiled, looking fresh and rested. She was not in her bathrobe. She was not in swimwear, anticipating a sweaty session in the sun. Rather, she was dressed to see Jazz, keeping an appointment, wearing nice slacks with a silk Hermès blouse that mimicked a cowboy shirt. She asked, "Can I get you something to drink before we sit down?"

We declined, Jazz adding, "But please, help yourself."

"I'm fine," she said, sitting near the end of an L-shaped sofa.

Jazz and I sat on the other extension of the L, pivoting to face her. Jazz said, "We noticed your pickup was gone. I wasn't sure if you were here."

"I wouldn't leave you in the *lurch*, Jazz." Heather laughed. "Brooke and Tyler wanted to go out and do some exploring. Näzh went along for the ride; he doesn't drive and was getting restless." She paused, then repeated, "*Restless*. It sounds rather like an infant, doesn't it? I'm twelve years older than he is, but sometimes, the difference feels more like forty."

Jazz opened a small portfolio she'd brought. "Do you mind if I take a few notes? And don't worry. Nothing you say will get back to... anyone."

"No problem, Jazz. Go right ahead."

I interpreted this permission as plenary, so I pulled out my phone to type notes of my own as Jazz prepared her pen and pad. I asked Heather, "Has Detective Madera already spoken to you at length?"

"On Sunday, when we all gave statements to her crew, she spent quite a bit of time with me—more than with the others, I thought. She mainly asked background questions about every-one *else* and never really pressed me for my own alibi. Once I confirmed that I had slept here in the guest house and had not been in the main house between midnight and three, that was that. She did say she would call me about a follow-up interview, but I haven't heard from her."

I turned to Jazz. "Anything from Arcie yet?"

She nodded. "I talked to her earlier today, and she had some initial findings from the medical examiner."

"Anything you can talk about?" (This was my veiled way of asking if she could discuss this in front of Heather.)

"There were no surprises," Jazz assured me. "Everything was in line with appearances at the crime scene. The medical examiner determined that Wendy died shortly after one o'clock that morning. And analysis of her stomach contents—including the vomit—revealed that she had in fact ingested honey. Results of routine toxicology are still to come, but even if she happened to have drugs in her system, it was the reaction to honey that killed her. Considering that she struggled to find her EpiPen, but couldn't, we can rule out suicide; she did not intend to die that way. All of this confirms our earlier conclusion that this was a homicide."

"Murder," Heather mumbled. "It doesn't seem possible. This whole ordeal has felt like a bad dream. I keep thinking: When we wake up, we'll discover that Wendy's death was a horrible accident, but nothing so sinister as *murder*."

With a sympathetic tone, Jazz said, "I share your mixed emotions, Heather. From everything I've learned about Wendy, it seems she was *not* a likable person—but we owe her an honest effort to name her killer."

Heather agreed soberly, "Of course."

While they spoke, I noticed that Max Hazer, the past-his-prime hippie pool guy, had arrived and begun his twice-weekly ritual, using a long-handled skimmer to remove a few leaves from the water's surface.

Sounding a happier note, Jazz said, "So *tell* me, Heather, what on Earth is an 'equestrian winery'? What do horses have to do with wine?"

Heather allowed herself a soft laugh. "Believe it or not, equestrian wineries are actually 'a thing.' For most people, when you mention wine, they think of Napa, but there are also some serious vineyards in Southern California, and Temecula's reputation has steadily grown. As for the horses, I assume that angle rose out of the notion that vineyards are associated with ranching, as well as agriculture. Nowadays, many vineyards have a tourist business on the side, so why not bring horses into the experience? Stables, riding, tasting, dining, a shop or two—it's a surprisingly natural mix, and our guests love it."

Jazz asked, "How did you get started with this?"

"My husband, Jason—he's gone now—he suggested it shortly after we were married. We were just getting started and feeling adventurous, so we borrowed some money and took the leap. Sometimes in life, things just have a way of working out. It did for us. For Brooke, too—she grew up at Trot-n-Tipple. How many kids can say *that*?"

Jazz laughed. "That's a far cry from where *I* grew up—in LA."

I had already heard some of this earlier from Keith, so my attention again drifted to Max as he worked on the pool. He lit a cigarette, then knelt to attach a thick blue vacuum hose to the filter intake recessed in the coping at the water's edge. I heard the pump rev higher as he began cleaning the bottom of the pool.

Heather told Jazz, "I realize that 'Trot-n-Tipple' might sound a tad cute, but I'm proud of the place. You'd enjoy it—you should drive over for a visit sometime."

"Good idea," said Jazz, nodding while scribbling a note. This was no idle comment, since she turned to me with a quick nod.

Joining their conversation, I said to Heather, "Do you mind if I ask when you lost your husband?" I recalled Keith telling me it was a few years ago, but he wasn't specific.

Heather gathered her thoughts, looking suddenly perplexed. "I'd like a glass of wine. Would you care for some?" With a smirk, she added enticingly, "It's Trot-n-Tipple's finest…"

Jazz said, "I'm sure it's wonderful, but I'm stuck on water."

I told Heather, "I'd be glad to join you, thanks."

She got up and moved over to the kitchen area, where an island for the sink served double duty as a breakfast bar. Jazz and I followed her, seating ourselves on stools facing into the kitchen while Heather pulled a bottle of wine from the fridge. She then set it on the island and opened it, speaking to us across the sink. "It's a dry Riesling, perfect before noon—and I love it *cold*, not just chilled. Try." She passed me a glass.

"Nice," I said. "Very nice."

She poured a glass of mineral water for Jazz and wine for herself, then drank, eyes closed, breathing deeply. "Ah," she said. "That's better."

After an awkward lull, I said, "If you'd rather not talk about your husband, that's fine. I didn't mean to ... intrude."

She waggled a hand. "Not at all—you didn't 'intrude.' It's a topic I don't often discuss, but under the circumstances, you probably need to hear about this."

Jazz gave me a look, then opened her notepad, telling Heather, "Fire away, girlfriend. Sounds like man trouble."

"Not exactly." Heather sipped more of the Riesling. "To answer your question, Dante, I lost my husband ten years ago. God, don't you hate euphemisms? I didn't 'lose' him. He didn't 'pass away' or 'pass on.' He didn't 'cross over.' He wasn't 'called home.' No. Jason *died*."

With a slow nod, I said, "I'm so very sorry."

Jazz added, "Our condolences, Heather. You're still hurting—it must've been awful."

As if she hadn't heard us, as if she were thinking aloud, she said, "Brooke was *barely* out of high school when her father was snatched away. How I wish she and Jason could have known each other as *adults*—two beautiful people who deserved more time together. But that was cut short. That was *stolen*."

There was a passion in Heather's voice that told me her husband hadn't died from a heart attack or a car accident or a fall from a ladder. I asked, "What happened, Heather?"

She tried to take another sip of wine, but the glass was shaking so badly, she used both hands to set it back on the counter. She closed her eyes and then, it seemed, a calm descended on her. She blinked. Looking first at Jazz, then at me, she said, "What happened? Wendy happened. Wendy killed Jason."

I was struck speechless.

But Jazz was too curious not to ask: "*How?*"

"Not with a gun. Not with a knife or a club or a crowbar."

I couldn't help thinking, *Candlestick?*

"Nothing like that," Heather told us. "Are you aware of Wendy's 'problem'?"

"Uh... several," said Jazz. "Help me out here."

I turned to her. "I'm guessing this has something to do with drugs."

Heather leaned across the counter to refill my glass. "Congratulations, Dante. Yes, Wendy had a *serious* drug problem. She was in trouble with a lot of people. If she wanted to fuck up her life—fine with me. But it didn't stop there. She was in so deep, she needed to spread the pain. She needed to hook others. In a moment of weakness, Jason let her into his life, and that was the beginning of the end—for him. It happened quickly, in the course of a few months. He went from successful businessman, loving husband, and devoted father—to become a hopelessly addicted fentanyl user. It broke our hearts and damn near destroyed the business. Wendy didn't actually inject him. Jason did that himself, once too often, because he was powerless to stop. But make no mistake: Wendy *killed* Jason."

In the silence that followed, Jazz scribbled in her pad while I typed on my phone, but we were both at a loss to speak.

After what felt like minutes, a lull that probably lasted mere seconds, Heather told us, "That was all in the past, of course. Long ago. Brooke got over it more quickly than I did—she's *young*—and I'm dealing with it better now, but I still have my moments." She grinned. "Sorry to go operatic on you."

I said, "We completely understand, Heather. Thank you for opening up to us—I'm sure it was difficult." My brow pinched. "But I'm wondering: Having been through such an awful experience—with your own brother's *wife*—how did you manage to maintain a familial relationship with Harold? I've seen the two of you interact, and you seem just fine together."

"Now, *that*," said Heather, "that's a very good question. At first—trust me—there was plenty of friction. More accurately, I was enraged. I did not hold back in blaming Wendy for Jason's death, and by extension, I openly blamed Harold as well. But... you know the old yarn: blood is thicker than water. Ultimately, Harold will always be my 'big brother,' and he still refers to me as his 'kid sister.' Harold and Heather. Back when we were growing up, everyone said it like one word, *Harold'n'Heather*. So I learned to forgive Harold and focus my hate on Wendy."

Jazz said, "I'm pretty sure of the answer, but did you ever find it in your heart to forgive Wendy?"

Heather barked a single, loud laugh. "*Forgive* Wendy? I'll *never* forgive her, dead or alive. And I'm glad that bitch finally got what she deserved."

Well now, I thought. *There's* a motive.

Jazz, I was certain, recognized this as well, but she didn't question Heather further about it. Instead, she changed topics, asking her, "What's it like, working in a family-owned business? I'm guessing the upside outweighs the problems, right?"

Heather nodded, smiled. "Absolutely. Sometimes when I get fed up, I need to sit back and remind myself that..."

I tuned out. Looking past Heather's shoulder, I was gazing at the double-door refrigerator a few feet behind her. The wider door displayed a seemingly random assortment of photos, perhaps twenty, most of them torn out of magazines and others that looked like postcards and snapshots. There was no apparent order to them—it looked more like a slapdash collage, attached to the stainless-steel door with colorful magnets and bits of blue painter's tape, reminding me of something a child might post on the refrigerator in the family kitchen. Except, there were no children staying here, and the photos—the ones I could make out from a distance—were anything but childish. The images included the bull statue on Wall Street, the front grille of a Rolls-Royce, a bearded man wearing a turban and sitting in the lotus position, a stack of shiny gold bricks, and an architectural rendering of a sleek, anonymous office building.

Heather's conversation with Jazz had petered out, and she now said, "You seem transfixed, Dante. Dreaming of a Rolls-Royce someday?"

"No," I said honestly. "They've never much interested me."

Heather said, "Really? That's refreshing. Näzh is enthralled by them. Whenever he sees one, he practically drools. I find it embarrassing."

"Have you talked to him about that?"

She shrugged. "Why intrude on his fantasies?"

Jazz asked her, "So that's what those pinups are about—his fantasies?"

Facetiously, Heather said, "Heavens, *no*. Näzh would positively *chafe* at describing all this as 'fantasy pinups.' No, my friends, *this*"—she stepped to the refrigerator and struck a Vanna White pose—"this is his 'vision board.' Or the travel version, at least. You should see the one at home. It covers a wall."

With a blank look, Jazz said, "You've lost me."

I said to Heather, "On Sunday, Näzh described himself as your spiritual adviser. So this must have something to do with 'manifesting,' right?"

Heather told us, "Vision boards have *everything* to do with the practice of manifestation. They're the principal tool in turning desired outcomes into reality."

Jazz snorted. "Sounds to me like wishful thinking."

Heather stepped back to the island for a sip of her wine. Then she told us, "Lots of people dismiss manifestation exercises as wishful thinking—and I get it. But the idea isn't new. The central concept goes back as far as the philosopher Lao Tzu, the transcendentalist Ralph Waldo Emerson, and more recently, Norman Vincent Peale's *Power of Positive Thinking*. Oprah herself has touted vision boards. Granted, it takes a certain, shall we say, *open-mindedness* to embrace the particulars, the nuts and bolts, of manifestation. It's not for everyone. Jazz, you're a detective, a just-the-facts kinda gal. I respect that. And I understand your skepticism."

Jazz asked, "And how do *you* feel about it, Heather? Vision boards and manifestation: The height of serene wisdom? Or a steaming crock of horse hokum?"

Heather suppressed a laugh. "Somewhere in between." Twisting an imaginary key, she locked her lips.

I told her, "We'd really like to talk to Näzh sometime. Do you know if he'll be around this afternoon—maybe two o'clock?"

"I'm sure he'll be here. After this morning's outing, he'll be worn out for the day. He can be rather delicate."

Confused, I asked, "No health problems, I hope?"

"God, no. Näzh is wonderfully virile; it's his disposition that can be delicate. I'll let him know to expect you."

Jazz asked me, "Can you handle it on your own? I have a meeting after lunch."

"No problem. The only Sunny Junket guests assigned to me this week are right here, so I should check back anyway."

Jazz and I spent a few more minutes talking to Heather, wrapping up our interview and thanking her for her insights.

She reminded us, "I truly *would* appreciate your keeping the details of our discussion in confidence. Please?"

I assured her, "Say no more, Heather."

And she slid the glass door closed behind us as we left.

Out on the terrace, I noted how brilliantly the pool sparkled in the late-morning sun. On the white limestone pavers, a faintly damp trail, still evaporating in the heat, led back to the concealed filter equipment, where Max Hazer had disappeared through the service gate.

We had time to run a few errands on our own before going to Huggamug, where Rebecca Jiang would join us at noon. Jazz and I agreed to meet there about ten minutes early.

When I walked through the door, Jazz had already secured a prime window table in the front corner, which would give us a full view of both the room and the street. She spotted me at once and waved me over.

"Hi there," I said, winded, as I'd parked my car behind Sunny Junket, then trotted the remaining block to get to the restaurant on time.

"Drink up," she said, having ordered lemonade for three. Menus were already in place. Jazz was seated in the chair nearest the window and indicated that I should take the one near-est the wall. The third chair, for Rebecca, would have her facing directly into the corner.

I sat and drank a slug or two of lemonade while Jazz placed her notebook on top of her menu and opened it. "It's sort of mind-blowing," she said. "I'm wearing two hats at this lunch—one as a private investigator providing services to Keith Gibkin, checking out Rebecca on behalf of his father's best interests."

Catching on, I concluded, "And wearing the other hat, you're providing investigative services to Keith's father, Harold, check-ing out all the suspects on behalf of Zola."

We both shook our heads as if clearing cobwebs—the whole setup was crazy.

"A few preliminaries," she said, glancing over her notes. "I heard from Arcie again, and she let me know that the EpiPen found in Zola's bag was, in fact, Wendy's—just as we thought. They had no trouble tracing the prescription back to her."

I said, "So that's just further evidence that the killer knew about Wendy's honey allergy, knew she had an EpiPen, and then deliberately took it, sealing her fate."

Jazz nodded. "Right. Also, Arcie reported that the only finger-prints found on the EpiPen were Zola's and mine. Same for the honey bottle. Makes sense—Zola and I handled both items when they were found in her purse. But the lack of anyone *else's* prints does *not* make sense."

"Which means," I said, "someone—the killer—wiped all finger-prints from both items before planting them in the purse."

"Exactly," said Jazz. "Still, that doesn't necessarily exonerate Zola. She *herself* could've wiped the earlier prints to cause con-fusion."

Ridiculous, I thought. (But yes, it was logically possible.)

Jazz marked a check next to something in her notes. "Now, then: your reactions to this morning's talk with Heather."

With a breath of a laugh, I noted, "Well, she certainly handed us one dandy of a motive for killing Wendy. She's *still* grinding an ax—you could practically see the sparks. Not that I blame her."

"Me neither. Heather had a fuckin' *fantastic* motive—almost a *noble* motive—avenging the death of her husband. But...?"

I completed Jazz's thought: "But Heather isn't stupid—far from it. She's smart enough to know that revealing this background is *not* in her best interest, but she told us anyway. Which *could* mean that she figured it was better for us to hear it volunteered directly from her, rather than having Arcie discover it through investigation. On the surface, that's a sign of innocence."

"Then again," said Jazz, "it could also be a sign of cunning—and guilt. So Heather is still on the list, maybe a half notch higher."

I shrugged. "Quarter notch."

With a laugh, Jazz said, "But *enough* of this hairsplitting. I think we should follow Heather's suggestion to visit Trot-n-Tipple. Are you up for a trip to Temecula tomorrow?"

"I *can* be, sure. My schedule is 'flexible' these days."

She looked concerned. "Your job—are you nervous about Sunny Junket?"

"I didn't *think* so, but maybe I should be. I dunno."

Jazz shot up from her chair and waved at Rebecca, who had just walked in from the street. I stood as well, and we greeted Rebecca with pleasantries (the ladies shared a lady-hug) before we all settled into our seats.

Lifting her lemonade, Rebecca told us, "Cheers."

We echoed the sentiment, then all of us opened our menus and studied them with uncommon interest, each of us hesitant to set the course of our conversation.

Finally, Jazz took charge. "You must be wondering, Rebecca, why I suggested this meeting."

"Well"—she hemmed—"you *said* you wanted to talk about 'the situation with Wendy,' which I interpreted to mean 'the murder.'" She grinned.

She was prettier than I had noticed before. I don't know if it was the ambience of the coffeehouse or the light angling in from the street, but away from the Gibkin crowd and the scene of the crime, she was far more poised and less harried. As before, she was beautifully dressed—heels, slacks, jacket. I've never cared for the word *classy*, but she had the look of a definitively classy businesswoman, capable and intelligent. Her Asian features were graced with a gentle, restrained smile.

Jazz said, "I'm sorry my phrasing wasn't more candid. Yes, I'd like to discuss the circumstances of the murder."

A waiter appeared. "Have we decided on lunch? I should mention that the soup today is butternut squash." Under his breath, he added, "A bit early for *that*, in my opinion."

Having wasted so much time staring blindly at the menus, we were not yet prepared to order. "Then let me bring you some bread," said the waiter. "No rush." And he was gone.

Jazz cleared her throat. "Rebecca, I hope you won't be offended, but the single question I most want to ask is this: What was your reaction to Wendy's death? And who do you think was responsible for it?"

"Purely in the interest of precision, that was two questions."

Jazz allowed, "A two-parter, I guess."

Rebecca thought for a moment. "The short answer to part one is: I'm not sure. The short answer to part two is: I don't know."

"Noted," said Jazz. "Please elaborate if you can."

Rebecca fiddled with her napkin, then dabbed her lips, leaving a pink smudge on the white linen. "My reaction to Wendy's death—let's see, now. I found it disturbing, of course. Scary stuff. That night, someone was murdered under the same roof where we were all staying."

Jazz reminded her, "But it wasn't just 'someone.'"

"No, it wasn't. It was Wendy. Harold's wife."

"And where was your bedroom, Rebecca? Anywhere near Wendy's?"

"No," she said. "The main house has two wings, each with two bedrooms, on opposite sides of the great room. Basically, we had the whole house between us that night."

I asked, "So you didn't *hear* anything from Wendy's room at any time during the night?"

Rebecca shook her hear. "Impossible. Plus, I was exhausted. Saturday was busy—traveling, shopping, putting dinner together, and *then* cleaning up. I was in bed before midnight and slept soundly till morning."

The bread arrived, with cruets of olive oil and vinegar. We took a quick second look at the menu and placed our orders.

After the waiter left, Jazz asked Heather, "On Sunday, when did you become aware that something was wrong?"

She shrugged. "Shortly past noon, same as everyone else, when you and Dante went to tell Wendy that brunch was ready—and then came back to tell us what you'd found."

Jazz asked, meaningfully, "And when you heard the news that Wendy was dead, what was the very first thing you *felt*—before you had time to think about it?"

Though Jazz had asked for an instant reaction, Rebecca did indeed take time to think about it. She said, "I'm not sure what you expect to hear from me. Was I happy or sad, that sort of thing? Now, look. It's no secret that Wendy and I weren't exactly best buds, so my first reaction to hearing she was dead—let's just say I wasn't grief-stricken. Stunned, maybe. We all were. It was unexpected."

I reminded her, "*One* person there was expecting it."

"Okay, point taken. But *I* was stunned, and to tell the truth, my overwhelming reaction—once I began processing it—was relief."

Jazz scratched a note while asking, "Why were you relieved?"

"Wendy was *not* a pleasant person. Working in the Gibkins' house—with her around, not to mention that damn monkey—was often hellish. All that carping about *food*. And anything she *was* willing to eat, she just threw up, so what the hell was the *point*? But then, suddenly, she was gone. You *bet* I was relieved. But most of all, I was relieved for Harold."

Jazz and I glanced at each other. She asked Rebecca, "Relieved for Harold—why? His wife had died."

Rebecca stiffened, pausing before she replied. "I'll tell you the same thing I've already told Detective Madera: Wendy was a shrew, a harpy, a crazy drug-addled bitch. And Harold is *far* better off without her." Offhandedly, she added, "Did you notice? He might have broken down at first—it was the shock—but he seems to be over it already."

Jazz and I had indeed noticed Harold's abbreviated grieving. Was he as "relieved" by the murder as Rebecca was?

Jazz asked her, "Are you aware that Harold has retained me to investigate the death? That's why Detective Madera and I are *both* conducting interviews."

"Yes, I know you're working for Harold. He told me about it. He also told me *why* he's doing this—to clear that Zola woman. What's the story with *her*?"

I said, "She's a *friend* of ours. She's also very fond of Richard

Gibbs, Harold's second cousin—which was the premise for this disaster of a family reunion."

"Yes, yes, yes"—she sounded bored by the details—"but why would Harold pay to get Zola off the hook?"

"First of all," said Jazz, getting annoyed by Rebecca's tone, "I've made it clear to Harold that I'm working to find out who *did* kill Wendy, not who *didn't*. If that happens to clear Zola, as I sincerely hope it will—great." Jazz took a deep breath. "Second, if you're wondering why Harold would pay me to do this, I gotta tell ya, I don't have a clue. So why don't you ask *him* about his motive?" Pointedly, she added, "I understand that you two are reasonably, shall we say, 'close.' Correct?"

Rebecca sat back in her chair and steadied herself, breathing deeply. She closed her eyes. When she opened them, she reached for her purse and fished out a tube of lipstick, then touched up her lips—a deep, dusty pink. She told us, "Harold and I have helped each other through more crises than I can count." She dropped the lipstick back into her purse and snapped it shut.

I said, "How have you helped each other?"

She looked at me as if I were dense. "We were *there* for each other—us against the world."

Jazz asked, "Don't you mean 'us against Wendy'?"

Rebecca smirked. "Your words, Jazz, not mine. But you raise a valid point. Harold and I have always shared a certain ... synchronicity. Though we never spoke of it, we both knew how *wrong* Wendy was for him. Whenever she'd create chaos, I'd restore the order in his world. We're kindred spirits. I suppose you could call us soulmates."

I asked, "Does he think of *you* as a soulmate. Has he told you that?"

"Not in so many words. But he hardly needs to say it—I already *know* it." She flipped her hands and smiled, as if the simple truth of her assertion should be self-evident.

"I dunno…," I said skeptically. "Every time I've seen you and Harold together, he's treated you like the *help*—the cook, the maid, the gofer."

She leaned over the table, telling me in a fierce whisper, "He was being *discreet*. He's a gentleman to the core, and he understands that appearances *matter*."

I thought, *Harold? Harold Gibkin?*

We were quiet as the waiter returned to the table and delivered lunch: a cheese thing for Jazz, a Tex-Mex thing for me, and a fruit salad for Rebecca. "Enjoy!" he said, then disappeared.

Calmly, Jazz said to Rebecca, "Unless I'm mistaken, it sounds like you love Harold. That's the bottom line, right?"

Again that look from Rebecca, as if we were dumb beyond belief. She actually rolled her eyes. "Of *course* I love Harold. I always have, and now we're free to express it."

Jazz glanced at me, then stared at Rebecca. "C'mon, honey. Woman to woman, just tell me this: Have you and Harold ever been…intimate?"

"Good heavens, *no*. We've been the very model of propriety."

Jazz raised a finger. "Just so we're on the same page here: I wasn't necessarily talkin' about, you know…*ruttin'* or whatever. So let's dial it back. I'm asking if you've ever shared a little stolen kiss, or a hug, or even words of tenderness. Either before or since Wendy's death, has Harold ever returned your feelings with an explicit expression of his 'love' for you."

Tears welled in Rebecca's eyes. "Well, *sure*. There were lots of—"

Jazz quickly added, "Holiday bonuses and pats on the back

don't cut it. We're talkin' about stuff that really says, 'I love you, and I want you.'"

Rebecca's lower lip quivered. She swiped a tear that slid down to the corner of her mouth, smearing lipstick on her chin and index finger. Sobs began to rise in her throat as she told us, "I think you're both ... you're both just *awful* ... and as far as I'm concerned ... you can both ... you can go *fuck yourselves*!"

Her last words were shouted, hushing the room and drawing glances. She stood, slapped her napkin on the table, and marched away, heels snapping, as she made her way through the crowd and out the door.

Jazz turned to me. "I have no idea what she sees in him."

I shrugged. "Love is blind."

And we divvied up her fruit salad.

Rebecca had never even gotten around to the second part of Jazz's initial question, which asked her to speculate about *who* Wendy's killer was. But we'd heard enough, and I felt that she'd risen a solid notch on our suspect list. When I mentioned this to Jazz, she raised my estimate: "Notch and a half."

Shortly before two that afternoon, I returned to the rental house in Rancho Mirage, where I planned to interview Näzh Hoyle. Parking at the curb as usual, I walked through the courtyard and noted that the Trot-n-Tipple horse trailer was still there, unhitched, but the pickup truck was gone, as before.

When I rang the doorbell, I was surprised—pleasantly—to be greeted by Tyler Evans, the bookish Black boyfriend of Brooke Ferris. "Hey, Dante," he said. "C'mon in."

Following him into the great room, I noticed a laptop open on the kitchen island with a printer next to it and some paperwork spread about. No one else was present. I didn't know if either Rebecca or Harold was in the house, and after what had happened at lunch, I didn't want to run into them. I asked Tyler, "Is Näzh here—in the guesthouse?"

"Yeah, he's expecting you. I thought I'd work over here this afternoon—and give you some privacy." He sat down in front of the computer.

Recalling that he was a freelance illustrator, I strolled over to glance at the screen. "*Hey*," I said, "you do some beautiful work. What a talent—congratulations."

"Thanks, man. It's a living. Won't make me rich, but I love it."

"Maybe we could talk about it sometime—later this week?" I handed him one of my cards.

He dug out one of his. Passing it to me, he said, "Anytime that works for you, just let me know. And I'm *guessing* you also want to talk about what happened to Wendy."

I admitted, "You're on the list. It needs to be done."

Focused on his computer screen, he shrugged. "Cool."

I moved toward the terrace doors at the back of the house, then turned to tell Tyler, "I noticed when I got here that Keith's little Mercedes wasn't parked in front. Do you know if he's around?"

"Far as I know, he's away for a few days—lawyer stuff, back in Rancho Santa Fe."

"Ah." I couldn't help wondering if last night's awkward dinner with Christopher Friendly had sent Keith packing for the coast. Probably not, I reasoned. I doubted whether his emotions were that fragile, and he had previously voiced his intention to return to his office occasionally. Perhaps I would send him a chatty text later, then try to gauge his response.

Meanwhile, the task at hand: I went out to the pool terrace, walked over to the guesthouse, and rapped on the frame of one of the glass doors.

It slid open. In the dazzling afternoon sun, reflections from the glass made it difficult for me to see anything but darkness within. I was greeted: "Welcome, Dante."

My eyes adjusted as I stepped inside, and there was Näzh, barefooted, dressed as usual in a gauzy Eastern-looking outfit, but this one wasn't as ascetic as the ones I'd seen before. While his previous getups included a jumpsuit and, alternately, something like pajama bottoms, today he wore what I'd call palazzo pants, bright orange and embarrassingly sheer. As before, he wore the rhinestone choker, which glittered in the light from the windows. The room smelled of incense—or maybe he was wearing patchouli. Whatever it was, it made my eyes itch.

When I stepped past him, he moved to slide the door closed, but I asked, "Maybe you could leave that open a bit?"

"*Certainly*, Dante. Please, come in. And make yourself comfortable. Would you like some green tea?"

At that moment, I'd have preferred something stronger, but I said, "Sure, thanks. Tea sounds good." As the afternoon had turned hot, I assumed the tea would be iced. But no.

Näzh fussed with a small black iron kettle on a grated contraption with a glowing lump of coal—a hibachi, I guess. While the water boiled, he grated twigs and spices into a mortar, added sprouts and (notably) a drip of honey from a glass jar, then pounded the whole mess with a pestle.

"Won't be a second," he said while adding loose tea to a clear glass pot. A gob from the mortar also went into the pot, followed by boiling water from the kettle. He covered the cloudy green stew with a cozy to let it steep, then set out a tray with two bitsy porcelain cups—and a sizable strainer. "Soon, soon," he said.

"Whenever. Good things are worth waiting for."

"So *true*," said Näzh, setting the tray on a low table in front of the sofa, where I was seated. Lithe and feline, he slid in next to me on the cushion. "The greatest pleasures should never be rushed. In fact," he added with an odd lilt, "they should be postponed and protracted—*teased*, as it were."

This was getting just a tad freaky.

He pulled one of his feet up to the cushion so he could pivot to face me, with his other foot planted on the floor. When I turned my head toward him, I found myself looking into the crotch of his diaphanous palazzo pants.

With a stretch of my imagination, I might've been able to concoct fantasy circumstances in which this display would be alluring, or even exciting. His long black ponytail and trim silver-flecked beard gave him an edgy look that would be easy to find attractive. And I had to admit that what I could see inside the palazzo pants piqued my interest. But the reality of that afternoon's circumstances had the opposite effect on me—Näzh simply gave me the creeps.

I asked, "Are you always this welcoming to your guests?"

"No," he said, locking eyes with me, "not always."

On Saturday, the day I met him, he'd addressed me as "dearest Dante," which seemed like an obvious come-on, but then, in the same breath, he asked if I had 'discovered the powers of manifestation,' so I simply dismissed him as a flake. Now, though, his intentions were unambiguous.

I said, "May I ask you something directly?"

"Please do." He pulled the scrunchie from his ponytail and shook his hair free, letting it cascade over his shoulders.

"Your relationship with Heather—you're not just her spiritual advisor, but the two of you are lovers, aren't you?"

"Her mindfulness is really quite remarkable." He smiled.

Huh?

Leaning to place the scrunchie on the table, next to the tray, he continued: "Heather has vision and focus and purpose. On top of which, she has an exquisite beauty, inside and out. Of *course* we're lovers. But more than lovers—we're truly soulmates."

Not two hours earlier, Rebecca had declared that she and Harold were soulmates, a delusional claim at best. Now Näzh was claiming the same bond with Heather, and I was inclined to think that he, too, was hallucinating. Which made me wonder exactly what was in the slimy swill in his teapot.

As he poured and strained it into the white cups, I said, "When I asked if you and Heather were lovers, I wasn't referring to a metaphysical connection on the astral plane, so let me be explicit: Do the two of you have sex?"

"Well, *duh*, Dante dearest. Heather and I often have sex—sometimes twice a day. Whyever would you ask?"

"Because you're *showing* me your junk. What kinda game *is* this?"

He paused, smirked, and handed me my tea. Settling back on the sofa, he raised his tiny cup, saying, "*Namaste.*"

"Yeah, whatever." We sipped. Though expecting the worst, I found it wasn't half bad.

He placed a delicate hand on my knee. "I can tell you're an open-minded sort of man, Dante. Surely you can appreciate pansexualism."

With a bored sigh, I said, "So you're telling me you're 'bi.'"

He withdrew his hand. "Such a crude expression, *bisexual*. It's so either/or ... so black or white ... so this or that. As a highly sexual person, I find erotic energy *everywhere*. It's fluid and ever changing."

I gave him a look. "And how does Heather feel about that?"

He shrugged. "She's fine. She has no interest in 'possessing' me, and vice versa. When you think of it, the very notion of possessing someone seems sort of *primitive*—doesn't it?"

He made a reasonable point. I'd had my own history of tussling with this issue, letting it destroy a relationship after nearly thirty years together. And now I had embarked upon only the second serious coupling of my life—with Isandro—and I was still reluctant to commit to it beyond insipid labels like "roommate" or "boyfriend" or "other half."

But this wasn't about me. It was about Näzh and Heather. I said, "I barely know Heather, but she's told me about her marriage to Jason—and how it ended. I can understand how the fear of losing someone might've left her with commitment issues."

Näzh sat up straight, cocking his head, as if intrigued by my words. "If, by 'commitment,' you're referring to marriage, then you're correct: Heather has no more interest in it than I do. However, in the more general sense of 'commitment,' she has no aversions at all."

I cocked *my* head. "What do you mean?"

He stood, beckoned me with his finger, and strolled us over to the kitchen area. Not far from the refrigerator, along an expanse of wall behind the dining table, stood an easel displaying a large architectural drawing of an anonymous-looking office building, artfully rendered. I had noticed it earlier, in the morning, while Jazz and I were there to see Heather, but I hadn't paid much attention to it because I assumed it was an illustration project of

Tyler's. I now realized that it depicted the same building shown in one of the small images posted on the refrigerator door—Näzh's so-called vision board.

Peering at the easel, I asked, "What exactly *is* this?"

Näzh furtively glanced about, as if someone might be lurking and listening. "Can I tell you something in confidence?"

Without knowing what it was, I couldn't answer with certainty. Even so, I told him, "Sure."

As I moved closer to the easel for a better look, he stepped up behind and put his hands on my shoulders, pulling us tight—I felt his warmth against my back. I felt him quiver (and hoped it wasn't an orgasm). I felt the bristle of his beard against my neck as he spoke into my ear with quiet, breathy excitement. "Look upon it and behold: the Institute of Manifest Visualization."

Hands on hips, I turned to ask, "And what, pray tell, is *that*."

"It will be the fruition of a dream long in the making. The Institute will become the nucleus of an entire campus devoted to the development of more powerful manifestation techniques—and spreading the practice to legions of new followers through the teaching of methods and philosophy. The world is *ready* for this, Dante."

"And let me guess: *you'll* be at the helm of it."

"Yes. That's the whole point."

"Impressive. But it sounds like a fairly expensive proposition."

Without compunction, he said, "And that's where *Heather* comes in. As I mentioned, she has no aversion to *commitment*—not when it involves a worthy cause. In essence, she's already agreed to underwrite the project, at least enough to get it off the ground. She's planning to set up a trust, but needs some time to quietly explore the options—since it might cause some ripples in the family."

I muttered, "I'll just bet it would." Then I asked him, "Does her daughter know about this?"

"*God*, no. Brooke would throw a shit fit."

"First," I said, "Brooke hardly strikes me as the type to 'throw a shit fit.' And second, even if she did, I can't say I'd blame her."

He shrugged. "That's a matter between mother and daughter—and has nothing to do with me."

Obviously, it had *everything* to do with Näzh, but instead of confronting him, I simply asked, "Where *is* Heather? Right now."

"Out somewhere with Brooke—bonding, I guess. They said something about a designer-outlet mall along the interstate. Cabazon? A bit of a trek from here. I'm sure they won't be back *soon*." Lasciviously, he added, "... if you catch my drift." Whatever it was he specifically had in mind, I could tell at a glance he was ready for it.

"Look," I lied, "you seem like a nice guy, and I'm flattered by your interest, but what you're suggesting could cause a *lot* of trouble and even cost me my job. In other words: back off."

He pouted, "Party pooper."

I told him, "I'm curious about something. Heather is fifty-two years old—I recall that because I'm just a year older. But you, Näzh, I think you're quite a bit younger, right?"

"Yes. I turned forty a few months ago, so Heather is twelve years older."

"Which means," I said, "that she's not old enough to be your mother, and you're not young enough to be her son. But I wonder how her *daughter* feels about your relationship. Is Brooke okay with it? Or is it awkward? I mean, what's the age difference between you and Brooke?"

"As it happens," he explained, "Brooke is twenty-eight, so there's a twelve-year difference between *us*, too. I'm smack in the middle between mother and daughter—a sandwich, of sorts."

Before I could blink away this unsavory image, Näzh mused, "Then there's Tyler—what a sweet kid, a little rough around the edges, not exactly my type, but what can I say? It's complicated."

I thought: *Complicated? It's horrifying.*

And then my eye drifted to the refrigerator, to the vision board created by this pansexual, hedonistic "spiritual adviser." The collage had been altered since that morning. And I quickly spotted what was different.

A new photo had joined the collection—a photo of me. It was one of the pictures Näzh had snapped in the main house after arriving on Saturday afternoon, when there was a crowd sorting through the pile of luggage in the great room. I stood in the midst of three or four other people, but they had all been scissored away from the sides of the print, leaving only me.

Just me.

CHAPTER
EIGHT

By the time I left the guesthouse, Näzh and I hadn't even broached the topics I had gone there to discuss: possible suspects and motives for Wendy's murder. But I did go away with a new realization: there were powerful undercurrents roiling the relationships of most of the reunion guests in Rancho Mirage.

At home that evening, after Isandro had returned from work and changed into a comfortable old pair of chinos and a soft chambray shirt (looking *very* huggable), I suggested, "Cocktails by the pool?"

And three minutes later, we were out on the terrace, seated near the Inca warrior, joking about the stone phallus—or rather, its shadow—which crept across the pavers in the rapidly setting sunlight. Instead of toasting each other, we shared a little kiss before sipping our drinks, and then, settling in, we recapped our workdays to each other.

His had been utterly routine, but mine provided plenty to tell, especially the story about Näzh, his vision board, and his gauzy palazzo pants. I told Isandro, "And in case you're wondering, I wasn't even tempted."

He laughed. "Not much to work with, huh?"

"*Au contraire*—he had quite a lot to offer. But I was so freaked by the situation, his come-on was a nonstarter."

Isandro laughed again, untroubled by my encounter. And although I was relieved by this seeming affirmation that he was not hell-bent on "possessing" me—a notion Näzh had dismissed as primitive—I also felt an unexpected tinge of disappointment that Isandro might think of me as "only" a roommate or boyfriend, which is exactly what I had wanted. But now…I wasn't so sure.

He asked me, "Did you see Keith today?"

Aha, I thought. Was Isandro checking up on me after all? No, I realized, he was merely looking for any feedback regarding the previous night's dinner for four.

I told him, "Keith's car wasn't at the rental house, so I asked if he was around. Turns out, he drove back to his law office this morning—not sure when he'll be back. Hope he wasn't offended by our attempted, and *failed*, matchmaking. Maybe I should text him." Fishing, I asked, "What do you think?"

"You don't need *my* permission. Go ahead."

And once again, I felt the slightest pang that Isandro had granted me total independence, exactly as I had always wanted.

"Sure," I said, "why not?" Pulling out my phone, I found Keith's number and opened a text, but I struggled with what to say. My purpose was simply to get a reading of his mood. If I was too apologetic and groveling, I might only convince him that he *should* be pissed. If I was too glib and cheery, he might be irked that I was too dismissive of what had happened. After giving this way too much thought—the evening had slipped into twilight—I wrote: MISSED YOU TODAY. HOPE TO SEE YOU AGAIN SOON.

Sending it, I told Isandro, "Well, *that* won't win any prizes, but at least I reached out."

"Yoo-*hoo*-oo." It was Zola, stepping out from the main house with Richard. "May we join you, boys?"

"Please *do*," "Of *course*," we answered in unison, standing to greet them as they approached.

Richard had his usual evening martini in hand; Zola carried her anytime Tom Collins. Richard gave hugs; Zola, kisses. They sat together on the extended cushion of a chaise longue as Isandro and I reclaimed our armchairs—all of the furniture upholstered in stylish, alternating circus stripes of dark putty and light mushroom. Zola really did know her stuff.

"*Well*," she said, "I don't know about *you* boys, but I've really been needing this drink." After a perfunctory raise of her glass, she tilted it back and downed half of it.

Richard explained, "I'm afraid milady has had a rough day."

Isandro and I exchanged a troubled glance. "How so?" I asked.

Zola set her glass on one of the short cigarette tables that were positioned next to each chair. (She firmly believed that one's cocktail, not cigarette, should always be within arm's reach, a sentiment I found admirable.) She told us, "I spent the latter part of the afternoon—it seemed like *hours*—with Detective Madera. We were in a seedy little office at gestapo headquarters."

Richard interpreted: "It was a sheriff's office in Palm Desert, where Arcie is stationed. As such places go, it seemed perfectly pleasant."

"It was hideous," Zola insisted. "Molded plastic chairs. Vertical blinds. Potted *plants*. One shudders to think of it. I'll have dreams..."

I asked, "How did the interview go?"

"It was frightful—all of it under the watchful eye of a khaki-clad Nazi."

Richard told us, "There was a deputy in the room. He was twenty if he was day, and he appeared far more intimidated by Zola than vice versa."

She gave us a sly wink. "I know how to stand up for my rights."

Which suddenly made me think: "Was a lawyer present?"

"Certainly *not*," said Zola. "I was told I could have one, but I have nothing to hide. Why bother?"

I cringed. "Zola, be careful." Looking her in the eye, I said, "Christopher Friendly has offered to represent you. Should I ask him to call you?"

Richard turned to face her, giving a stern nod.

Zola's gaze drifted to the darkening sky. "I suppose it wouldn't hurt."

"I'll let him know, then."

Isandro jumped in, sounding concerned: "So tell us, Zola. How did it go with Arcie? What did she want?"

Picking up her glass again, fingering it, she explained, "It was really just a rehash of everything we already talked about on Sunday at the rental house—the 'crime scene,' as *she* referred to it. Naturally, we talked about the items found in my purse—the honey and that allergy gizmo. And we talked *endlessly* about the logistics on Saturday—where the purse was and when; where *I* was and when; who had access to it when I *didn't*; and on and on. It was mind-numbing. I answered everything I could, but that day was so frantic that all the details became blurred."

I asked, "Could you read Arcie's reactions?"

"To be fair," said Zola, "she seemed to understand that it was impossible to account for everyone's actions that day. And at no time did she actually *accuse* me of spiking the posset and stealing the shot gadget. I pointed out to Arcie that if I'd done those things, I wouldn't have left the evidence in my bag the next day, only to have it spilled in front of everyone. She agreed that such reasoning was a strong point in my favor, but she also pointed out that it could have been a clever ploy—on my part."

"Huh?" said Isandro. "How would *that* work?"

Though I'd never wanted to voice this possibility, now seemed to be the right time: "If Zola had committed the deadly deed, she could've guessed that her Friday-night food fight and screaming match with Wendy would eventually come to light, casting her under suspicion. So I'm assuming the 'clever ploy' suggested by Arcie is that Zola could've decided to plant the evidence in her own purse, and when it was found, it would appear to be an obvious, inept frame-up—casting suspicion *away* from her."

"Christ," said Richard, wagging his head.

"And *I* need a refill," said Zola, standing. "What a day."

Richard stood. "It's getting chilly. Let's go inside."

Zola reminded me to ask Christopher to phone her. Then we said our good-nights, and they made their way back to the house.

When they were out of earshot, Isandro asked me, "Do you think things are actually heating up for her?"

"Hard to tell. I hope not, but—" And I was interrupted by the ring of my phone. With a glance at the readout, I answered the call: "Hi, Jazz."

"About tomorrow," she said. "Still up for a drive to Temecula?"

"Count me in. Sounds interesting—an equestrian winery."

"I did some checking. They take reservations, but they're not necessary. I'd rather just show up." This was her usual technique —visits without warning. She continued, "I'm thinking if we leave around nine, we'll be there by eleven. Then we do some scouting, have lunch there, and we're back by late afternoon."

"Good plan. I assume you're driving?"

"Natch." With that settled, she changed topics: "I heard from Arcie."

"Regarding Zola, I assume."

"That's not what I was getting at, but yeah, she mentioned talking to Zola today. Said it was inconclusive."

"That makes me nervous, Jazz. By now, I'd like to see Zola moving *down* the list, preferably *off* the list, but it seems Arcie hasn't reached that conclusion. Just now, I was talking to Zola and convinced her that it's time for a consultation with Christopher."

"Right, probably a good idea. Want me to ask him to set it up?"

"That would be great. So, what *else* did you hear from Arcie?"

"It's about your friend—Näzh Hoyle."

I laughed, having already reported the events of my afternoon to Jazz. I asked her, "What about him?"

"Would you believe he has a record?"

"Him? I'd believe just about anything. What'd he do?"

"Fraud. Garden-variety huckster stuff—tried to soak a rich widow in Orange County. Something to do with his 'manifestation' gig. He didn't get very far, though. The old gal got suspicious when he asked her to write another check. She called her lawyer, who called the cops. He did a few nights in jail, then made a plea deal. Since there wasn't much cash involved—yet—he ended up paying it back, paying a fine, and doing some community service. But the record stands: he's a swindler."

Although this came as little surprise, hearing it as fact gave me cause for concern. I asked, "When do we clue Heather in? According to Näzh, she's ready to write him into her trust—but he did seem to feel she was dragging her feet."

"In that case, let's leave it alone for a bit. The fallout from something like that could really complicate the murder investigation. Fortunately, Heather struck me as nobody's fool—I can't imagine she'd let herself be scammed by the likes of Näzh Hoyle. Wonder what she sees in him."

I reminded Jazz, "I *saw* what Heather sees in him. Näzh may be a chiseler without a nickel to his name, but trust me, he has *other* assets."

Isandro was laughing over my end of the conversation as I rang off with Jazz. He said, "Come on, *coração*. Let's go upstairs. Getting cold out here."

It still amazed me that, in the desert, anything below seventy could feel "cold."

Later that night, up in the loft of the coach house, we turned off the lights in the living room, set up the coffeemaker in the kitchen, and made our way back to the sleeping area and the bathroom, where we were now undressed, taking turns at the sink, brushing our teeth.

While waiting for me to finish, Isandro said, "Know what?"

"What?" I said, spattering a few bubbles of toothpaste on the mirror.

Isandro used a washcloth to wipe it clean, reminding me, "Last night, we had a bet—and you lost." He grinned as I looked up at his reflection in the mirror.

Hmmm. I rinsed my mouth, dried my chin with a towel, and turned to him. "It seems you've been giving some thought to payback."

With a nod, he told me matter-of-factly, "It's overdue. With interest."

Wrapping him in a loose hug, I said into his ear, "But you never sent a bill."

"Oops, my bad. Now, where did I leave it...?"

I followed as he switched off the bathroom light and led me out to the sleeping area, where we turned off the remaining lights, except for a dim lamp on one of the nightstands, next to our phone chargers. Moving to opposite sides of the bed, we pulled back the covers, plumped the pillows, and hopped in.

As we rolled together into a full-body embrace, I said, "So tell me, now. What—*exactly*—do I owe you?"

He snuggled with his head on my shoulder, licked my ear, and whispered into it.

"Wow," I said. "Pretty stiff—your rates have gone up."

"Inflation. Live with it."

He was *always* ready, and after my strange but tantalizing afternoon, I wasn't far behind, so it didn't take us long to get into it. No doubt about it, Isandro really enjoyed lovemaking, and his joy usually surfaced in laughter. First came the giggles, accompanied by his mumblings in Portuguese, and now came his first full-throated guffaw, sounding more like a shout of delight, when—

One of our phones buzzed, vibrating on the nightstand.

We froze. (How sick that we'd both become so conditioned, so obsessed, so *mastered* by those damn things.) Staring at each other in the near darkness, we sputtered a sigh of resignation. Since I was on the side of the bed next to the phones, I said, "Should I check that?"

He kissed the tip of my nose. "*Por favor.*"

Rolling over, I saw that the intrusion had come from my phone, not his. It was a text from Keith: BUSY WITH COURT DATES, MIGHT COME BACK FOR WEEKEND.

After reading it to Isandro, I said, "Well, his message was no more revealing than mine was."

"Tit for tat, *coração*."

I continued, "But he sure took his time getting back to me. Maybe he *is* pissed after all."

Lying next to me, Isandro shrugged—I felt the bed wobble— as he told me, "If Keith is pissed, he'll just have to stew. There's nothing we can do about it *now*."

I chuckled. "I love your sense of practicality."

And he purred as we got back to business.

A year ago, I'd have discouraged Jazz from taking a daylong trip to a winery. Back then, she was still in the process of kicking the booze habit that had wrecked her marriage and had played a role in dooming her career with the Palm Springs police. She had also struggled with anger issues, but the anger had surely been fueled by the alcohol. During the first year of our friendship, I was always watchful for any "slips." And along the way, she had one. So a winery tour would have seemed like a very bad idea.

Since then, however, Jazz had fully reformed and "conquered her demons," as they say. She was still cautious enough, and wise enough, to describe herself as a *recovering* alcoholic, but she had also learned to be her own harshest judge. So I knew that if she considered a visit to a vineyard to be in the best interest of her work, I could trust her decision.

On Wednesday morning, when she pulled up to the curb of the side street behind the coach house, I opened the door of her black SUV, but before I could get in, she told me, "Stop. I wanna get a look at you."

"Uh, *why?*" I asked, stepping back to improve her view.

"I thought so," she said pensively. With a grin, she added, "Dante, you've got that *glow*."

Hopping in, I shut the door and buckled up, marveling at her sixth sense. "Wrong," I said.

"Don't bullshit *me*, honey. It's written all over you: somethin' *good* happened last night, prob'ly in bed. And I *hope* it was with Isandro."

"Okay," I admitted, "it was fabulous."

She squealed—along with the tires—while blasting away from the curb.

The drive would last nearly two hours, taking us out on I-10, heading west through the Banning Pass, which separates the San Bernardino and San Jacinto mountain ranges. We would then leave the Interstate and head south on state highways to the rural wine district lying just east of Temecula.

Along the way, Jazz and I caught up with news of the investigation. She had already spoken to Christopher, who would set up a meeting to strategize with Zola.

Jazz said, "Christopher also asked me to remind you about the fundraiser for Emma's school—Saturday night, Wasi'chu Hills clubhouse."

"It's on the calendar," I assured her. "Isandro and I dusted off our tuxes and sent them out for pressing. Did Christopher have any updates about the ballet performance—and the visiting dance master, Servando Ureña?"

With a hoot, she said, "Christopher cannot stop *talking* about that dude. Must admit, I can't wait to get a look at this guy."

"Me neither." I tried to mute my enthusiasm, but I had already Googled the *premier danseur* and found myself starstruck. He would definitely be worth seeing in the flesh.

Returning to less frivolous matters, Jazz said, "Wendy's murder."

"What about it?"

Hands on the wheel, watching the road, she breathed a little huff of a sigh, sounding frustrated. "I just don't sense that we're *getting* anywhere with this. We've talked to nearly everyone, and it seems they *all* had a reasonable motive, but they *all* had exonerating circumstances. And now Arcie Madera is making Zola squirm because, objectively, she had motive, means, and opportunity. You and I *know* that Zola didn't do it—or hope to God she didn't—so we need to take a fresh view of the guests staying at the rental house."

"And all of *them*," I said, "have check marks in both the 'guilty' and 'innocent' columns. It's a mess."

Jazz nodded. "So think with your gut for a moment. Consider everything we know. If, for some reason, you were *forced* to name the guilty party—here and now—who would it be?"

I turned to look at her. "Do *you* have someone in mind?"

She glanced over at me. The SUV swerved. "Yes, I do."

"Then say it with me." I counted down: "Three, two, one."

"Harold," we both said.

She elaborated, "It's no accident the spouse is always the first suspect."

"Except," I noted, "the motive is flimsy. Granted, he had ample means and opportunity, but if he's been truthful about expecting no inheritance, *why* would he kill her? He won't get a windfall. And despite Rebecca's fantasies about building a life with him, he's just not interested—so there's *no* reason to think he murdered his wife in order to play house with his secretary."

Jazz said, "You're absolutely right on all counts. Still, if I *had* to pick the killer—right now—I'd say it's Harold."

"Sorry, Harold," I said over my shoulder, as if he were sitting in the back seat. "I agree."

Jazz drummed the wheel with her fingers. "Who *haven't* we interviewed yet?"

"Just Brooke Ferris and boyfriend Tyler Evans. Also Keith Gibkin, in the sense that we haven't directly questioned him about motives and alibis. But he's a lawyer, so attempting to do that would get dicey. Plus, I've already had *lots* of less-pointed conversations with him, and my gut tells me to scratch him off the list."

Jazz nodded, thinking. "So—maybe tomorrow—let's try to follow up with Brooke and Tyler. Are you available?"

"Seems so. No new assignments from Sunny Junket."

The dashboard navigation alerted us to an upcoming turn. Jazz slowed the SUV and took a left exit from the highway onto a county four-lane, and a few miles later, we turned onto a two-lane rural blacktop. It was hard to believe we were midway between Los Angeles and San Diego. Only thirty miles from the coast, we were surrounded by lush farmland, scrub, and the arid foothills of halfhearted mountains that had shrunken with the passing of forgotten eons.

"I think," said Jazz, slowing down, "we're getting close."

And just ahead we saw the sign, with an arrow pointing right: TROT-N-TIPPLE, ½ MILE.

The dusty gravel drive took us along a split-rail fence to a swung-open entry gate and a sign announcing we'd arrived. Another winding drive led into the property, which now struck me as immense.

We could see the fields of grapes stretching off in all directions as we merged into a large roundabout with parking spaces radiating from its outer perimeter. Inside the roundabout was a circular pasture, fenced, with a few horses dawdling in the breeze, manes aflutter. Jazz parked—perhaps two dozen visitors' vehicles were already there.

Emerging from the SUV, I noticed at once that the bright October morning had the nip of fall, some twenty degrees cooler than it was in the desert. The air carried the scent of agriculture—grasses, fodder, soil, manure—while the gentle snorts and whinnies of horses drifted from the pasture as well as the stables beyond. On a whim, I'd worn cowboy boots, an old pair from the back of my closet (pure affectation from my earlier years, as I'd never been on a horse, let alone herded cattle). Jazz wore a pair of red high-top Keds. Locking the SUV, she told me, "Let's take a look around."

There was no admission fee—we were free to wander. Heather had explained to us that the tourist element of the enterprise was written off as public relations and name recognition, although the shops, bar, restaurants, and stable services generated a handsome revenue stream, in addition to the profits from the wine itself.

A quick self-guided tour confirmed my initial impression that the property was huge. We saw the stables and corrals, the barns and outbuildings, the fleet of trucks and equipment, the meandering horse paths and service drives, and the quaint "village" of structures where tourists ate, drank, and shopped. Behind the barns, I saw what appeared to be a large employee parking lot. Farther out, the vineyards themselves extended beyond our field of vision. That much land—in Southern California—suggested that Heather Ferris was indeed a *very* wealthy woman. Her home, I surmised, was the expansive "rustic" manse atop a distant knoll (rustic, that is, in the elevated style of Ralph Lauren), surrounded by acres of manicured turf and a gleaming white post-and-rail fence.

During our wandering, we found an exhibit that displayed sample plantings of the grape varieties and an explanation of how they were cultivated. A young woman wearing a cowboy hat, a vest, and a name tag—TRACY—told us that our visit coincided with the peak of their harvest season, which began in July and extended into November. When a group of visitors moved on, we were left alone with Tracy.

Jazz said to her, "What a beautiful place to work. I'll bet you love it here."

"Yes, ma'am." She flashed a merry smile. "I used to be part-time, summers only, but when I finished college last spring, they asked if I wanted to stay on, full-time, and learn the ropes of management." She laughed. "I mean, why would I want to be anywhere *else*?"

I said, "It must be a massive operation. Any idea how many people work here?"

"Oh, gosh …" She paused for some quick calculations. "We have about fifty full-time, another thirty part-time, and during harvest—it varies—up to a hundred seasonal workers."

Jazz and I glanced at each other with raised brows.

Tracy asked brightly, "And where are *you* folks from?"

"Palm Springs," I said. "Just drove over for the day. We've heard great things about Trot-n-Tipple and wanted to take a look."

"Well, isn't that *nice*! How'd you hear about us?"

With a turn of my head, I deferred to Jazz.

She explained, "Actually, we're acquaintances of Heather Ferris. She's visiting the desert for a while and told us about the place—suggested we come for a visit sometime."

"Oh! Hold on just a minute. Let me tell the ranch manager you're here. Okay?"

Jazz flipped her hands. "Okay!" We shared a grin while Tracy pulled out her walkie-talkie.

"Frank?" said Tracy over the static. "There's a couple of nice folks here from Palm Springs, friends of Heather, and she asked them over for a visit." The radio crackled with a garbled response. Tracy turned to ask us, "What's yer names?"

After we told her, she said into the walkie-talkie, "The man is Dante, and the woman is Jazz. Right, 'Jazz,' like the music. Okay, Frank, I'll let them know. Thanks."

Returning the gadget to its holster, looking pleased with herself, Tracy told us, "I *thought* he'd do that—you're invited for lunch, on us."

"Oh, *heavens*," said Jazz, "that's not necessary."

I reminded her, "But we'll need to eat."

"Yes... I suppose so." Turning to Tracy, she said, "Since you're so gracious to offer: thank you, we'd be delighted."

"*Good*," said Tracy, checking her watch. "They'll be expecting you at The Bistro anytime after noon, but no rush. And if Frank gets a chance—Frank Dillon—he'll pop in to say hello sometime before one."

As a fresh group of tourists wandered over from the parking lot, Tracy told us, "Have fun." Then she cleared her throat and welcomed the newcomers, starting her spiel from the top.

Jazz and I continued our walking tour, but by now, we had the gist of it: grapes, more grapes, horses, more horses. As we strolled past the stables, I looked into each of the stalls, taken by the beauty of these magnificent creatures. Jazz, however, kept her distance, walking along at about an arm's length away from me.

With a laugh, I told her, "I take it you don't ride."

She snorted. "Get serious. I grew up in LA, and *not* in the toniest part of town. I never even *saw* a horse till I was eighteen—

and they *still* scare the crap out of me."

In the little tourist "village," which had a theme-park feel, we did some window shopping but weren't in the market for wine, souvenirs, or riding crops, so we didn't browse inside the shops. As expected, I saw that The Tasting Room was essentially a bar, which left the two restaurants. We discovered that The Bistro, our destination, was clearly a notch above The Grill Room, which was more pedestrian.

When we stepped inside The Bistro, the hostess looked up from her podium with an earnest smile, greeting us, "Jazz! And Dante! We've been expecting you. Welcome." Grabbing two menus, she said, "This way, please."

While following her, Jazz leaned to tell me, "Ten to one, Tracy alerted them that they would know who I am because I'm Black."

"Oh, come *on*," I said dismissively—but she was probably right.

We were led to a prime window table with a perfectly framed view of—what else?—horses. The table was set with white linen, good china, a tidy arrangement of yellow roses, and an array of four different-shaped wineglasses for each of us.

While I seated Jazz, she told the hostess, "I'm the designated driver, so I'm afraid I won't be needing these."

With a snap of her fingers, the hostess summoned a busser, who removed Jazz's stemware. He poured water for both of us while the hostess explained, "You're welcome to explore the menu, if you wish, but Mrs. Ferris has asked us to roll out the red carpet. If you don't mind, our chef would be *delighted* to select a sequence of special courses for you this afternoon."

Jazz said, a tad too graciously, "Then we'd be *delighted* as well."

"*Delightful.* Hope you've brought your appetites. Enjoy." The hostess took our menus, bobbed her head, and disappeared—as if in a puff of smoke.

From the corner of my mouth, I said to Jazz, "Well, this is unexpected—and a bit much, don't you think?"

She leaned back in her chair, lolling elegantly while lifting her water goblet. "A bit much, indeed. But the price is right."

Glimpsing her red Keds under the table, I suppressed a laugh.

Rather than finding it "a bit much," we were disappointed to find that our lunch was, more accurately, a bit *precious*. I've often felt that chef-driven cuisine is more about the chef than the diners, and our experience at The Bistro was no exception. While there were many courses, each beautifully presented, they were *very* sparse and oddly sauced—a single shrimp, a scallop, a dab of paté, a paper-thin shaving of Wagyu—and on and on. Although, collectively, they did not leave us hungry, they were a far cry from the belt-busting feast implied by the hostess. And the many wines I was served, though lovely, amounted to little more than a sip of each—barely enough to justify washing so many glasses.

During dessert, described as "An Explosion of Chocolate" (but consisting of a gigantic white plate dotted with four brown cubes no bigger than dice), a man in Western wear approached our table, Stetson in hand. "Excuse me," he said. "Dante and Jazz? I'm Frank Dillon."

I started to rise to greet him, but he insisted, "Sit, sit. May I join you?"

"Of course," we told him. When he sat, we shook hands over the table and thanked him for lunch.

Eyeing the big plate, he asked us wryly, "Enjoying the 'Explosion'?" He broke into laughter with us, then lowered his voice while confiding, "Not quite my cup of tea." He raised a pinkie, and we laughed again.

He had already signaled a waiter, who now brought coffee to the table—no delicate demitasses, but three hefty mugs. We tasted the steaming brew, and it was damn good.

"*There*," he said, "that's better. Now, tell me: What do you think of Trot-n-Tipple?"

I said, "Well, we're *amazed*. Who wouldn't be?"

Jazz told him, "What an *operation*, Frank. And you're the man in charge?"

He laughed again. "That's what they tell me. But I don't exactly look at it that way. Never much cared for being boss or giving orders—I figure it's *my* job to make sure *their* jobs are not only productive, but satisfying. That way, they like what they're doin', and Mrs. Ferris likes the results. Plus, I get *paid* for working the best job in the world."

"Sounds like a win-win-win," said Jazz.

Sounds a little too happy-happy-happy, I thought.

"It sure is," said Frank. "I've been here since the early days, right after Heather and Jason—God rest him—started setting things up. Back then, *none* of us really knew what we were doin', but over the years, we figured it out, all right, and now we've got a sweet, smooth-running system in place. Safe to say, we're all proud of it—at least *I* am." He laughed again, but this was more of a thoughtful chortle, as if reflecting on a life's work well done.

I asked, "Do you *live* here—on the property?"

"Yup, I do. Got a little house, other side of the parking lot—not real big, but nice. Some folks joke that I spend too much time here, but *that's* the job. It's not just full-time; it's *all*-the-time, seven days a week. Tried a vacation—once. Didn't like it."

Jazz exhaled a low whistle. "Now, *that's* dedication."

He winked at her. "Wouldn't have it any other way."

I said, "We noticed the *big* house, up on the knoll. I assume Heather lives there?"

"Yup. She and Jason built that, once the wine business really took off—*swell* place. And Brooke grew up there—lucky kid!"

Jazz asked, "Is Heather usually *here*, running things?"

"Used to be, all the time, especially right after Jason passed on. Kept her busy and occupied, I guess. But she's adjusted."

"How do you mean?"

Frank explained, "We all miss Jason, always will. Heather will probably never get over the loss, not completely. But that initial grief has passed, slow but sure, and she's back among the living, as they say. So now, she's away from here a *lot*. Travels. Cruises. Goes to conferences. Visits friends. And—as you know—she's spending a month in Palm Springs."

"Actually," I said, "Rancho Mirage, but close enough."

Jazz said to Frank, "You told us you've got a smooth-running system in place. Now that Heather is away so often, how does that system work?"

"If you've got all day, I can tell you all about it, and you'd be bored stiff. But the system I've got with Heather *starts* with the daily phone call. Whenever she's away, anywhere in the world, she gives me a call each morning, ten sharp, and I always make sure I'm ready for it, somewhere quiet where we can talk—weekdays and weekends alike. I tell her what she needs to know about the business, and we decide how to proceed. But it's also just a chance to catch up."

Jazz said, "Sounds kinda pleasant—civilized. But what about time zones? Ten o'clock here isn't necessarily ten o'clock *there*."

Frank nodded. "Good point. Since she's the boss, the call is at ten in the morning wherever *she* happens to be, and it's up to me to figure it out. So if she's in Timbuktu, I'm up and waiting to hear from her in the middle of the night."

Jazz laughed. "Most accommodating of you."

"Hey, it's the least I can do. I can call her anytime I need to, but the call *from* her is like keeping an appointment. She's always on the dot, and she never calls more than once a day."

Consistent with this, I remembered the day before, shortly past ten in the morning, when Jazz and I went to interview Heather at the guesthouse. When we arrived, she mentioned that she'd just wrapped up her daily check-in call with the vineyard.

Jazz was saying to Frank, "... and I can't help wondering about Heather's house, up on the knoll. Jason is long gone now, so does she live there *alone*? I mean, it's *huge*."

"It's big, all right," said Frank, "and from time to time, Heather *has* been alone up there. When Brooke went off to college, and even after nursing school, when she started working, she would stay at the house during vacations and visits, but she wasn't *living* there—so Heather had the whole place to herself."

I asked, "But now?"

"Well"—Frank hedged—"things are different. Brooke changed nursing jobs, and now she's working as a full-time caregiver to patients dying at home, meaning, she lives with *them*. But those 'clients' never last long, so in between, she's back at the house with Heather." Frank paused. In a different, reticent tone of voice, he said, "Plus, we've got the boyfriends now."

My brow reflexively arched with interest. "Tyler and Näzh," I said.

Frank nodded. "Don't get me wrong. Both Brooke and Heather deserve every happiness, and it's good to know that they each have someone special. That Tyler, what a swell guy—hardworking and grounded. He really seems right for Brooke."

I prodded: "And Näzh?"

Frank asked, under his breath, "Have you met him?"

Jazz and I nodded, poker-faced.

"Then you know what I mean." Frank tossed his hands. Unconvincingly, he added, "But it's not my place to judge. As far as I'm concerned, they're just one big happy 'family'—in a makeshift sorta way."

Less diplomatically, Jazz said, "To each his own. But I don't think Heather should settle for Näzh. She could do *so* much better."

I reminded her, "Heather hasn't 'settled' anything with Näzh."

"Yeah," she agreed without enthusiasm. "In light of everything that's happened, it's better that she's not alone." Jazz turned to Frank: "I assume you heard what happened—to Wendy."

He sighed. "Yes, Heather told me the news right away when we talked on Sunday. What a mess—for all concerned."

I asked him, "There was some friction between Heather and Wendy, correct?"

"Friction?" He laughed at the understatement. "Sorry. Like I said, not my place to judge. Whatever Heather and Wendy might have thought of each other, that was strictly between them."

Jazz said, "Understood. But may I ask: What did *you* think of Wendy?"

He shrugged. "Never met her. She wasn't welcome here."

On a more upbeat note, Frank suggested, "How about some dessert before you go? I mean, *real* dessert." Without waiting for an answer, he summoned a waiter and ordered, "Mud pie for three."

Some twenty minutes later, when we were fully sated (and afflicted with sugar jitters), Jazz and I thanked Frank again, said our goodbyes, and strolled back to the roundabout—immersed in thought, but not speaking.

Jazz unlocked her SUV. We got in and thumped the doors closed. She switched on the engine and shifted into reverse, but held her foot on the brake as she turned to ask me, "Did you catch that?"

I grinned. "Heather told Frank about Wendy's death on Sunday."

Jazz said, "And Heather's daily call is at ten sharp."

"But *we* didn't discover the body till after twelve."

CHAPTER
NINE

Driving back to Palm Springs, Jazz and I spoke of little other than the revelation that Heather had known about the suspicious death at least two hours before Jazz and I emerged from Wendy's bedroom and announced the tragedy to everyone who had gathered for brunch.

I said, "Heather and Näzh were sunning themselves at the pool when we arrived that day, as if nothing had happened. When we broke the news, she seemed as surprised as anyone."

Jazz recounted, "And when we interviewed her—just yesterday at the guesthouse—Heather said the whole ordeal felt like a bad dream. She said she expected to wake up and learn that Wendy's death was just 'a horrible accident,' not murder."

"But then," I said, "after Heather told us the whole story of her husband's death—and how she blames Wendy for it—she concluded, 'I'm glad that bitch finally got what she deserved.'"

Gripping the wheel, Jazz looked pissed. "Not sayin' she *lied* to us, but Heather omitted *plenty* of critical information. Bottom line—she deceived us."

I calmly posed the question: "What do we do about it?"

We both pondered this briefly. Then Jazz said, "Not sure."

I reasoned, "Even though Heather didn't let on that she had early knowledge of the murder, that doesn't mean she *did* it."

Jazz nodded. "Several possibilities: She could've somehow discovered the body on her own, then said nothing because she didn't want to be found suspicious. Or, she could've learned about it from the killer and wanted to protect that person. Or, by simply badmouthing Wendy and venting her hate, she could've inspired someone else to do the deed, without even knowing it. Any way you slice it, yes, she was at some level 'involved.' But I'm not ready to believe she's the killer."

I agreed, "Me neither."

"So," said Jazz, "I'm inclined to let this ride for a while. Even if our hunch is wrong and Heather *is* the killer, I don't think she's a flight risk—if she suddenly took off, that would be seen as an admission of guilt. Better for us to say nothing for a few days. She's obviously comfortable with the status quo, and she might be in a position to help lead us to the truth."

"And what about Detective Madera?"

Jazz bit her lower lip for a moment, then said, "I do *not* like being less than forthright with Arcie, but for the time being, let's keep it to ourselves."

I nodded. Although I, too, was uncomfortable keeping Arcie out of the loop, I was relieved that Jazz had decided to do so. As if thinking aloud, I said, "We now know that Heather was somehow involved in what happened. And if *she* was involved, that probably means that someone *else* was also involved." I turned to Jazz, asking, "Who?"

She turned to look at me—the SUV swerved on the highway, prompting an annoyed honk from someone in the next lane. Ignoring that, Jazz said, "Once again, instincts point me to Harold. He was not only Wendy's husband, but also Heather's brother. To me, that sounds like a natural, plausible alliance for some conspiring."

"My thoughts exactly." I listened to the sleepy thrum of the tires for a minute or so, then broke the lull: "If we're going to play dumb with Heather for a while, then what's next?"

Jazz said, "We haven't interviewed Brooke or Tyler yet. Maybe we could set that up for tomorrow."

"Sure. I saw Tyler yesterday and mentioned we might want to talk—he was fine with it."

"Good." Jazz added, "But I'd rather not meet them at the rental. Heather might be around, and we should probably avoid her till we have a better understanding of her role in this. Talking to her now, even casually, might make her curious about what we do—or don't—know."

"So," I said, "any bright ideas for some neutral ground where we could have a heart-to-heart with Brooke and Tyler?"

Jazz shook her head. "Sorry. Not thinkin' straight. Must be the mud pie slowin' me down."

I had to laugh—she was now doing eighty on the Interstate. "No problem," I told her, "because I have a *perfect* idea for where we should meet."

Sunnylands is the name of a sprawling two-hundred-acre estate in the middle of Rancho Mirage, developed in the 1960s by Ambassador Walter Annenberg and his wife, Leonore, as their winter home. The estate's centerpiece is the main house, a mid-century pink-and-white fantasy designed by architect A. Quincy Jones, then decorated and custom-furnished by the legendary Hollywood actor-turned-designer, Billy Haines. The grounds encompass guest cottages, a golf course, several lakes, and even a mausoleum enshrining the Annenbergs' remains. Their philanthropic gifts totaled more than three billion dollars.

While they lived in the house, they frequently entertained royalty and heads of state, including presidents from both parties. After their deaths, the estate transitioned to a conference center, often dubbed "the Camp David of the West," hosting high-level meetings of global leaders in relaxed, posh privacy—earning Rancho Mirage the moniker "playground of the presidents."

Most recently, a fifteen-acre visitors center was developed as an extension of the grounds, offering artful desert gardens, walking paths, and an expansive lawn used for events or the restful appreciation of a jaw-dropping mountain vista. Anchoring this tasteful serenity, a sleek, contemporary building, Sunnylands Center, houses exhibitions, a café, gift shop, and a spacious lounge area with a wall of windows, perfect for contemplating the benign possibilities of vast wealth. It's also a great place for just hanging out.

And all of this happened to be located about two miles away from the rental house currently occupied by the Gibkin-Ferris family. I was certain that the storied, art-filled past of Sunnylands would be of special interest to Tyler Evans, a talented artist himself, but it was a worthy destination for *any* visitor to the area—and then I learned that Jazz herself had never been inside the gates.

"I guess the invitation musta got lost in the mail," she said with dry sarcasm.

"Don't be nuts," I told her. "You don't need an invitation or, for that matter, a reservation. You don't even need to *pay* to get into the visitors center—you just go."

Tours of the actual house and its grounds were another matter. Those always sold out, well in advance, so we didn't have a prayer on such short notice. It didn't matter, though, because our immediate purpose had nothing to do with touring—we simply needed the right setting for a significant, honest conversation.

"Plus," I told Jazz, "I'll drive. Trust me, you'll enjoy making your entrance in an open convertible."

"Fine by me. Set it up."

When I phoned Tyler that evening, he seemed genuinely pleased to hear from me. And when I told him what I had in mind, he said, "*Great*. I've been wondering about that place." I suggested eleven o'clock, and he okayed it with Brooke. Their quiet exchange of words made it apparent that they were together when I called—seemingly inches apart.

By Thursday morning, only four days had passed since the murder. But so much had transpired, it felt dizzying—little of which was directly related to my job at Sunny Junket. I had checked in with the office each day, by phone, but wasn't needed for new clients. So that morning, I skipped the call.

As planned, I did the driving and picked up Jazz. She'd taken Emma to school that morning, then visited Blade Wade at his loft, so she was waiting outside his door when I pulled up to the curb in the strip mall. It was just past ten thirty, a truly postcard-perfect October day in the desert, seemingly made for a jaunty little outing in the Karmann Ghia. The car was not technically a roadster because it had a back seat (sort of), a cramped space that was impossible for adults, so I would not be picking up Tyler and Brooke, who planned to meet us at Sunnylands.

Jazz was in good spirits. When I commented on this, she said, "Well, *yeah*—I'm not driving for a change."

I laughed. "I thought you *loved* to drive. You're a take-charge sorta gal, captain of her own ship, always in control..."

"Sometimes," she said, discreetly lowering her voice, "it can be refreshing to, uh... to just 'let go,' if you catch my drift." She smirked.

"Huh?" But then I noticed: "My God, now *you've* got that glow."

She primped, but said nothing.

"*Out* with it, girlfriend. I want details."

She threw back her head and laughed merrily in the breeze as we sped out of town.

When we drove through the Sunnylands gate to the visitors center, we were ten minutes early, and as we parked, I noted that the Trot-n-Tipple pickup had not yet arrived—I'd have easily spotted it among the ritzy assortment of gleaming sports cars and tricked-out land yachts.

Walking with me from the car to the building, Jazz was duly impressed. "I can't *believe* I've never seen this," she said. "Who *knew*?"

"I did," I reminded her.

Inside the building, we were immediately drawn to the rear wall of glass in the vast lounge, which had the feel of a quietly modern hotel lobby. The furnishings of the room were understated, allowing maximum impact from the view beyond the windows—a panorama of green turf, ruddy granite mountains, and a sapphire sky embellished with a few friendly cotton-ball clouds. At the far edge of the lawn, the members of a tai chi class, clad in black, practiced their silent moves, looking like a ballet troupe in slow motion.

Voices called to us: "Hey, Dante." "Hi, Jazz."

We turned from the windows to find Tyler and Brooke stepping across the room. Our greetings included hugs—a new development that seemed warm and spontaneous. While they gabbed with Jazz, I noted that they were easily the youngest members of the Gibkin-Ferris party staying at the rental house. I was old enough to be the father of either of them; Jazz could have passed as a young aunt. And because Jazz and Tyler were Black—Brooke and I, white—we made a wholesome, handsome quartet.

Though I had frequently visited Sunnylands, it was new to the others, so we spent some time going through two galleries. One was a permanent exhibit covering the overall history of the estate. The other was a changing exhibit that currently displayed a collection of table settings, complete with handwritten place cards, which had been used for various events in the main house over the years. Reading the cards was truly an eye-popping exercise in name-dropping.

On a weekday in early autumn, the seasonal crowds had not yet arrived, allowing us to move about at our leisure, as if claiming all of this lordly space as our own—enough to put anyone in a pleasant state of mind. So the true purpose of our meeting (to talk murder) was held at bay while we explored the nearby grounds and eventually settled at a shady terrace table near a reflecting pool in a manicured cactus garden.

It was still a bit early for lunch, so I popped into the adjacent café and returned with iced tea for all of us. We tasted it, and Brooke commented, "You can always tell when they actually brew the stuff fresh—this is great."

Her comment reminded me of my later years of college, when I was living in my first apartment on a budget so slim that it was virtually nonexistent. I always had a big, bargain-size jar of instant tea in my meager pantry—and a pitcher of it, mixed and cloudy, in the refrigerator. I drank a *lot* of it, and to this day, I'll recognize it at once and nearly gag when a restaurant has shown the faulty judgment to serve instant tea. But Brooke was right—this was great.

Jazz got quiet, then softly cleared her throat. "I hate to broach this in such beautiful surroundings, but Dante and I want to ask you a few questions about last weekend—when Wendy died."

Brooke and Tyler glanced at each other, sharing the trace of a grin, as if acknowledging that it was time to get down to business—the ugly business of murder in our midst. Brooke said, "Sure, Jazz. How can we help?"

"Wendy's death is a police matter," said Jazz, "and Detective Madera is working on behalf of the people of Riverside County to help bring justice and closure to your whole family. But Harold, your uncle, has also engaged Dante and me to explore the matter on our own—he feels that Zola Lorinsky has been framed for the crime, and he wants to prove otherwise. Now, if you think about it, that's pretty remarkable, isn't it?"

Brooke cocked her head. "Why?"

"Because the victim was Harold's *wife*. If I were put in his position, I'd want to get to the *truth* of the matter—wherever it might lead. I can't help feeling it's strange that his first instinct is to protect Zola."

I jumped in: "Don't get us wrong. Jazz and I are thoroughly convinced that Zola had nothing to do with Wendy's death. So we welcome the opportunity to help get her in the clear. But it *does* seem strange that Harold himself puts such a priority on this."

"Well"—Brooke shrugged—"I guess that's just Uncle Harold being Uncle Harold. He marches to a 'different drummer,' the drummer in his *head*. But that's why I've always felt so close to him."

Looking surprised, Tyler asked her, "Really?"

She laughed. "Of *course*, sweets. Harold is a bit of an oddball, I admit, but I've always admired his offbeat sense of vision, his willingness to 'risk it all' in the pursuit of a goal he finds important. In my book, that's admirable." A wrinkle crossed her face as she added, "*Less* admirable, by far, is the smoking—and that god-awful whiskey he swills—but that's all part of the package. He is what he is."

With a sputter of a laugh, Tyler asked, "Would you still love me if I took up smoking and Old Nine-Tails?"

Through a stern look, she told him, "Absolutely *not*. That was never part of *your* package. I had no choice in inheriting a crazy uncle, but I can be very picky when it comes to the man I love."

He leaned in his chair to kiss her lips. "Thanks, baby."

I smiled. And I couldn't help asking, "So it *is* love?"

Brooke held Tyler's shoulders at arm's length, as if examining the goods. "Yes," she said with slow deliberation, "now that you ask, I do believe I love him." Turning to Jazz and me, she added with a silly laugh, "I mean, who *wouldn't*?"

I thought it best not to answer—especially since Jazz was flashing me a look that warned, *Down, boy.*

Getting back to business, Jazz said to Brooke, "So, then. You've always felt affection for your so-called crazy uncle. Can I assume Harold feels the same way about you?"

Without hesitation, she said, "He does. Sure, he *adores* Keith, but a son isn't a daughter, and I've always had the impression that Harold might've wanted to raise a little girl. Naturally, when I was young, he probably saw me as the next best thing, a niece. So we've always been close."

Treading carefully, I said, "Brooke, when your father died, how old were you—just out of high school?"

"Right." She nodded. "I was eighteen. Ten years ago."

Pushing further, I said. "What an awful loss for both you and your mother. When Jazz and I talked to her two days ago, she told us the whole story. I assume you're aware that your mother blames Wendy for your father's death."

"Of course," she said soberly.

"Did *you* blame Wendy, too?"

"Sure." Brooke shrugged. "Why wouldn't I? What happened, happened."

Perplexed by this, and muted, I didn't know how to continue.

So Jazz forged ahead: "If you and Harold always had such a close, warm relationship, didn't Wendy's involvement in your father's death cause a rift between you and your uncle? I mean— talk about throwing a *wrench* in the works."

"It was ... yes ... a problem. At least at first. But at eighteen, I wasn't a kid; I was old enough to understand that Harold wasn't accountable for his wife's actions. And he *certainly* never tried to defend what she'd done. In fact, he was bereft. I thought they'd probably split up, and I admit, I still have to wonder why they didn't. Maybe he pitied her. She *was* sick, after all."

Jazz said, "That's putting it mildly: Hard-core drug addiction. Bulimia. Lethal food allergies. And that monkey? Now, *that's* sick."

Tyler nudged Brooke with his elbow, saying softly, "That's not the end of it. Right, babe?"

With bowed head, she slowly nodded.

Jazz and I glanced at each other. She asked Brooke, "Is there something we don't know?"

Brooke looked up, telling us, "Yes, there's more. Or at least there *was*. But it doesn't matter—not anymore."

Jazz's notebook was in front of her on the table, but it had remained closed till now. She opened it while reminding Brooke, "Any information you have could be helpful. But we won't know unless you share it with us."

Brooke hesitated. "It's no big deal. Really."

Gently, I nudged, "Come on, Brooke. What's going on?"

She mustered a weak smile. "All right—but nothing's 'going on,' okay? It's just that Wendy's list of maladies had a more recent addition. It was sorta hushed-up."

Jazz took a stab: "Cancer?"

Brooke shook her head. "Wendy had contracted Flassman syndrome."

Jazz and I shared a confused look. She told Brooke, "Sorry. I'm not familiar with that."

"Let me back up," said Brooke. "I used to work as a nurse in a physician's practice at a large medical center in San Diego County. This doctor had a long history with both the Gibkin and the Ferris sides of our family. About a year ago, I was leaving the practice to begin hospice work, so the office threw a little going-away party for me. At the party, the doctor—I'd rather not specify his name—he mentioned in passing that he wished my aunt well. I was confused by this because I'd never thought of Wendy as my aunt; she was just 'Uncle Harold's second wife.' So the doctor clarified: Wendy Gibkin. And I sorta thumped my forehead and thanked him for his kind wishes. And he said he was sorry about the terrible diagnosis, but then as soon as he realized I had *no* idea what he was talking about, he clammed up and made an excuse to leave the room."

"Yikes," I said. "That does *not* sound good."

"Yeah, *tell* me. So a week later, when I wasn't working there anymore, I called one of the receptionists—we were good friends—and I asked if she could *possibly* take a peek in the files and let me know what was going on. An hour later, she got back to me: Wendy had Flassman syndrome. I couldn't find much about it, but it did sound serious—a degenerative disease."

Jazz asked, "How far along was it? Was Wendy suffering from it, or was that still to come?"

Brooke tossed her hands. "I simply didn't know, and in fact I still don't."

I asked, "Have you talked to your uncle about it?"

"Well"—she waffled—"that's sorta the crux of this story."

Tyler crossed his arms and turned to tell Jazz and me, "I haven't heard *this* part myself."

Brooke drank more of her iced tea—the glass was nearly empty now—then said to us, "Uncle Harold and I were always close, right? And from time to time, we'd meet for lunch, just the two of us, and catch up. But after I started in-home nursing for terminal patients, it seemed impossible to plan social lunches, so Harold and I lost touch for a while. Suddenly, though, I had a gap 'between patients,' and I called him. Next day, we met for lunch."

Jazz said, "When was that?"

"About a month ago. First thing I asked, of course, was 'How's Wendy doing?' And he was like, 'Whataya mean? Status quo. The *monkey's* fine.' And he laughed. So I took his hand and said, '*No*, Uncle Harold—the Flassman syndrome.' And that's when I realized: This was total news to him. He'd never heard a thing about it."

Tyler was wide-eyed. "Holy Christ."

She conceded, "It was a monumental 'oops' moment."

After lunch, Jazz and Brooke wanted to do some browsing in the gift shop, so I said to Jazz, "Tell you what: I'm going to take Tyler on a stroll through the gardens. We can catch up with you gals out front at the entrance.

She gave me a thumbs-up, understanding that I wanted to ask

Tyler a few questions away from Brooke.

Tyler seemed to understand this as well. I had no intention of giving a lecture on the natural habitat of agaves, paloverdes, or barrel cactus—and the only comment *he* made in that regard was that he enjoyed the "linearity" imposed on the plantings by the landscape architect.

Walking along a shaded pathway, I said to him, "You and Brooke seem to have settled into a nice comfort zone together. Congratulations—you make a great couple."

"*Thank* you, Dante. I appreciate that. We're both still sorta new to 'serious' relationships, so we're taking it slow. Not sure where it's headed, but we don't want to mess it up."

"A wise approach," I said. But I was confused. "By 'taking it slow,' you mean..."

He laughed. "I *mean*: we're in no rush for rings or vows or babies. But sure, we're intimate."

"Ah. It was none of my business, but thanks for sharing."

"No problem." And he got quiet. As we strolled along, he had nothing more to say. He seemed suddenly preoccupied. Troubled.

I asked, "Anything wrong?"

"Well"—he stopped walking—"it's that *family* of hers."

There was a bench a few feet ahead along the path, so I gestured that we should sit down. Once settled, I echoed, "That *family* of hers—I hear ya, Tyler. In my job at the rental agency, I've come across some odd characters in some odd situations. I thought I'd seen it all, but the Gibkin-Ferris clan is uncharted territory."

He was leaning forward, elbows on knees, burning off energy by pumping one foot, which made his whole body shake. His owlish good looks, his puppy-dog sweetness, his laid-back and grounded demeanor—all of that vanished as he sat up and turned to face me with creased features and anger in his eyes. His simmering rage wasn't directed at me, though.

"That racist *bitch*," he said. "Wendy. Fourth of July. When I went to their fuckin' barbecue in Rancho Santa Fe, she sauntered over to us and told Brooke, 'If you want a monkey for a pet, you should get one in a cage, like Koo-Loo. They're *far* less trouble.'"

I cringed as he continued, "And dear Uncle Harold? That old slob heard it all—but he didn't have a single word to say about it." Drained, Tyler slumped.

I wrapped my arm around him and pulled him close, rocking him like a baby, trying to ease his pain.

CHAPTER
TEN

Back in the Karmann Ghia, returning home from Rancho Mirage, Jazz and I compared notes.

"By my count," I said wryly, "the list of possible suspects with compelling *motives* just grew by two."

"And one of them," said Jazz, "was fairly predictable. We might have guessed that Brooke blamed Wendy for her father's death, but now we *know* it. Brooke couldn't have been more blasé in admitting to the grudge."

"Right," I said. "But today's *other* revealed motive came out of the blue. The loathing in Tyler's voice caught me off guard as he told me about the incident with Wendy—and her vile 'monkey' slur." I paused before adding, "Good thing she's not still around. I'd be tempted to—"

Jazz stopped me: "Cool it, Dante. We've got more than enough suspects—as is. Plus, we've got a whole new wrinkle to consider."

I nodded. "Flassman syndrome. Interesting, yes, but it didn't *kill* Wendy. Her death was the result of anaphylactic shock."

"But...," said Jazz.

"What?"

"For the sake of argument, the Flassman diagnosis might've been more than Wendy could handle. If so, she could've knowingly eaten the honey-laced posset, killing herself. Except"—Jazz growled a sigh of vexation—"the totality of evidence has already ruled out suicide."

"This *case*...," I muttered. "One step forward, two back."

I fell silent for a while as we drove through Cathedral City, approaching Palm Springs.

"You know," I said, "there's still *one* potential suspect we haven't questioned."

She chortled. "Keith Gibkin, stepson of the deceased. Think he did it?"

"No, of *course* not—at least I hope not. But he's part of the whole messy dynamics of that family, and he might be able to help sort things out."

She asked, "He's coming back from his office this weekend, right?"

"Last I heard. But then he'll be right here in the thick of all this craziness again. If you're up for a drive tomorrow, maybe we should pay a little visit to Rancho Santa Fe."

Jazz turned to me with a decisive nod. "But I don't think we should just pop in unexpected."

I reminded her, "That's your usual technique."

"True. But Keith is a lawyer, and he's not likely to slip up just because we paid a surprise visit. So we might as well extend the professional courtesy of *asking* to see him there. For all we know, he might be in court tomorrow."

Nodding, I said, "I was hoping you'd say that. He's a nice guy, and I wouldn't want to... rub him the wrong way."

Jazz gave me a knowing look. "Just set it up, okay?"

That evening, I texted Keith, asking if he had time to see Jazz and me at his office the next day, and I was surprised that he

responded so quickly: FABULOUS. ANYTIME AFTER ELEVEN IS
GOOD. LET'S DO LUNCH. If Monday's attempted matchmaking dinner with Christopher Friendly had miffed Keith, it now
seemed he was over it. So I informed Jazz of this, and our plan
was set.

Our Friday logistics were similar to Wednesday's, but the drive
would take us beyond Temecula, another forty minutes south
to Rancho Santa Fe, just five miles inland from the coast. Once
again, Jazz drove, as the gladiator conditions of the freeways
were better suited to her muscular SUV than to my vintage convertible.

A few minutes past eleven that morning, we rolled into the
quaint historic district of downtown Ranch Santa Fe. It had
been many years since I'd last visited the exclusive little community of some three thousand residents, but it looked instantly
familiar, as not much had changed. White stucco Spanish-style
buildings with red tile roofs—most of them with a single story,
a few with two—lined the walkways of tree-studded streets that
had lazy intersections unencumbered by stoplights. Tourists and
locals drifted into and out of the shops, offices, and tiny branch
banks, like actors creating a storybook tableau of life well lived
in Southern California.

We had no trouble finding Keith's office, located just a half
block off the main street, wedged between an antiquarian book-
store on one side and, on the other, a tiny, tiny shop specializing
in thimbles. In keeping with this fantasy setting, we slid into a
vacant parking space directly in front of Keith's door. Over it was
a discreet sign in raised bronze letters: KEITH GIBKIN, ATTORNEY.

When we walked through the door, I expected a bell on a
spring to jangle, but no. The old-timey character of the street
scene disappeared as we entered a contemporary interior, styled

in a neutral, masculine palette of grays, brown, and cream. A receptionist looked up from her desk. "Good morning," she said with a smile. "May I help you?"

I said, "Mr. Gibkin is expecting us. Dante and Jazz."

She peered at her computer, looking confused.

"That's all right, Yolanda," said Keith, stepping out from a doorway to greet us with handshakes and hugs. "Please—come in." And he led us into his office, closing the door behind us.

Jazz blew a soft whistle. "Nice digs." I detected a note of envy in her comment. The room was not much bigger than Jazz's own office in Palm Springs, but it was impeccably furnished and well organized, an inspiring workspace. By contrast, her private-eye office still needed a serious makeover.

Keith thanked her for the compliment, then told us, "Sorry for the lame reception out front. My original office manager helped me set up the practice and worked here for eight years—but she retired a few months ago. I've been 'auditioning' a series of temps ever since, and this one won't be here much longer."

With a showy sigh of sympathy, Jazz told him, "It's *such* a burden—good help can be *so* hard to find." (I, of course, was the only help she had—and not much more than a temp myself.)

Keith laughed. "Before we sit down, can I get you anything. Water? Coffee?"

"Thanks," I said. "I'm fine."

Jazz lowered her voice to ask him, "Can you point me to a restroom? Long drive."

"Of course." He pointed. She left.

In addition to the desk and a pair of chairs facing it, the office had a conversation area with a sofa and armchairs. Keith gestured for me to choose a seat, and when I settled at the end of the sofa, he sat in the nearest chair.

He told me, "I was so surprised to get your text last night." His tone seemed delighted.

"And I was surprised by *your* quick reply." With a laugh, I added, "Were you waiting to hear from me?"

He shrugged. "Guess I was. I've been wanting to apologize for the way things ended on Monday night."

"You have *nothing* to apologize for. I should *not* have 'ambushed' either you or Christopher with a surprise meeting. And I'm sorry that Christopher got so frosty with you—the setup wasn't *your* doing."

"No worries. He's already..." Keith paused for a tantalizing moment before completing the thought with a twitch of his brows: "Christopher has already 'made amends' for his snarky behavior on Monday."

"Really? How?"

"He was here Wednesday night. Well, not *here*, in the office. But at my condo, on the shore." He grinned.

I howled, "No *way!*"

Returning to the room, Jazz asked, "What'd I miss?"

"Oh, not much," I said, struggling not to blurt the news. "It seems your ex paid a visit to Keith—Wednesday night."

Her turn to howl: "No *way!*" Then she grilled Keith: "Was it, like, *dinner*—or the whole shebang?"

Keith weighed his words. "Oh, there was dinner, all right, but also a bit of shebang."

Jazz pivoted to high-five me, but I fumbled it, having never been adept at the rituals of sport.

Although Jazz and I had made the trip that day with murder on our minds, Keith's news about Christopher instantly became the hot topic, and we hadn't even mentioned Wendy yet when Keith said, "If we're going to keep our lunch reservation, we'd better leave."

His little Mercedes would have been uncomfortable for three, so Jazz again played chauffeur, driving us to a nearby inn with a charming terrace and an enviable table under an ancient eucalyptus, a spot that was always Keith's for the asking.

After we'd placed our orders, Keith asked us, "Is there anything I need to know about the investigation in the desert? Out here this week, I've barely even thought about it."

I was tempted to make a friendly crack about his thoughts being preoccupied by Christopher, but I let that slide.

Jazz said, "First, Keith, a bit of business. You've hired me to investigate Rebecca Jiang in the best interests of your father—suspecting she's a gold digger and a threat to his marriage. But now, with Wendy gone, those dynamics have changed entirely. Point is, I haven't spent much time on Rebecca's background, not enough to compile a report, so I'd like to consider that investigation canceled, terminated, no charge."

"That's kind of you, Jazz, and I'm fine with calling it off, but I should pay you for whatever time you've—"

She cut him off with a wave of her hand. "Don't be nuts. If I thought you owed me something, I'd bill you for it, but it was nothing, and that's that. Besides, what matters now is the investigation of Wendy's death, right?"

He nodded. "Of course."

Jazz told him, "Detective Madera is making progress with forensics and with leads of her own, but Dante and I have been focused on getting better acquainted with the guests at the rental house. We'd *love* to pin the murder on an outsider—and save your family any extended anguish—but sorry to say, all the evidence is pointing to *someone* who was at the rental on Saturday night."

Warily, Keith asked, "Have you found any... 'direction' yet?"

I said, "We haven't been able to zero in on one suspect." I was fudging on a technicality, of course. Both Jazz and I had expressed a hunch that Keith's father, Harold, was most likely responsible for the crime, but we also had reason to believe that Harold's sister, Heather, might have been involved—so we were not looking at "one suspect," but two.

"Keith," said Jazz, "are you familiar with a medical condition called Flassman syndrome?"

I could tell from Keith's expression that he wasn't familiar with it—and that he had no idea why Jazz had asked about it. With a confused shrug, he said, "Never heard of it."

I told him, "Neither had I—until yesterday."

Jazz explained to Keith, "Your cousin Brooke shared a fascinating story with us, but we're not quite sure what to make of it—if anything. She used to work for a doctor who had treated Wendy, and he let it slip that he regretted having given her a terrible diagnosis, which turned out to be Flassman syndrome. It's a degenerative disease. Months later, Brooke had lunch with your father, and she expressed her concern over Wendy's condition."

Keith told us, "Dad never said a word about this."

"Because," I said, "he, too, was unaware of it. Brooke was mortified that she'd dropped the bomb over casual chitchat at lunch."

"Speaking of lunch," said our waiter as he shimmied up to the table, "enjoy."

We picked at our salads. Keith said, "This Flassman syndrome —is it fatal?"

"Always," said Jazz, "at least I think so. I haven't been able to learn much about it."

Keith floated an idea: "Maybe suicide, then?"

Jazz shook her head. "Probably not. In Wendy's bedroom, there was clear evidence that she'd frantically tried to find her Epi-Pen, which then turned up in Zola Lorinsky's bag. I'd bet my life that Zola didn't steal it, but *someone* obviously did—meaning, Wendy didn't kill herself."

"Well," said Keith with a quizzical look, "that *is* weird. Sorry I can't be of more help."

"Actually," said Jazz, "you've helped a lot. Now we can assume that Wendy's condition was *not* common knowledge within the family, and we can also assume that your father's surprise was an honest reaction when he heard about it from Brooke."

"But," I said, "we still don't know if the Flassman angle was relevant to the murder."

Jazz agreed, "Not a clue."

Keith had pulled out his phone and started making a few notes. "As I understand it, then, the field of suspects is still wide open—everyone at the rental house that night had the *opportunity* to spike the posset and steal the Epi-Pen, also giving them the *means* to kill Wendy. As for a *motive*, it's safe to say that everyone disliked Wendy—some even hated her—except my father, who seemed to love her, inexplicably, despite her *many* faults."

I said with a grin, "An accurate summation, counselor."

Jazz said to Keith, "Help us brainstorm a bit. Yesterday, Dante and I did a little exercise, speaking from the gut, taking everything into account, and forcing ourselves to just lay it on the table and name the most likely killer. As it happens, we agreed. So, do the same thing right now and tell us: Who killed Wendy?"

I had no reason to think that Keith would name his father—as Jazz and I had—but Keith surprised me. Sort of.

"Well," he said, leaning back in his chair, "a spouse is usually the first 'person of interest' in any murder investigation, and objectively, Dad can't be conclusively *cleared* at this point, so he's probably at the top of the list. But he *is* my father, and I think I know him well enough to be confident that he couldn't have killed his wife. Setting him aside, then, my suspicions naturally flow to someone else. As it happens, I'm now in a position to provide some additional background on that person."

Jazz and I both asked, "Who?"

Rather than answering us directly, he asked, "What's your impression of Näzh Hoyle?"

Jazz and I exchanged a look. "Christ," she said, "where do I fuckin' start?"

I volunteered, "I'll start." Turning to Keith, I said, "Näzh is flat-out strange. He's got weird ideas and crazy goals."

Keith said, "By 'crazy goals,' are you referring to the Institute of Manifest Visualization?"

"In fact, I am. So you *know* about that?"

"Aunt Heather told me about it. She's skeptical."

Jazz said, "Thank God."

Keith added, "But she enjoys his company. And here's the thing: From the moment I met Näzh, when he arrived at the rental house on Saturday, I sensed that I already knew him. And yesterday, it finally clicked."

I grinned. "You've captured our attention."

He elaborated: "This was nearly twenty years ago, while I was in college at Berkeley. I came out during my sophomore year. Not that I'd ever been closeted—I simply hadn't figured out 'who I was' till then. The worst of the AIDS crisis was waning, but its impact on the Bay Area was profound and lasting. The school had various gay organizations, some of them purely social, but most had a political bent, dedicated to gay rights or AIDS action or both. So, as part of my coming-out process, I joined one of these groups—it went by an acronym, which I can't remember. And that's where I met Näzh, a name that I *definitely* remember. I mean, who'd name a kid *Näzh*, right?"

"Frankly," I said, "I'll bet he made it up."

With a quiet laugh, Keith said, "You're probably right. Anyway, he was a senior that year, two years ahead of me, and then he was gone. But while he was around, he had this reputation of being *way* out there, and I mean like 'interplanetary.' This was at *Berkeley*, remember, where counterculture is a major thing anyway. But trust me, he stood out—and not in a flattering way. With his crazy clothes and weird-ass philosophy, he earned the nickname 'Swami' from some members of the group, which struck me cruel, or at least immature. Oddly, it didn't seem to bother him in the least. In fact, I think he liked it."

I said, "This might seem like ancient history, but do you mind my asking: Did you ever have sex with him?"

"No, I don't mind. And no, the two of us never connected. He was into this 'tantra' thing, which involved withholding and prolonging and *mind games*, for lack of a better word. Bottom line: what he was into, most guys weren't."

I asked, "But just to clarify: He was, in fact, openly gay, right?"

"Definitely. And that's my whole point in dredging this up. Right *now*, you see, he's my aunt Heather's main squeeze, and he has these major plans to spend her money on his wacky Institute for Wishful Thinking—as I like to call it. So he really can't afford to let Heather find out that he's gay or 'bi' or anything not focused on *her*. And if I recognized *him* on Saturday, he probably recognized *me*. Does he feel threatened by this? I don't know. But you asked me to think with my gut. And my gut tells me that Swami is up to something."

Keith then crossed his arms, as if resting his case.

"But," said Jazz, "Heather already knows that Swami swings both ways. She knows that he thinks of himself as pansexual, finding erotic energy *everywhere*. He described sex as 'fluid and ever changing.' At least that's what he said Tuesday when he showed Dante his junk."

Stunned, Keith asked me, *"Really?"*

I nodded.

Keith leaned near and lowered his voice: "Back in the day, word on the street was: Watch out for Swami. He's hung like a horse."

I couldn't argue with that.

After lunch, rather than returning to Keith's office, Jazz drove us over to the neighborhood where Keith had grown up. He sat in the front passenger seat, guiding Jazz through the winding roads—the dashboard navigation map of the community bore no resemblance to a grid, except for the several blocks of the downtown area, about two miles away.

From the back seat, I asked Keith, "You no longer live here in town, correct?"

"Right. You'll see the house where I grew up, but I moved out on my own before Dad married Wendy. My condo has an ocean view—nice bachelor pad—and I can get to the office in fifteen minutes from there."

Jazz told him, "Sounds like a sweet setup."

He said, "Okay, just a couple more curves, then slow down on the right shoulder." A half minute later, he said, "Stop... *here.*"

We were on the edge of the road at a closed gate to a long driveway that led up the hillside. The surroundings were heavily wooded, but the trees thinned at the gate, affording a clear view of the house itself. "My God," I said, "it's *huge.*"

Jazz asked, "That's for *one* family?"

"Plus a monkey," Keith reminded us. And he pointed out some caging that had been added to a porch, visible from the road. I didn't see the monkey, though.

I said, "Pardon my asking, but I'm curious: What was the source of the Gibkins' wealth?"

Keith chortled. "I assumed you already knew. The money dates back to before the split in the family. We made buggy whips."

I wasn't sure he was serious. Jazz said, "You have *got* to be kidding."

"Nope," he said. "*Somebody* had to make them—when there was actually a demand—and a couple of shrewd brothers found-ed Gibbs Whips. Not overly clever branding, I admit. Neither was the slogan: 'Best in the West.'"

"You are *making* this up," Jazz insisted.

"If you want, I can open the gate, take us up to the house, in-troduce you to Koo-Loo, and show you the whip room. It's a collection in a closet, dedicated to the history of what *was* the family industry. Way back when, Model GW200 was a real barn burner. But alas, times have changed."

Jazz said, "I think we can skip the tour."

I asked Keith, "Who's minding the monkey?"

"There's help, one live-in—and I've lost track of how many service people." Keith's phone rang. He looked at the readout and told us, "Excuse me. I *really* need to take this."

The lilt of his voice made me wonder if maybe—

"Christopher!" he said into the phone. "What's up?"

Jazz stretched her neck to look at me in the back seat. We both arched our brows.

Keith continued, "Hey, that's *perfect*. Thanks so much for making room for me. Tomorrow at six—can't *wait*." Then he mumbled something with a hand covering the phone. Clearly, it was not meant to be heard by Jazz and me, but Keith's secretive tone was laced with schoolgirl giddiness.

When he rang off, we sat in suspended silence for a few moments, until Jazz said to him, "I *take* it you'll be joining us at the fundraiser tomorrow night."

"Indeed I will." He beamed. "Christopher managed to boot someone from the table he's hosting, so I guess I'll need to dust off the tux."

"Well, well, well," she singsonged. "Ought to be fun." Gone were her prior misgivings about a dreary evening with a bunch of stuffed shirts.

Keith brought the conversation back to the present, asking us, "Are you sure you don't want to go up to the house?"

Jazz scrunched her face. "Monkeys… aren't my thing."

I laughed. "Monkeys, horses—what *else* gives you the creeps?"

She snorted. "As if I would tell…"

Keith asked, "Know what still gives *me* the creeps?"

"Uhhh"—Jazz whirled a hand—"I doubt if it's trouser snakes."

Keith ignored that. "What still creeps me out is Heaven's Gate."

Jazz and I paused for a moment, struggling to recall.

"My God," I said. "The mass suicide—that was in Rancho Santa Fe—late 1990s—there was a comet."

Keith nodded. "The Hale-Bopp comet, 1997."

Jazz said, "I was just a kid. It was *weird* shit—with that mansion called Heaven's Gate."

"Actually," said Keith, "the *cult* was called Heaven's Gate, a

New Age religious movement. They were renting a mansion they called The Monastery, and it was located"—he pointed—"right next door, on the hill just over from our house. From my bedroom, you could see into their backyard. I was eleven. And our neighbors, thirty-nine of them, they poisoned and asphyxiated themselves, believing they'd be transported from Earth on a UFO trailing the comet. People here were in *shock*."

I said, "People *everywhere* were shocked by the tragedy—and mystified by the absurdity of it. I was in my mid-twenties, living in LA by then, and I thought, *Woo-hoo! Welcome to California!*

Keith said, "I *saw* them. And I saw the TV crews surrounding the emergency responders as they came down the long, curved stairway with the tiled steps, carrying out the shrouded bodies on stretchers. It's insane—the crap that people can be bilked into believing."

Sitting there in Jazz's SUV, gazing at the tranquility of the hills and the trees, I pondered the dangerous power of cults and their leaders.

Which also brought to mind: Näzh Hoyle's manifestation racket.

C H A P T E R
ELEVEN

Saturday night would be a welcome diversion from the daily grind of the murder case, which seemed unlikely to be solved anytime soon. One week ago that night, I had attended the freestyle dinner gathering that led directly to the wee-hours demise of Wendy Gibkin. Tonight, though, I drove Isandro in my convertible—top down—to the hallowed grounds of Wasi'chu Hills Country Club in Rancho Mirage.

Over the years, the fabled golf community had drawn celebrities and titans of industry as its members, who built sprawling custom houses there. Members like that expected fine dining, and invitations to the clubhouse were highly coveted by outsiders—so that evening's fundraiser for the expansion of Gilded Palms School was a sure sellout.

With cocktails and auction beginning at six, dinner at seven, and the program at eight, it would be a long slog, so we didn't need to arrive on the dot. We pulled up to the gatehouse just as the sun was setting, around six twenty. Since we were both wearing tuxes, the guard didn't bother to check us in—he simply pressed his magic fob to roll back the gate, telling us, "Have a wonderful evening, gentlemen."

I'd had occasion to visit here a couple of times before, but it was new to Isandro, who gaped as we cruised toward the clubhouse. The plantings and fountains, the date palms and paving stones, the attention to detail, the sheer luxury of space—everything said, *You have arrived.*

"Welcome, gentlemen," one of a pair of valets told us as we circled under the porte cochère. They opened the car doors for us and closed them after we got out. One of them whisked the car away while the other rushed ahead to open the lobby door for us. "Have a splendid time."

"I'm *sure* we will, thank you."

Guided by a merry din, we easily found the ballroom used for the opening reception. An attendant at the door asked for our names, then told us our table number, adding, with a wink, "Best in the house."

"*That* sounded promising," said Isandro as we stepped into the crowd.

"Stick with me, kid—you can't go wrong."

Spotting our arrival, a waiter approached us with a tray, offering, "Champagne? Or would you prefer cocktails?"

"This will be lovely, thank you." And we each plucked a frosty flute from the tray.

There was a crowded bar area along one side of the room, while the opposite side had rows of tables for the silent auction. Most of the guests mingled and gabbed in the middle.

Seemingly out of nowhere, Jazz appeared, striding toward us as she blew a wolf whistle. "Don't *you* guys look special!"

We did, in fact. It was the first time Isandro and I had seen each other in black tie, and we were both duly impressed—it had taken considerable restraint for us to leave the coach house on time, as we were tempted to simply stay home and get down together. But I spared Jazz these details and told her, "You're lookin' pretty good yourself."

"*This* old thing?" she said facetiously. I didn't know if her little black cocktail dress was old or new, but *I'd* never seen it, and she was an absolute knockout in it. She stepped close to Isandro and me, lowering her voice to tell us with a grin, "They're here."

Before I could ask for clarification, her ex-husband, Christopher, moved quickly in our direction with Keith Gibkin at his side. Christopher told Isandro and me, "I'm *so* sorry for being such a pill on Monday night. And I'm *so* grateful for meeting Keith—can't thank you enough for the introduction." Keith echoed these sentiments as well.

We assured them there was no need to apologize—or thank us—for anything. I said, "We're just glad to know that you two seem to have clicked."

It was ridiculously early to make any assumptions regarding what the future might hold for them—they barely knew each other—but it was plain, just looking at them, that they were off to a strong start. Physically, they really did seem to *belong* together. In their formal attire, they looked like two very handsome middle-aged grooms on a gay wedding cake.

Jazz said, "And *I'm* glad we lost another stuffed shirt at Christopher's table."

I said, "I assume Blade is with us—that's six. Anyone else?"

"Two more," said Christopher. "Patricia Cubbins, director of Gilded Palms—she does *not* like the term 'headmistress.' And one of the board members."

Jazz said, "That last one is our only stuffed shirt. One in eight—at least we've got him outnumbered." She looked over my shoulder. "And speaking of Blade…"

We turned as Blade Wade approached our group. "*Hey*," he said, big grin, "it looks like a *party* or something." Isandro and I hugged him; Christopher introduced him to Keith.

Keith said, "I understand you're a painter?"

Blade shrugged. "That's what they tell me."

Christopher laughed. "Mr. Humble." Turning to Keith, he explained, "Blade Wade is a *huge* name in the world of contemporary abstraction. And in fact, he's contributed a new work to tonight's auction. The school is *thrilled* about this."

Blade dismissed the praise: "Happy to help." Then he said, "I'm old news, but a rising *new* artist has also contributed a work tonight. C'mon, take a look." And he led us over to the auction area. It was clear that Christopher, who'd helped organize the event, did not know about this.

Blade led us around the auction tables to a side wall that displayed one of his dynamic eight-foot abstractions, predominantly red. "There!" he told us, pointing beyond his own work to a smaller painting, about thirty inches square. I knew at a glance that little Emma had painted it, and it must have been very recent. At only five years old, she had already transitioned from her earlier, representational compositions to a purely inventive style that was rooted, incongruously, in both naive innocence and a deep understanding of imagery.

Christopher hugged Jazz, telling Keith, "Our *daughter* did that, and I have no idea where she got the talent. It wasn't from *me*, so it must've been Jazz."

Through a warm smile, Jazz told Keith, "He's *so* fulla shit."

Our attention to Emma's painting had been noticed by others, who now grouped around us for a better look. From the comments I heard, I suspected that bidding would be brisk.

"So," said Blade, "little Emma is making *two* debuts tonight— her first ballet performance onstage, and the first public exhibition of her painting."

Both Jazz and Christopher seemed a bit overwhelmed, in a joyful way, and the evening had scarcely begun. The six of us moved away from the auction area to make room for those who were writing bids.

Returning to the middle of the reception room, which had grown louder and more crowded, I spotted Detective Arcie Madera and her husband, Cooper Brant, a local architect. I nudged Jazz, asking, "What's Arcie doing here?"

"I thought you knew," said Jazz. "Cooper designed the addition to the creative-arts building. He'll be speaking about it tonight."

"Ahhh," I said, "then the project is in good hands."

They spotted us as well, and we moved to greet each other.

While Cooper and I made small talk about the proposed building, Jazz and Arcie discussed the case. I heard Arcie say, "Nadig is getting impatient."

This was no surprise. Peter Nadig, the district attorney, was a hotdog prosecutor who chased headlines with zeal, especially when a potential death penalty was involved. With Wendy's murder case reaching the one-week mark, he was doubtless itching for less investigation and more action.

Arcie reminded Jazz, "The incriminating evidence was found in Zola Lorinsky's *purse*. Granted, it looked like a frame-up, but at this point, that's all we've *got*."

"I have a few ideas," said Jazz. "Later this evening, let's put our heads together."

"Sure." Then Arcie said to Cooper, "Ready for a drink?"

"I thought you'd *never* ask." Taking her arm, he waltzed her to the bar.

I stepped aside with Jazz, asking, "Are things heating up for Zola?"

"Yeah. So tonight could get awkward. I think Zola and Arcie are at the same table."

"Zola's *here*?"

Jazz told me, "She came with Richard Gibbs." When I looked even more confused, Jazz said, "Richard and Zola are *living* together, right? Just across the pool from you and Isandro, right?" I nodded, still confused. Jazz explained, "Richard is on the Gilded Palms *board*. He's a big donor to the school. He popped for the table next to ours tonight, hosting the board president, Simon Wormley. Arcie and Cooper are also at that table."

"Oh, boy..."

"They're right over there," said Jazz, discreetly pointing into the crowd. I saw Richard and Zola gabbing with another couple, a man and woman I didn't recognize. Jazz and I walked over to them.

Zola barked with delight, "Dante! *Dah*-ling! I didn't expect to see you tonight."

"Likewise," I said lamely as we pecked cheeks.

During our round of greetings, Richard introduced us to the other couple: "Please meet my esteemed guests, Dr. Luciana Ortiz, my cardiologist for *too* many years, and her son, Noé."

Luciana was a bright-eyed, energetic woman who must have been well into her sixties, possibly older, as her son seemed only a few years younger than I was, in his forties. This led me to assume that Luciana's husband was now out of the picture—in any event, he wasn't with us that night.

While we stood together gabbing pleasantly, I noticed that Luciana and Zola had already bonded, laughing like old chums, even though the doctor was more restrained in manner and more subdued in dress than the decorator was. In truth, *no one* could be expected to rise to Zola's level of pizazz.

At seven o'clock, we were interrupted by the sound of chimes as several pairs of large double doors were opened to the main ballroom, where tables were set for dinner under the warm glow of chandeliers. The crowd began shuffling out of the reception room.

Tapping Luciana's shoulder, I said, "Dr. Ortiz, if you don't mind, could I possibly have a word with you?"

"Why, certainly, Dante." She asked Noé to go on without her, then stepped back from the crowd with me. With a soft smile, she looked deep into my eyes—as if examining me—and asked, "How can I help you?"

I began, "Dr. Ortiz—"

"Please, Dante. Call me Luciana."

"Thank you, Luciana." Awkwardly, I explained, "Now, don't get me wrong—I'm not asking for medical advice. I'm not ill, and I'm not 'asking for a friend' who's ill. But I'm wondering if you've ever heard of a condition called Flassman syndrome."

She blanched, backing off a few inches. "Why do you ask?"

"I'm not sure what Richard might've already told you, but my friend Jazz and I are investigating the murder of a woman at a rental house here in Rancho Mirage."

"Good heavens," she said.

"And due to purely circumstantial evidence, our friend Zola is under suspicion—which is ridiculous, of course."

Luciana nodded. "Of course. But why are you asking about Flassman syndrome?"

"Because it has a bearing on the motive for the victim's death, a week ago. Her name is Wendy Gibkin, and about a year before she died, she was diagnosed with Flassman—but it wasn't common knowledge among a large circle of suspects."

"Just so I'm clear," said Luciana. "Wendy didn't *die* from the disease, correct?"

"Correct. She died from anaphylactic shock, and the evidence indicates this was not accidental. We thought we'd ruled out the possibility of suicide, but with the recent revelation of the Flassman diagnosis, we're not so sure anymore."

With a slow, gentle shake of her head, Luciana told me, "I'm afraid this poor woman could have indeed considered suicide—*if* her doctor had painted a clear picture of the prognosis. When I was in medical school *many* years ago, I was taking a seminar that focused on extremely rare and fatal diseases. It was led by a panel of senior physicians and surgeons. During the final meeting of the class, one of the students posed an interesting question to the panel: 'What is the single worst diagnosis you would never want to give?'"

I drew a breath, sure of what was coming.

Luciana continued, "We had already covered Flassman syndrome during the course of the seminar, learning that it was related to ALS, but even worse and—thank God—much more rare. While diagnosis of ALS is a lengthy ordeal, Flassman syndrome leaves distinct markers in various blood tests that allow a fast and definitive diagnosis. The degenerative disease is devastating, untreatable, and progresses rapidly after the first year or two."

I guessed, "And your panel picked Flassman as *the* worst."

"They didn't even need to discuss it. The four of them just looked at each other and nodded. Then the panel's moderator told us that Flassman syndrome is such a hopelessly morbid condition, if he himself were to be diagnosed with it, he wouldn't hesitate to get his affairs in order and end his own life."

"Jesus," I mumbled.

Luciana added, "Hearing this, I wondered if the moderator's words were exaggerated for effect—but then the other three doctors somberly *agreed* with him."

While this was sinking in, Luciana must have read the terror in my face. Placing a hand on my arm, she said, "If you had any interaction with this poor woman, don't worry—it's *not* contagious."

I wiped my brow with the back of my jittery hand, telling Luciana, "That was more than I bargained for, but I can't thank you enough."

"Happy to oblige. I hope you'll solve your riddle. And now, on a lighter note, shall we dine?"

Taking her arm, I escorted her out of the now deserted reception room.

In the main ballroom, most of the crowd—numbering perhaps two hundred guests—had located their tables and were settling in. Adding to the soft glow of the chandeliers, votive candles flickered at each place setting on the heavily draped white linen. Someone had underwritten centerpieces of pink and white roses for the two dozen round tables, filling the room with a cheerful fragrance that I couldn't help but associate with weddings.

At the far end of the room was a shallow stage, with a screen on the back wall showing a projected image of Cooper Brant's design for the building project. It was sleek and modern, with an artful Palm Springs vibe, exactly what I would expect from an architect of his caliber.

I didn't need to check table numbers. I saw Jazz, Isandro, and the others in our party, hosted by Christopher, at one of the two tables directly in front of the stage. Next to it, at the table hosted by Richard Gibbs, I saw Zola, Arcie, and Richard's other guests. Each of these two tables had one remaining open seat—one for Luciana, one for me. After making our way through the room, we hugged, then parted to join our respective tablemates.

I ended up seated between Isandro on my right and Blade on

my left. On the other side of Blade was Jazz, followed by Christopher, Keith, and at the head of the table, the school's director, Patricia Cubbins. She was a matronly character—queenly, one might say—whom I'd met once before when little Emma was interviewed for admission to the school. Jazz had left that meeting with a decidedly sour impression of the woman, who later redeemed herself by consulting Jazz on a revision of the elite school's diversity statement.

Finally, the eighth at our table, seated between Mrs. Cubbins and Isandro, was one of the school's board members—the stuffed shirt dreaded by Jazz. I didn't quite catch his name when we were introduced, and I didn't hear him say another word all evening.

Over the chitchat, I leaned past Blade to tell Jazz, "I had an interesting conversation with Dr. Ortiz."

"Anything I need to know?" she asked.

Blade signaled a time-out. He asked Jazz, "Wanna trade seats—so you and Dante can talk?"

Jazz was practically out of her chair before pausing, leaning to Christopher on her left, and asking, "Mind if I switch seats with Blade, honey? Don't want you feeling 'abandoned.'"

Christopher glanced over for a moment—having been thoroughly engaged with Keith—and told Jazz, "No problem. Have fun." And he immediately turned back to Keith, picking up where they'd left off, leaning nose to nose.

After Blade seated Jazz in the chair next to me and moved next to Christopher, she asked me, "What about Dr. Ortiz?"

"She gave me the complete scoop on Flassman syndrome. Long story short: it would be a dandy motive for suicide."

Jazz nodded. "But none of the evidence points to that."

"I know. But by the time Wendy died, her *husband* knew about the diagnosis—Harold heard about it from Brooke—so I think that creates an angle worth exploring. Plus, we found out during our visit to the winery that Heather, Harold's *sister*, knew about Wendy's death before you and I 'discovered' the body. Something's going on. Exactly what, I don't know, but the answer almost certainly lies somewhere between Harold and Heather."

After mulling this for a moment, Jazz said, "Maybe it's time to get Arcie involved."

I had to laugh. "After all, it's *her* investigation."

The meal was lavish and beautifully served, but slow. In a lull before dessert, the president of the school's board of directors, Simon Wormley, got up from the next table, climbed the three or four stairs to the apron of the stage, and stepped to a lectern. Tapping the microphone, he drew the attention of the crowd, then prattled words of welcome and a seemingly endless list of thank-yous, naming every member of the various committees who had worked on the event. Then he called Mrs. Cubbins to the stage, who recited a welcome of her own before introducing Cooper Brant, "the man of the hour," to speak about the design of his ambitious addition to the school's creative-arts complex.

By this point, many of the guests had turned their chairs at the tables so they could face the stage, but Isandro and I were fine where we sat. We listened attentively to Cooper's presentation, but my attention started to drift—the beautiful projection of the architectural rendering didn't require much explanation.

I leaned to ask Isandro, "Are you having fun yet?"

Under the tablecloth, his finger traced circles on my thigh. "Of course. I'm here with *you*." And I wondered why I'd ever been reluctant to settle down with him.

After Cooper ended his presentation — to energetic applause—board president Wormley resumed the stage. He reminded everyone that there were pledge cards at our places, then exhorted us to "invest in the future of our precious students at Gilded Palms School for the Gifted." Volunteers passed among the tables, picking up written pledges, but most of the guests simply tucked the cards away for consideration at home.

"And I have a few figures from tonight's silent auction," said Wormley, fluttering a sheet of paper. "With huge thanks to those who contributed items to the cause—and special thanks to the bidders who so generously opened their hearts and their wallets—I'm delighted to announce that, during the cocktail hour alone, the Gilded Palms building fund was enriched by more than two hundred *thousand* dollars."

As the crowd cheered, Jazz leaned to tell me, "Well, that might pay for the doors and windows—but it's a start."

Wormley continued, "I must say—assuming these figures are correct—I find one of these purchases *quite* astonishing. A student from our kindergarten class donated a painting of her own making to the auction ..."

Jazz, Christopher, Blade, and I all exchanged sudden, high-alert glances.

"... her name is Emma Friendly, and her painting fetched a winning bid of ten thousand dollars. Not bad, huh? Thank you, Emma! And thanks to the anonymous donor."

More cheers, more clapping. And needless to say, the guests at our table were gobsmacked. With a hearty belly laugh, Blade told me, "That's more than *mine* went for."

I assured him, "It's just a fluke. Not everyone has the right space for a big, dynamic 'statement' painting like yours."

"Thanks, Dante, but I don't need consoling. I couldn't be prouder of Emma—and that painting of hers was worth every penny, if only as an investment. Between you and me, that's why my gallerist, Marc Albré, bought it. I sent him a photo, and he asked me to place the winning bid for him. Believe me: Emma has a future. If she sticks with this, there's no stopping her."

"Well," I said with a shrug, "she's had *excellent* instruction."

Another belly laugh. "So true, Dante. So true."

Wormley had turned over the program again to Mrs. Cubbins, who now stood at the microphone. "Ladies and gentlemen, the stage needs to be reset for our *very* special dance feature. While that's being taken care of, please enjoy your coffee and dessert—and you're welcome to mingle and gab a bit, if you like. Thank you for your patience."

A crew appeared, removing the podium from the stage. They then wheeled in a grand piano and positioned it on the floor in front of the stage apron. Someone checked its tuning while others, onstage, rolled painted scenery out from the wings. A techie with a headset stood center stage, running lighting cues with someone unseen.

Meanwhile, many guests stood and drifted from their tables.

Detective Madera had risen from her seat at the table next to us and was passing time in conversation with the dowdy wife of the board president. I nudged Jazz, telling her, "Arcie might appreciate being rescued—and that would give us a chance to compare notes." Jazz nodded.

We rose, standing only three or four steps away from Arcie and Mrs. Wormley. Proving my prediction correct, Arcie eyed us with a pleading look.

Jazz and I approached them with gracious smiles and interrupted their conversation to introduce ourselves to Mrs. Wormley, praising her husband's stewardship of the school. (Jazz might have spoken from knowledge of his tenure, but I was blowing smoke.)

Mrs. Wormley bubbled with gratitude for our accolades.

Then, a curious look crossed Jazz's features. She leaned close to Mrs. Wormley and discreetly tapped her own face near the edge of her lips—as if alerting the other woman to a sprig of something green in her teeth.

Mrs. Wormley whispered, "*Thank* you, my dear," then rushed off to the ladies' lounge.

"Wow," said Arcie. "Why didn't I think of that?"

Jazz smirked. "Because *you're* not so devious."

"I'll take that as a compliment—I guess."

"Arcie," I said, "Jazz and I have been talking about—what else?—Wendy Gibkin's murder. And we have some information you might find of interest."

Her brows arched. "Then let's hear it."

Jazz said, "We've learned that Wendy had been diagnosed with a fatal disease. It's called Flassman syndrome."

With a quizzical look, Arcie said, "Never heard of it."

"You're not alone," I said. Then Jazz and I told Arcie the whole story: the nature of the disease, how it was diagnosed, who knew about it, and when. I concluded, "Obviously, this raises the possibility of suicide, even though the evidence doesn't point to that. At the very least, though, the Flassman issue suggests there might've been a tangle of motive-related dynamics. If so, we think it involved Wendy's husband, Harold—and Harold's sister, Heather."

Jazz added, "Another news flash, Arcie: we've learned that Heather probably had knowledge of Wendy's death before Dante and I found the body." Jazz then related to Arcie our visit to Heather's vineyard and our conversation with her ranch manager.

Pausing to take all of this in, Arcie shook her head, as if clearing cobwebs. "Jeez," she said, "you two have been *busy*."

I was tempted to ask, *And what have you been doing?* But I knew Arcie too well, and respected her too much, to indulge in such a glib and groundless comment.

As if having read my mind, however, she told us, "I might've gotten further with the investigation if I didn't need to waste so much time fending off Peter Nadig and filing useless reports. He's got it in his craw that the 'evidence in the purse' is adequate—and he'd rather make headlines than make sure. He's like a dog with a bone."

I suggested, "Maybe the best way to change his mind is to toss him a bigger, better bone—like an airtight arrest of the *real* killer."

"Well, *yes*," she said with a facetious tone, "that might do the trick. But that's assuming we can, in fact, name the real killer."

Jazz told her, "It is *not* Zola. It *has* to be either Harold or Heather or a conspiracy between the two of them. And I think I know how we can sort it out."

Arcie crossed her arms, then grinned. "I'm listening."

"I know you were off duty when we summoned you to the rental house last Sunday. Up for some more overtime tomorrow?"

"I might be persuaded—if duty calls."

Jazz explained, "Dante and I can go to the house tomorrow morning and gather everyone for a 'little talk.' I'll let them know in advance that we're close to solving the case—that'll make sure no one skips out."

Arcie said, "And you want me there."

Jazz hesitated. "Yes—but I think it might be best if you're waiting at the curb in your car, maybe with a deputy. I have a feeling that the meeting will be more productive without a police presence, at least at first."

"Sure. What time?"

Jazz glanced at both Arcie and me, suggesting, "Eleven?"

We nodded just as Mrs. Cubbins began clanging her water goblet with a spoon. "Could everyone now return to their seats, please?"

A few minutes passed as people disengaged from their conversations and settled back at their tables. Before Jazz and I sat down again, we went to Christopher and Keith's side of our table and hunkered between them.

I asked Keith, "Will you be staying at the rental house tonight?" When he hesitated, I added, "Or maybe not?" He gave Christopher a questioning look.

With an air of disappointment, Christopher told Keith, "Maybe that's best. Emma will be back at the house tonight. After a week away, she should 'reclaim her space,' so to speak."

"Perfectly understood," said Keith. With a wink, he added, "I'll be around for a few days—we'll find the right time."

Returning the wink, Christopher said, "Count on it."

Jazz said, "We're not just bein' snoopy. We actually *need* to have Keith at the rental tomorrow morning."

He assured her, "I'm all yours. But what for?"

"A showdown," I said. "We're hoping to wrap up the murder case."

Christopher's lawyerly antenna went up. "Should *I* be there? I agreed to look after Zola's interests."

Jazz and I glanced at each other, shook our heads. She told Christopher, "No, that shouldn't be necessary. If things go as planned, Zola's off the hook." She reminded him, "And besides—you'll have Emma."

With that settled, Keith asked, "When will this happen?"

I said, "I'll drop by around eleven—just a friendly concierge check-in to be sure our valued guests are happy. Jazz will happen to be with me." I didn't mention that we'd have the cops at the curb.

"So," Jazz said to Keith, "your role in this is simply to make sure that everyone will be there. Tell them we're coming, and if anyone tries to wriggle out, tell them you think we *might* have news about Wendy's murder."

"Got it," said Keith. "And I assume my *other* role in this is to represent my father's interests."

He was right, of course, but this was a sensitive point. Jazz told him, "That's strictly between you and your dad. Since we hope to compel a fair amount of truth-telling tomorrow—truth regarding the circumstances of Wendy's death—I'm sure Harold will appreciate your emotional support."

Keith chuckled. "That was *very* cautious phrasing."

Jazz shrugged. "Maybe I shoulda been a lawyer."

Mrs. Cubbins clanged her glass again. "If I could have everyone's attention, we're about to begin."

Jazz and I skittered back to our seats as the crowd hushed and the lights in the room dimmed.

Mrs. Cubbins said, "For the entertainment portion of our festivities, we're so very honored to have with us tonight the visiting dance master of our ballet program at Gilded Palms. He wants to tell you what we have planned for your enjoyment, so please welcome—the one and only—Servando Ureña."

And we were all on our feet as the world-renowned *premier danseur* strode out from the wings to meet Mrs. Cubbins, center stage. He kissed her hand, took her microphone, and made a deep, elegant, well-rehearsed bow as Mrs. Cubbins retreated into the shadows. He was wearing a long velvet cape that fell to his knees—not far enough to conceal that he wore tights and was dressed to dance in an unannounced but much rumored encore.

"My friends," he said. Isandro and I glanced at each other. While his dancing and his artistry, not to mention his drop-dead physique, were judged among the finest in the world, his speaking voice... not so much. He had uttered only two words, but they were high-pitched, nasal, and heavily accented with a Castilian lisp that only further eroded his manly image. When he spoke of "the sensational students of this inspiring institution of arts and letters," Isandro and I had to grab each other's hands beneath the tablecloth, squeezing so hard that it hurt, forcing each other not to laugh.

When a fierce-looking woman with a buzz-cut and a tuxedo came out and seated herself at the piano, cracking her knuckles, Ureña said, "So I present to you the young corps de ballet of Gilded Palms School of the Gifted, performing three of the dances from Tchaikovsky's *The Nutcracker*." He added, "I know it might seem sort of early for this, but the selected dances are the least Christmassy ones." The more he talked, the more he sounded like Truman Capote.

He walked from the stage to the sound of anticipatory applause, but as the lights dimmed to black, the crowd became silent.

We heard the scurry and patter of little feet taking their places, and then, when the lights went up full, the pianist began plunking out the rhythmic, energetic strains of the "Miniature Overture"—and the entire troupe of twelve dancers flew into action. Emma was among the youngest three; the oldest might have been eighth-graders. I noted two brave boys among the ten girls. Their formations changed fluidly with the music, but Emma, being smallest, usually wound up at one end or the other.

In her tutu and tiara, which resembled a sparkly princess dress, she looked adorable—but then, she *always* looked adorable, even in overalls. I saw Christopher leaning over Keith's shoulder, whispering in his ear, pointing out his daughter. Jazz and Blade held hands, leaning forward in their seats, as if another six inches would improve their wide-eyed view.

The pause between selections was very brief, meant to discourage applause (to be saved for the end), as the troupe then performed the "Dance of the Reed Flutes." Though they were clearly young students, some of them mere beginners, their energy was impressive, and Ureña's choreography played to their strengths, as opposed to their technique or precision. Still, they managed to remain in unison throughout. And—thank God—no one fell.

The first two selections were quite short, just two or three minutes each, but the third dance was considerably longer as the program concluded with—of course—"Waltz of the Flowers."

And it was lovely. I didn't know if any of these young dancers would ever beat the odds and perform professionally, but they were *doing* it. They were getting an early taste of this spirited art form and the discipline of working in an ensemble—a lesson in teamwork that rivaled any sport. They were beautiful, every single one of them, and their joy was palpable as they waltzed and swayed and *leaped* into the closing measures of the music.

And at last, pent-up applause burst from the room as if the well-educated, highly cultured audience had never heard this chestnut—as if they had just seen it danced for the very first time. Tears filled many eyes, and not just the women's. I'd have sworn I heard the snap of checkbooks being opened.

After a series of jubilant curtain calls, the dancers began an orderly exit from the stage, but a few of the youngest, including

Emma, skittered down the stairs to the floor of the ballroom and rushed out to the eager arms of their parents.

Jazz and Christopher smothered their daughter with kisses. Blade and I got in on the act, and Mrs. Cubbins blubbered with jolly emotion. Christopher introduced Emma to Keith, who offered a warm hug, and then, as the lights dimmed to half, Emma came over to sit on Jazz's lap.

The pianist turned to speak loudly to the crowd, without a microphone: "And now, a little surprise." Everyone laughed in anticipation of the announcement. She said: "The drunk solo, act two, *Don Quixote.*"

A collective gasp rose from the room with eager applause as the lights went black.

When silence reigned, the lights went up again, and there stood Ureña, center stage, without his cape, in a rustic-looking costume that included a snugly cinched suede vest—along with tights and a mesmerizing, tasseled codpiece. He held two pewter wine goblets aloft and, with a nod to the pianist, began the one-minute solo, which gave the illusion of drunken staggering that required, at the same time, virtuoso leaps and timing.

The bawdy, raucous accompaniment suggested a peasant dance hall. For that seemingly endless minute, the bejeweled and tuxedoed gentry in the Wasi'chu Hills ballroom—*all* of us—were transported to a faraway place in a long-forgotten time when a simple story, and a man in tights, could make magic.

Servando Ureña lived up to the legend, a wonder to behold. It was a once-in-a-lifetime experience, seeing him perform after his retirement from the stage. Everyone in the room—or, *almost* everyone—watched him, agog.

From where I sat, I could see silhouettes of those who sat facing the stage from the far side of our table. Everyone's gaze was

fixed on Ureña—except for Christopher and Keith, who dream-
ily stared at each other.

And then, glancing to my side, I found Isandro watching me.
When he winked, the room erupted with wild applause and cries
of "Bravo!"

By any measure, the evening had been a resounding success.
The pledge drive for Gilded Palms School had launched with an
auspicious start. Those attending the gala had witnessed a bit of
ballet history. And little Emma Friendly had sold her first painting—for five figures, at that.

After the return drive to Palm Springs, Isandro and I climbed
the stairs to our loft at the coach house. I unlocked the door,
asking, "Have a good time?"

"Mm-*hmm*."

Stepping inside with him, I asked, "Tired?"

"Nope." He pulled me close. "But I'm ready for bed."

I reached both arms around his waist, under his jacket. "Let
me help you out of that cummerbund."

Our antics didn't end till well past midnight, and when we finally called it quits, we quickly fell into a deep, sated sleep.

Sunday morning, we got up later than usual, around nine
o'clock. Over coffee, I told him about my plans with Jazz that
day. "The showdown begins at eleven."

He asked, "Do you want me to be there?"

"Not unless you want to be. You're certainly not an active suspect for Wendy's murder. Even though you were there last Sunday when Jazz and I found the body, you weren't there at all the
day before—when the posset was made and then spiked with
honey before it congealed that night."

"Good. That'll give me some lazy-time by myself."

I wondered aloud, "Pedicure and a box of chocolates?"

He looked suddenly inspired. "Green! What would you think of green toenails?"

I called his bluff: "If it works for you, it works for me."

When I arrived in Rancho Mirage and parked at the curb in front of the rental house, it was just two or three minutes before eleven. I didn't see Jazz's SUV—on the street or inside the courtyard—so I waited, thinking we should share any last-minute thoughts before entering. Then I looked up from my watch, glanced in the mirror, and saw her drive up behind me.

I hopped out of the car and met her on the street. As we nodded a quick good-morning, she asked, "Ready for this?"

"You bet—let's wrap it up."

She looked around. "Zola and Richard—are they coming?"

"I talked to them about it last night, before leaving Wasi'chu Hills. Said they'd be here—anxious to get everything settled." While speaking to Jazz, I sent Zola a text.

She replied at once: ON OUR WAY.

"They'll be here soon," I told Jazz.

Walking with her through the courtyard to the house, I noted that all of the visitors' vehicles were accounted for. After we stepped up to the front door, I rang the bell—and instantly heard the click of the latch, as if someone had been waiting inside.

"Dante, Jazz—good morning," said Heather, looking freshly made-up and put-together to greet company. "We've been expecting you."

I asked, "So Keith has spread the word?"

"Oh, indeed he has. But a Sunday-morning roundup sounds rather ominous, don't you think?" She laughed—as if she found it not the least bit ominous, but amusing. "Please. Come in."

Walking through to the great room, I noticed that the place looked reasonably (but not obsessively) tidy. Brooke and Tyler sat at the kitchen island, lingering over their breakfast plates. Rebecca Jiang fussed near the sink, loading the dishwasher, looking dressy in a silk pantsuit and kitten heels—forever in uniform for her role as Harold's loyal (and doting) gal Friday.

Keith strolled out from his bedroom, groomed and dressed for the day in khaki shorts, Top-Siders, and a polo of subtle green—the color of creamy pistachio gelato. He gave both Jazz and me a hug, offering, "Can I get you something? Coffee, maybe?"

We both declined. I told him, "Richard and Zola should be here soon." Looking about, I added, "Is your father around? And Näzh?"

He nodded. "Dad's been busy in his room, at the desk. I saw Näzh at the pool earlier." Then he asked Heather, "Could you let Näzh know we're about ready?"

"Sure," she said as she stepped out to the pool terrace, then over to the guesthouse.

Dingdong.

I told Keith, "That should be Richard and Zola."

He nodded and went to greet them.

Jazz nudged me. "Arcie just texted. She's out front whenever we need her."

Heather returned with Näzh in tow. He'd been spending too much time in the sun since Tuesday and now had an unhealthy red glow. Fortunately, today's harem pants were more opaque than Tuesday's orange palazzos. He carried a glass of unappetizing breakfast slop that appeared to have seaweed in it.

Keith brought Richard and Zola in from the front door, and they greeted everyone—but without much enthusiasm. When

Zola leaned to kiss my cheek, she said in a croaking whisper that anyone could hear, "Last time we tried this, it didn't end so well."

I suggested that everyone might like to get comfortable in the conversation area. As they began drifting toward the sofas and chairs, I said to Keith, "We still need Harold."

Since Rebecca was finishing up in the kitchen and was nearest the bedroom wing used by Harold, Keith asked her, "Could you try to coax Dad from whatever he's doing?"

She nodded and dried her hands before stepping away.

Jazz told everyone, "Sorry if we've seemed all *mysterious* in gathering you here this morning, but we really do need to sort out a few things."

Näzh raised a hand. "How long will this take? Because—"

A garbled scream stopped us cold.

We all froze for a long, uncertain moment—unsure of what we'd just heard.

Rebecca's second scream, louder and more terrified, left little doubt.

As if on cue, everyone rose, moving toward the bedroom.

"Stop!" Jazz commanded. "Stay right there." And she began rushing across the house.

Then she turned back, looking at me. "Not *you*. C'mon!"

I ran, catching up with her as we entered the bedroom.

Rebecca stood a good eight feet from the desk, having backed off, whimpering, after discovering the body.

Seated at the desk, Harold Gibkin had collapsed, face down, while working at his laptop. His head was smooshed sideways on the keyboard with eyes and mouth open. Vomit—*lots* of it—covered the keys and most of the desk, dripping to the wet carpet, filling the room with a putrid smell that carried heavy overtones of rotgut whiskey. That, and the smoky stench of cigarettes that still filled the air, triggered a gag reflex in my throat that I was barely able to suppress.

On the desk, in the mess, was an open bottle of Old Nine-Tails, about a fourth empty, and a smudgy glass of it, half full. A wadded, spent pack of cigarettes was tossed into a cereal bowl containing six or eight butts.

Oddly, he was *not* unshaven, barefooted, and wearing the frumpy bathrobe I'd seen before. Instead, he was well groomed and wore a nice Sunday outfit of tailored slacks, an open-collared dress shirt, and well-polished shoes—what some people might describe as "church clothes," although I had no reason to presume he'd had worship on his mind.

Being careful not to disturb anything, Jazz reached inside his collar to check for a pulse. "Well," she said, "so much for our big showdown." She grabbed her phone and alerted Arcie.

My mind was spinning.

Harold's death had thrown the entire investigation back to square one.

PART THREE
WISHFUL THINKING

CHAPTER
TWELVE

Arcie and her deputy were soon joined in Harold's bedroom by the same medical examiner, photographer, and forensics team that had visited the house just one week earlier. The irony of the situation was only too apparent, but everyone had the tact to skip the comments and stick to business.

As next of kin, Keith was brought into the room to formally identify the victim. "Yes," he said, "that's my father, Harold Gibkin." Then Jazz and I walked him out to the hall.

I put my hand on his shoulder. "Keith, I'm *so* sorry—what a terrible shock for you."

Wagging his head, he told us, "This is absolutely unreal. I don't even know how to react."

Jazz said, "It'll sink in soon enough. Stay strong."

"Thanks, Jazz. But Christ, what a mess. His estate—and Wendy's estate—the business, the house, the taxes, not to mention *funerals*. That's the sort of stuff I deal with every day, but I have to admit: this hits a *little* too close to home."

"Of course it does," I said, hugging him.

He took a long, deep breath. "Okay. No more tears."

(I had seen no tears. Or was this just another way of saying, "Pull yourself together"?)

He continued, "What should I tell the others while you're busy back here?"

Jazz said, "Have everyone stay put. Arcie's running the show now, but I know she'll want to talk to everyone."

Keith nodded. "Sure." And he walked out to the great room.

When Jazz and I returned to the bedroom, Arcie was sitting on the edge of the bed, taking notes while questioning Rebecca, who had remained there since discovering the body. She sniffled into a hankie between responses to Arcie as they pieced together the timing of the morning's events.

"Detective?" said the medical examiner. "A word?"

Arcie excused herself and went over to confer with him.

Jazz sat on the bed next to Rebecca, and I pulled a chair over to sit with them. Jazz told her, "My deepest sympathies for your loss today. And I also want to apologize for Tuesday's lunch—which ended badly. I'm sorry."

To my way of thinking, if apologies were in order for the emotional breakdown at lunch, they shouldn't have come from Jazz but from Rebecca herself. Now that Jazz had graciously extended the olive branch, I wondered if Rebecca might acknowledge her own shoddy behavior.

Balling the hankie, she stared at Jazz. "You really don't *understand*, do you?"

"Maybe I don't. Care to tell me about it?"

"You tried to convince me that Harold had no feelings for me—no *real* feelings. You tried to steal his *love* from me. And now, today, someone has stolen Harold *himself* from me." She rolled her swollen eyes, adding, "This has been one *hell* of a week."

Jazz turned to me with a blank expression—now was clearly not the time to pursue truth-telling with Rebecca. Jazz stood and told her flatly, "Again, our condolences."

Jazz then stepped over to Arcie, who'd finished with the medical examiner, near the desk. I joined them. Before speaking to us,

Arcie asked a deputy to escort Rebecca back to the great room.

When they left, Arcie explained, "I don't want any of *them* to know what we have here—not yet." With a latex-gloved hand, she gestured toward the whiskey in the glass that sat on the desk. It dazzled in a shaft of sunlight angling in from tall windows. Lifting it, she told Jazz, "Smell."

Doing so, Jazz wrinkled her nose. "Curious," she said.

Arcie passed it under my nose as well. I said, "The strong whiskey smell is obvious. But it's also slightly"—I struggled for the word—"*fishy*."

Nodding, Arcie set down the glass. "The medical examiner noticed it. From all appearances, the victim died from drinking this, and whiskey *alone* wouldn't kill him, so there's a reasonable chance the liquor was poisoned. And the poison that produces a slightly fishy smell in a warm solution—such as this, sitting in the sun—is nicotine extract. It's brown, like whiskey, which would mask its appearance as well as its taste. We'll still need to *test* for nicotine, but it's a very promising place to start."

Jazz said, "Harold was a heavy smoker. Would that make any difference?"

Arcie shrugged. "It might make him slightly less susceptible, but nicotine extract is highly toxic. If the solution was strong enough, it could be fatal within five minutes. It has a history of use as an insecticide."

Jazz and I glanced at each other. I marveled, "Who knew?"

The forensics team took a sample from the glass, then bagged the glass itself and the bottle of Old Nine-Tails. Vomit samples had already been taken from Harold's mouth and from the desk. The laptop had been bagged as possible evidence, as had Harold's phone, which he'd left on the desk.

230

The gurney was rolled in. And a few minutes later, Harold made his final exit, feet first, wheeled through the great room and out the front door, followed by the unbelieving gazes of the assembled guests—all of them now suspects in a *second* murder.

When the response team had departed with the body and the bagged evidence, Arcie and her deputy remained. Stepping over to where everyone was seated, she said, "Where to begin? It seems we just did this. We were starting to make some progress with *Mrs.* Gibkin's case, but now, with *Mr.* Gibkin's death, we'll need to start over. And if you were wondering: yes, we're treating both of these deaths as homicides."

Predictably, this caused a stir. Keith asked Arcie, "Are you treating the two cases as related?"

"We're assuming the two cases are almost certainly related, but at this point, we have no idea *how* they're related. It's possible that the same person is responsible for both deaths. But even if there's more than one killer, there's clearly some connection— both victims died here, under this roof, seven days apart, while the same group of people were staying in this house. That can't be a coincidence."

The visitors—the suspects—murmured while eyeing each other as if *no one* could be trusted. And they were probably right.

Arcie continued, "It's the same basic procedure as last time. We won't need to take fingerprints again, but we'll need to collect a new set of statements from all of you. Let me begin, though, with a few questions for the group." Checking her notes, she said, "First of all, I noticed that the victim looked rather 'dressed up' for a Sunday morning at home—in fact, most of *you* are looking sort of snazzy, too. Was something planned? Anything special?"

Heather, in her finery, told Arcie, "We were going to the Ritz-

Carlton for brunch. Harold invited us, his treat."

Making note of this, Arcie said, "Your brother was very gener-ous. Was this typical of him?"

Keith said, "When he was in the mood, yes, he could be very generous. He thought today called for it."

"Why today?"

"Because," said Keith, "he thought Wendy's murder would get wrapped up this morning—with Jazz and Dante—at least that's what he told us."

"So," said Arcie, "he was planning to celebrate the anticipated closure of his wife's case."

Everyone nodded. Keith said, "Exactly."

Arcie suppressed a smile. "I'm delighted to know he had such confidence in the investigation. Did he mention a specific time when he thought the riddle would be solved?"

Rebecca, standing behind the others, leaning against the kit-chen island, raised a finger. "He seemed sure it would be over by one, so he asked me to reserve a table for twelve at one thirty." When everyone started counting heads, Rebecca added, "He wanted to include *you*, Detective."

Dryly, Arcie said, "How nice of him. Can I assume you pro-ceeded to *make* this reservation."

"Of course. I took care of it right away."

I suggested to Arcie, "Maybe I'd better cancel that."

She gave me a knowing nod—the point of this was simply to find out if the hotel was in fact aware of these plans. I took out my phone, called the Ritz, and asked for the dining room. The story checked out, and I canceled the table.

Arcie asked everyone, "How was Harold coping with Wendy's death?"

Keith said, "As well as can be expected, I guess. Nothing could

be done to undo what happened to Wendy, and Dad was prac-
tical enough to realize that—to begin letting go of it. He was
never what I'd call an emotional man."

Rebecca insisted, "He was a *passionate* man." When her words
were met with incredulous looks, she clarified: "He had a passion for *ideas*."

Yeah, well, maybe, I thought.

Richard and Zola were perched on the same settee where, a
week earlier, they had spilled her purse. Richard politely asked
Arcie, "Detective, considering that Zola and I have not been
here since last Sunday—and we arrived here today mere *minutes*
before Harold's body was found—can I safely assume that neither of us is under suspicion for what happened today?"

Considering this for a moment, Arcie said, "Barring something unforeseen, I think that's a safe assumption, yes."

"Well"—Zola leaned to tell Richard, but her words were intended for all—"at least this time, they can't try to pin it on *me*."

Arcie said to everyone, "Help me brainstorm this. Did any of
you notice anything that made you think Mr. Gibkin might be
in danger?"

They all shook their heads.

Arcie tried again: "Can you think of *anyone*—here at the house,
or anywhere else—who might have wanted to harm Harold?"

"No," said Keith. "We all loved him. He was my *father*."

"He was my big *brother*," said Heather.

"He was my *uncle*," said Brooke.

"He was my employer, my *rock*," said Rebecca, heaving a loud,
pent-up sob.

I noted that the only two people staying at the house who did
not respond to this were Näzh Hoyle and Tyler Evans, the Ferris
ladies' "boyfriends."

Arcie noticed this as well. "Mr. Hoyle? Mr. Evans? Can you think of anyone?"

They both shook their heads.

I didn't know what to make of Näzh. Although he struck me as flighty, dishonest, and possibly deranged, I couldn't fathom any motive he might have for killing Harold.

On the other hand, Tyler had openly expressed to me his seething contempt for Harold, who had not stood up for him when Wendy called him a monkey—because he was Black. I knew him to be a talented, intelligent, soft-spoken puppy of a young man who had done nothing to deserve the wounds inflicted on him by Wendy's vile words. I also thought the prospects were good that he would become a devoted soulmate to Brooke. So I did *not* want to believe he was capable of murder. Objectively, though, he had a motive.

Jazz, I noticed, had stepped aside with Arcie, and they were huddled in a private conversation. Arcie nodded, then turned to tell us, "A few days ago, Jazz acquired some information that might be relevant to this inquiry." Then she stepped back so Jazz could speak.

"On Wednesday," she said, "Dante and I had the pleasure of driving over to Temecula, where we visited Trot-n-Tipple. I assume you've all been there, correct?"

With the exception of Zola and Richard, they all nodded. Speaking for the Ferris party, Brooke noted, "We *live* there."

Jazz smiled. "And what an idyllic setting it is. You actually grew up there—right, Brooke?"

Brooke returned the smile, nodding.

Jazz continued, "And I really need to thank *you*, Heather, for the royal treatment we got, once the word got out that Dante and I are friends of yours. Lunch was unbelievable."

Warmly, Heather said, "No need to thank *me*, Jazz. The special lunch was my way of thanking *you*—both you and Dante—for everything you've been doing on behalf of the family." Heather turned to tell Arcie, "When all this is over, Detective, I hope *you'll* visit the winery, too. We'd love to welcome you there and show our gratitude for your tireless efforts."

Arcie replied, in a neutral tone with no apparent enthusiasm, "I'll remember that, thank you."

Jazz said to Heather, "And I must say, the people working there are truly a credit to your management skills. What a team. Tracy, the tour guide, was so sweet and knowledgeable. And *Frank*— Frank Dillon, I think—he seems to keep everything running like a well-oiled machine, even in your absence."

Heather agreed, "I'd be *helpless* without Frank. He's been ranch manager since the start."

"He told us about the system you've developed."

"System?" asked Heather.

Jazz explained, "The daily phone call. You call him once a day, without fail, whenever you're away."

"It's a simple setup—nothing genius about it. But it works."

Jazz turned to me with a quizzical look, asking, "What else did Frank have to say?" (I was certain she hadn't forgotten any details; she was simply inviting me to jump in.)

I stepped toward the group, telling Heather, "Frank asked us to 'look after' all of you in the aftermath of Wendy's death." (I couldn't recall if he'd actually said that—probably not—but it seemed plausible.)

"He's such a sweetheart," said Heather. "Next phone call, I'll report to him that you and Jazz have *more* than lived up to his request."

"Thank you," I said. "But I'm wondering: How did he react

when you first told him that Wendy had died?"

"Aside from the shock of the news, he seemed to be most concerned about its effect on *me*—and whether that might have any effect on operations at the vineyard. I wanted to reassure him, so that's why I gave him the news right away."

"Meaning, you told him about it last Sunday?"

"Of course."

"During your regular daily briefing call?"

"Sure. I knew he'd be waiting to hear from me."

Keith caught my attention by clearing his throat. I asked him, "Yes?"

He said, "Excuse me, Dante, but I can't help being curious. What does Heather's ranch manager have to do with any of this?"

I recalled that when Jazz and I had visited Keith in Rancho Santa Fe, we'd shared plenty of updates with him, but we had *not* told him about our conversation with Frank Dillon.

I now told Keith, as well as everyone in the room, "Heather and Frank have a standing appointment for her to call him at ten o'clock every morning, seven days a week, whenever she's not at the vineyard."

Heather's eyes widened as she froze, but when I glanced around the room, I could tell that the others had not yet grasped the significance of the timing. I said to them, "In other words, Heather told Frank about Wendy's death at least two hours *before* Jazz and I discovered the body."

The room erupted with boisterous expressions of shock, confusion, and dismay. Jazz leaned to tell me, "It seems you've caught their attention."

Arcie tried to take over. If she'd had a police whistle, I'm sure she would've used it, but she was stuck with clapping her hands and calling for order, which had zero effect. Jazz came to the rescue with a well-practiced, piercing finger whistle—which brought the clamor to a dead halt.

Arcie stepped to within three feet of Heather's chair. "Mrs. Ferris," said the detective, "I need to have a conversation with you, and I think you might be more comfortable talking about this at the station." With the inflection of an order, not a question, Arcie added, "Would you come with me, please."

Tentatively, Heather stood. "Detective Madera, I'd much prefer to air everything right here, in front of everyone—if you don't mind, please. It could help my family to dismiss any doubts they might have about this. And let me be clear on the one crucial point: I did *not* kill Wendy."

Arcie asked the deputy to retrieve a recorder from her briefcase. When she had it in hand, she asked Heather to move to a quiet corner of the room, where they sat on opposite sides of a small game table with the recorder placed between them.

Jazz and I—and everyone else—moved toward them, where we could stand and listen.

Arcie made some introductory remarks into the recorder, then said to Heather, "On Sunday, October third, while you were staying with others at a vacation house in Rancho Mirage, California, Wendy Gibkin died in the early morning hours, not long after midnight. Her body was found in her bedroom by private investigator Jazz Friendly and her assistant, Dante O'Donnell, shortly after noon that day. They then alerted me, and I came to the house, followed by a response team. So my question to you, Mrs. Ferris, is this: Did you have knowledge of Mrs. Gibkin's death prior to noon that day?"

Heather hesitated, but nodded. "I did, Detective."

"How did you become aware of this?"

Everyone reflexively leaned an inch or two closer, hanging on Heather's next words.

She answered, "My brother told me about it."

As we reacted, Arcie commanded silence with a wave of her hand, asking Heather, "And for the record, when you say 'my brother,' you're referring to Harold Gibkin, correct?"

"Yes, Harold's my brother. Rather, he *was* my big brother, and I was his kid sister. He was fifty-nine; I'm fifty-two."

Arcie asked, "When did he tell you that Wendy was dead?"

"Around seven o'clock that morning. Last Sunday."

"Tell me about the circumstances of that conversation. How did it come about? Where exactly were you?"

"We were here at the house, of course. It was the first morning after our first night here. I'd slept in the guesthouse; he and Wendy had separate bedrooms in the main house. I've always been an early riser—working at a vineyard. Harold, not so much. In fact, I was surprised to see him up and about so early when I walked over from the guesthouse to get coffee—I didn't want to wake the others, still sleeping there. Here in the main house, there was no action, either—except Harold in the kitchen. When he saw me, he pulled out another mug, filled it for me, and said, 'I need to talk to you.' Then he led me out to the terrace, where we sat on a bench at the far side of the pool." Heather pointed out the window. "There," she said, "that's the bench. It doesn't match the other furniture, like it was sort of an afterthought, stuck well away from the house. Going there gave me the impression that our conversation was meant to be private."

"Private," said Arcie, "as in 'secret'?"

"As it turned out, yes. The moment we sat down, he told me, 'Wendy died last night.'"

"How did you react to that?"

"I was totally *stunned*, naturally. But he just seemed sort of... numb. I asked him, 'Shouldn't we be *doing* something?' And he said, 'Like what?' So I was even *more* stunned."

Arcie asked, "Did he tell you how she died?"

"Not at first. Not that I didn't ask—I mean, of *course* I wondered what had happened. Eventually, he did tell me, 'It must have been something she ate,' but he seemed to dismiss this as a minor detail, assuring me that everything would get sorted out later."

"Did he tell you *when* his wife had died?"

Heather shook her head.

Arcie reminded her, "For the microphone, please."

"No," said Heather, "Harold didn't tell me when she died. Now, in retrospect, I think he didn't know for sure. He said that he'd gone into her bedroom to check on her an hour or so earlier—and found her dead."

Astonished, Arcie asked, "And then he waltzed out to the kitchen to make *coffee*?"

"I share your confusion, Detective. It struck me as strange, to say the least."

"If he didn't want you to *do* anything, Mrs. Ferris, why was he even *telling* you about it?"

"He said that, just then, I was the only one he could turn to. He also said that he completely understood why I'd never liked Wendy, but against all odds, he still loved her and was now grieving her loss. Honestly, I didn't know *what* to make of all this—I wasn't even sure if I believed that Wendy was dead."

Arcie pointed out, "At ten o'clock that morning, you told your ranch manager that Wendy was dead. When you told him about it, I assume you believed it."

"By then," said Heather, "I believed it. As Harold and I continued to talk, he *begged* me—asked me to *swear*—that I wouldn't say anything about this 'until everything comes out.' He said I would understand the whole story 'in due time.' And that's why I was less than forthcoming with *you*, Detective, when you questioned me later that day. I'm really sorry about that. But like I said, Harold assured me that the truth would come out at the right time."

Restraining her anger, Arcie said, "Let me get this straight: That afternoon, you lied to me about a suspicious death in the house. But you blabbed about it to your ranch manager that very *morning*?"

"Well, I *had* to tell Frank. We wouldn't talk again till Monday, and I *had* to keep him in the loop—he's sort of my alter ego. To my thinking, he wasn't covered by my oath to Harold."

Arcie reminded her, "And now Harold's *dead*. Good God, he was reluctant to tell you how Wendy died. Didn't you even *suspect* foul play? That same day, by the time the response team left the house, we *knew* Wendy's death was suspicious, we *suspected* it was a homicide, and with the evidence collected since then, we're *sure* of it. This is an active *murder* case."

With surprising calm, Heather told her, "And now you can figure it out. Now we can *all* know the truth."

Arcie glanced at Jazz. Jazz glanced at me. And the others glanced at each other.

Again restraining herself, Arcie asked Heather, "*What*, pray tell, are you talking about?"

Heather leaned back in her chair with a relaxed sigh. "I'm talking about the *letter*. That morning, when Harold assured me that everything would get sorted out later, 'in due time,' he explained to me that he had written up all the details in a letter—to be opened only after his death." As if responding to our incredulous stares, she added, "And now he's dead, rest his soul."

Unable to mask her skepticism, Arcie asked, "I don't suppose you actually have this letter, do you, Mrs. Ferris? Because, if you do, I would most definitely appreciate having it."

Heather tossed her hands. "Nope. He didn't give it to *me*."

Arcie stood. Turning to the rest of us, she asked, "Does anyone know *anything* about this?"

No one answered.

I asked Keith, the lawyer, "Did your dad give you anything last week to be held in confidence till his death?"

"Nothing. Nada. Zilch. I'm as bewildered by this as anyone." Turning to his aunt Heather, he asked, "Are you *sure* about this?"

"That's what he told me, Keith. Granted, it sounds a tad like a parlor-game whodunit, but at the time, he seemed truthful, and I still have no reason to doubt it."

Keith turned to Rebecca Jiang with a questioning look.

"What?" she asked him, indignant.

"You were Dad's personal assistant for years, Rebecca. I assume that included some secretarial duties. Did he give you a sealed letter? Did he even *say* anything in this regard?"

She crossed her arms. "No. If he wrote such a letter, he didn't give it to me. Nor did he dictate such a letter or have me transcribe one or have me file one. If you're determined to pursue this, you might check his computer for it—I saw the police take the laptop out of his bedroom. But you'll be wasting your time. The very notion of a secret letter strikes me as absolutely ridiculous."

Arcie asked her, "Why is it ridiculous?"

Rebecca laughed, as if her reasoning should be self-evident. "To believe any of this nonsense about a 'letter from the grave' is to suggest that Harold had something to hide. I worked *closely* with him for seven years. I knew him better than *any* of you. He was a man of principle and vision—not a killer."

Jazz caught Arcie's eye with a subtle jerk of the head, as if asking, *Can we talk?*

Arcie rose from the game table and approached us. With lowered voice, she said, "What do you make of this—the letter? Heather could've invented that on the spot. In fact, the whole story about Harold and the coffee could also be a flat-out lie—now that he's not around to deny any of it."

"Or," said Jazz, "Heather could be telling the truth about everything. But even if she is, we don't know if *Harold* was lying about the letter."

"Remember," I said, "Heather has a known, plausible motive for wanting Wendy dead: retribution for her husband's drug-related death. On the other hand, we have no clear idea of what would compel Harold to kill Wendy."

Arcie said, "Presumably, if there *is* a letter, it would answer most of those questions. But c'mon—it does seem farfetched."

"Still," I said, "there's only way to find out if there *is* a letter: by looking for it."

Jazz and Arcie eyed each other for a moment, then nodded.

Arcie stepped over to confer with her deputy. She took out her phone and began speaking to someone while the deputy took notes. I assumed they were coordinating their logistics for both physical and electronic searches for the letter from the grave.

When Arcie returned to the game table, she removed the recorder and slipped it into her jacket. She told Heather, "I'm taking no action—*today*—with regard to your false statements of last week. But I must caution you, Mrs. Ferris, that if any of your statements during today's interview prove to be false, you will find yourself in serious jeopardy. For that reason, I must insist that you not leave the Coachella Valley without consulting me first. Am I clear?"

Heather nodded, hand on heart. "Yes, Detective."

"All right." Arcie then told the others, who were still standing around the game table, "Please return to your seats—I want to review a few matters with all of you."

When they had settled where they'd first sat, Arcie said, "We'll still need to take statements from each of you today—except Mrs. Ferris, who's already been questioned at length. We won't *solve* anything today, since we're now dealing with what appears to be a second homicide, so I need to ask all of you to remain available for the investigation as it progresses."

Brooke Ferris raised her hand. "Do you know how long this is likely to take, Detective? My schedule is wide open for a while, but soon enough, I'll be back on call for hospice."

"At this point, Miss Ferris, I have no idea of our time frame, but I'll give every consideration to your nursing duties. Just keep me informed." Then she turned to Keith. "As before, counselor, you're free to come and go as necessary, but please let me know."

Brooke and Keith both nodded their understanding.

Arcie said, "We'll be breaking into groups for the interviews, but are there any other questions first?"

Rebecca had returned to the kitchen island but now sat on one of the barstools. She said to Arcie, "Surely you can appreciate, Detective, how Harold's sudden death has shaken this family to its very core..."

Unless I was mistaken, her phrasing implied her own membership in "this family," a claim that would doubtless be disputed by Keith, Heather, Brooke, and Richard—actual blood relatives of the victim. Telltale glances and sour expressions made it evident that they were nettled by Rebecca's presumptuous words.

She continued, "... none of us even had a chance to say good-bye to Harold..."

I was tempted to remind her that no one had said goodbye to Wendy, either. Both had been wheeled out the door in zippered bags.

"... so I'm wondering, Detective, if you could give us *any* information regarding what happened to Harold. I saw him at his desk, and I'm certainly no expert, but it looked as if he might've been *poisoned*."

This produced no discernible reaction from the others, except that they swiveled their heads toward Arcie, as if hoping for more information. But they did not seem shocked—or even surprised—by the mention of poison. During the initial alarm and confusion following Rebecca's screams, details of her discovery had apparently escaped the bedroom and made the rounds.

I was curious how Arcie would handle the question. She'd already told Jazz and me that she wanted to keep the suspected nicotine angle hush-hush for now. So she obfuscated:

Arcie told Rebecca, and everyone, "Yes, we believe that Harold Gibkin was poisoned to death. It did not appear to be accidental. Our next step, forensically, is to try to establish the exact nature of the lethal agent, which could help to identify who was responsible. But in cases where no specific poison is suspected, toxicology can be an arduous and lengthy process, with no guaranteed results."

Arcie, Jazz, and I all knew that a specific toxin was indeed suspected, which would considerably speed up the testing.

The others, of course, were clueless. Or rather, the ones who hadn't poisoned Harold—*they* were clueless."

Näzh fluttered a hand. "Detective? Can you tell us how the poison was administered?"

This struck me as an odd question. If the group already knew that Harold was poisoned, wouldn't they also know he'd been drinking whiskey? Both Rebecca and Keith had been inside the bedroom and had surely noticed the bottle. Word would get around eventually.

So Arcie didn't hesitate to tell Näzh, "The poisoning agent was apparently added to the whiskey that Mr. Gibkin was drinking at his desk." With that out of the way, she asked everyone, "Anything else?"

Most responded with shrugs, but Rebecca got off her stool and stepped closer to us. "Detective?" she said. "The whiskey Harold was drinking this morning, Old Nine-Tails—that bottle was a gift from his long-lost cousin, Richard Gibbs."

Zola, getting suddenly defensive on Richard's behalf, asked Rebecca, "So *what*?"

"When he gave the bottle to Harold last Sunday, its seal had been broken."

Richard stood and faced Rebecca, explaining to her, as if to a child, "I opened it at home to *try* it—horrible stuff. Then I recapped it. I told Harold about that when he offered me a sample from his own bottle." Richard crossed his arms, having fully dismissed Rebecca's insinuation. Or so he thought.

Rebecca told Arcie, "Harold put the gift bottle away until the one he had was empty—this morning. The gift bottle was still full when he took it into the bedroom today. If you want to know who tampered with it, I know where *I'd* start."

CHAPTER
THIRTEEN

Zola was furious with Rebecca. Richard was pale with fear. Arcie had a new lead that required follow-up. And Jazz turned philosophical.

"You know," she told me while walking through the parking court, toward the street, "I had two clients staying in that house, Keith Gibkin and Harold Gibkin. For Keith, I was doing a background check on Rebecca Jiang because he thought she was scheming to end his father's marriage. I cancelled Keith's account when Wendy died because the home-wrecker worries were then moot. For Harold, I was investigating Wendy's death to help clear Zola, but now Harold has cancelled *that* account— by dying. So I guess it's all been *pro bono*."

I asked her, "Throwing in the towel?"

"No way. We've got to untangle this."

Monday morning is probably most people's least favorite time of the week. But older friends, retired friends, have told me they are no longer affected by the Monday icks, as if their latter years have morphed into a continuous Sunday tea dance (which, nonetheless, is slowly but surely unspooling toward one final spin around the floor).

Though I was still among the working class and not yet freed from the rhythm of the calendar, I found that my last two Sundays had not qualified as days of rest—not by a long shot—so I greeted this particular Monday morning with a sense of calm. Deep down, though, I might have suspected that it was merely the calm before the storm.

Isandro and I awoke at dawn and lolled awhile in our warm bed, cuddling, easing into the day, before I slipped away to the kitchen and switched on the coffeemaker.

A few minutes later, we were settled at the table in the front room of our coach house, facing the orange-hued vista that rose from beyond the pool terrace. Isandro said, "I know what *I'm* doing today—up to my elbows with Dr. Gastro—but what about you?"

"Good question. I still have no idea how things are shaking down at Sunny Junket, so I thought I'd go in, maybe talk to Ben."

Isandro said, "As bosses go, he's always backed you up, right?"

I nodded. "None better. But if the business is falling apart, who knows?" On a more enthusiastic note, I added, "Jazz and I need to put our heads together regarding what's next with the investigation."

Isandro, of course, had already heard the whole story of what had happened on Sunday—Harold's poisoning and the suspicion that Richard was responsible. Isandro now reached across the table to rest his fingers on my hand, asking, "You don't think there's any chance that Richard actually *did* it, do you?"

With a warm smile, I assured him, "Of course not. But my God, what irony: Richard and Zola showed up yesterday blithely thinking she was about to be dismissed as a suspect in Wendy's death. Instead, Zola's still on *that* list, and now Richard finds himself heading a new list for a *second* murder. Fortunately, Jazz is still committed finding the truth."

"And so are you, *coração*." Isandro stood and stepped behind my chair. Placing his hands on my shoulders, he bowed his head. I felt his lips rustle my hair as he said, "Richard and Zola have nothing to worry about—not with friends like you and Jazz on their side."

I appreciated his confidence. But I wasn't so sure.

When I walked through the street door at Sunny Junket and approached the reception desk, I braced myself for a round of Gianna's usual snark.

"Good *morning*," she said—perfectly pleasant, with no overtone of sarcasm.

Surprised, I returned the friendly greeting: "Good morning, Gianna."

"Oh?" she said, taking off her glasses. "Have we met?" And she leaned toward me for a closer look.

Okay. Now I got it. She hadn't seen me in a while. I asked, "Is Ben here?"

"If you're bringing him the bad news that another guest in Rancho Mirage won't be checking out alive—he's already heard about it. And how's *this* for a news flash? When we made the latest round of charges to Harold Gibkin's credit card this morning, they bounced back 'denied.'"

"Christ. I'd better talk to Ben."

"Good luck with that."

I headed straight for his office, where the door was open. Looking inside, I didn't see Ben, but I saw ... disarray. Not that a bomb had exploded, not exactly. But there were a few boxes on the furniture and the floor, and Ben's desk looked more tidy than usual. In fact, it was bare.

Turning around in the doorway, I called back to Gianna with a quiver in my voice: "What's going on?"

"Why ask *me*? I'm the *last* to know. But I think he's on his way in."

With an out-of-body feeling, I wandered through the maze of workstations to my own desk and realized that there was *no one* else in the building—just Gianna and me, a harrowing thought at best. I flumped into my chair, booted up my computer, and went to the company website.

At least *that* looked normal. All the contact information was current and active. The rental listings seemed to be intact. And the online reservation system was working. A prospective guest who might be considering us would have no reason to suspect that Sunny Junket's corporate ship was sinking.

Or was I leaping to unfounded conclusions?

Ben had already *told* me that we were facing a rough patch, that there would be some belt-tightening ahead. As for the mess in his office? Maybe the bigwigs, the money guys, the number crunchers—maybe they'd decided to move us to a smaller office space. That would actually make sense, as so many of our in-house functions had moved online in recent years. *Yeah*, I thought. Maybe the experts had decided to take advantage of the lull created by the recent defection of our principal agent, using this downtime to retool the organization and assure its profitable future for many years to come.

But when I saw the look on Ben's face as he trudged through the front doors, I knew that everything had gone haywire. When Gianna started pelting him with a list of messages, he simply raised a hand and shook his head without looking at her.

He wasn't even wearing "the uniform." I'd always hated the dad jeans and acid-yellow polo I'd once been forced to wear, but at that moment, I'd have given anything to watch Ben strutting in, proudly wearing the Sunny Junket colors. Instead, he wore an old gray fleece sweatshirt with a faded maroon school logo, MINNESOTA. But he looked as far away from his carefree college days as a guy can get.

In spite of this, he'd always managed to find a smile for me, and that day was no exception. He paused in front of his office door—plump and dowdy, no longer jolly, but defeated—and he faced me with a feeble trace of his Midwestern smile as he waved me over, saying, "Let's talk, Dante."

Following as he waddled into his office, I found that my concern for *him* far outweighed whatever I feared he might tell me. I closed the door as he removed the boxes from two chairs, and we sat a few feet apart in the middle of the room—not across his desk from each other, as in the past.

"Ben," I said, "whatever's going on, I'm sorry."

"Nah"—he waggled a hand, brightening—"nothing to be sorry about. Nothing lasts forever, and times have changed, *circumstances* have changed. Long and short of it: the company's being restructured and will probably be sold. Sunny Junket will remain, though. There'll still be an office in town, probably smaller. Maybe under the same name, maybe not. But know this, Dante: I put in the strongest possible recommendation for them to keep you on board. We've had no one better at schmoozing top-end guests at our most profitable properties. So whoever ends up running this place, they're going to need you."

"But what about *you*?" I asked.

He shook his head. "Middle-aged. Middle management. Dime a dozen. Plus, I happened to be in charge when everything went south."

"*Stop* that, Ben. That's not true."

He grinned. "Unfortunately, it *is* true. But I'll find something else. Maybe here, maybe someplace else, not sure yet. But I'll miss you, Dante."

I couldn't remember many instances in my life when I felt that I was on the verge of tears—but this was one of them.

He must have seen that I was getting misty. He laughed. "No worries, Dante. You'll be fine. And Gianna will still be here—the place couldn't run without *her*." And he broke into a hearty laugh. Good ol' jolly Ben.

I heaved a long, uncertain sigh. None of this appealed to me. But I needed the paycheck.

"Thanks, Ben. I'll do my best."

I didn't even bother checking out with Gianna—just sailed past her as I headed out the door and walked down the block toward Huggamug. Jazz and I had work to do that day, and needless to say, any duties at Sunny Junket now felt like a *very* low priority.

When I climbed the stairs and entered Jazz's front office, she called out, "If that's you, Dante, we're in the conference room."

I wondered, *We?*

"Oh—hi, Arcie," I said as I walked into the room. Detective Madera sat with Jazz at the black Parsons table with notes spread out between them. Jazz had brought her laptop over from her desk across the hall, and Arcie was typing on her phone.

She looked up from the phone long enough to say, "Good morning, Dante." Then she resumed typing.

Jazz gestured: "Have a seat."

I asked, "Any test results yet?"

"In fact," said Arcie, setting her phone aside, "I just received confirmation that Gibkin died of nicotine poisoning—enough to kill a horse."

Jazz asked, "The report said *that*?"

"Well, no." Arcie grinned. "The language in the postmortem report was a bit more technical, but that's the upshot. Also, forensic testing of the whiskey—in the bottle and in the glass—revealed the strong presence of nicotine, as expected. So we know exactly *how* Gibkin was killed."

I asked, "In order to do this, where would someone *get* the nicotine extract?"

"It's easier than you'd probably think," said Arcie. "Concentrated tobacco juice is commercially available, used mainly to kill rose aphids. But in a pinch, it's easy to make a home-brewed extract. Just crumble loose tobacco into boiling water, let it steep for a few hours, then strain it. *Voilà*. Strong enough to kill an aphid—or a horse—or just about anything in between."

Jazz asked, "Time of death?"

"Late yesterday morning, about an hour before the body was discovered. It had just happened. The stomach contents, as well as the vomit, included that morning's breakfast—nothing suspicious about that—plus the whiskey, plus residue of the nicotine 'tea.'"

"Clearly," said Jazz, "this wasn't an accident—someone deliberately spiked the booze."

"Right," I said, "and I think we can safely rule out suicide. He was planning on brunch at the Ritz—he was dressed for it, and he had Rebecca reserve the table. Meaning: he was murdered."

Arcie nodded. "That's the only logical conclusion. This was a homicide. And it resembles *Mrs*. Gibkin's murder the week before in two ways: Both crimes were essentially poisonings. And both crimes could have been committed by anyone staying at the rental house—and sorry to say, we still need to include your friends Richard and Zola in that circle of suspects."

Not what I wanted to hear. But I asked Arcie, "What about fingerprints—the bottle, the glass? Can anyone be eliminated?"

She shook her head. "No, not definitively. As expected, there were *many* fingerprints on the bottle, and we could identify those of the victim and others staying at the house, as well as prints from Richard, who'd given the whiskey as a gift. The glass was mostly smudged with the victim's prints, but there were a few others from people in the house—who could've handled the glass while putting away dishes after cleaning. Taking all of that into account, we can't identify the killer on the basis of prints that *were* found—or were *not* found—because it's certainly possible that the bottle was spiked without touching it, or by wearing gloves. Bottom line: the fingerprint testing tells us nothing."

"Shifting gears," said Jazz, "we've got this nutty-sounding story from Heather, the victim's sister, regarding a letter he wrote the week before, when his wife died."

Arcie said, "I agree: that does sound farfetched. But it also sounds, at the very least, *plausible*. And if, in fact, such a letter *does* exist, it would explain a great deal, so the search has begun. The bedroom where the victim died—where he had his desk and most of his belongings—that was sealed off yesterday, and we have a forensics team conducting a thorough search there today. If he left a document in that room, we'll find it. If not, we'll broaden the search. But realistically, how far can we go with it?"

I asked, "What about Harold's laptop?"

Arcie paused. "Well... this is *interesting*. We thought that if Mr. Gibkin had left an important letter, he might have written it on the computer, printed it, then signed it."

I said, "The group had at least one portable printer with them—I saw one on the kitchen island when I was at the house on Tuesday."

"Yes," said Arcie, "our team took that, as well as the laptop. You'll remember that when we found Gibkin's body, he'd collapsed on the keyboard, which was covered with vomit. We weren't even sure if we'd manage to get the computer to power up. But we did, and that's when we discovered that it had been wiped."

"Meaning," said Jazz, "someone cleaned up the puke?"

Arcie shook her head. "The computer's drive and memory had been wiped clean—erased—there was nothing on it."

I said, "That *is* strange. Rebecca said that Harold was working at his desk most of the morning. When his body was found, he certainly *looked* as if he'd been busy at the keyboard."

Arcie said, "I think he was trying to selectively *restore* the computer from the ground up. It was in the process of reinstalling the operating system when it shut down. My guess is, sometime earlier, he'd wiped it—which suggests he wanted to prevent something in particular from being found."

Jazz said, "Something like … the *letter*."

Arcie shrugged. "Possibly. That would fit the story he told his sister—and it's consistent with his pressure for an oath of secrecy. We also checked his phone, which had *not* been wiped, and it contains no files appearing to be a recent letter. Our next step will be an attempt to retrieve lost data from the wiped laptop, but we'll need assistance with that." Arcie's phone buzzed, and she lifted it to read a message.

Jazz said, "Nearly lunchtime. Care to join us?"

"Sorry." Arcie stood and began packing her briefcase with the files she'd brought. "The DA just called a meeting—in Riverside. I've *really* gotta run."

And a moment later, she was out the door.

After Jazz had locked up the office, the two of us went downstairs and exited the side of the building. Stepping around to the front, we entered Huggamug.

Mondays were usually slow for lunch, and we got a good table—in fact, the same corner table by the window where, last week, we had met with Rebecca Jiang. While the server was handing us menus, he asked, "Are we expecting a third today?"

He seemed greatly relieved when Jazz informed him, "Just us."

During the lull while perusing our menus, Jazz said, "Something's been nagging at me."

I set my menu aside. "What's on your mind?"

"Yesterday, at the rental house, after Arcie and her team arrived, she called Keith into the bedroom for a formal ID of the body. When that was taken care of, you and I took Keith out to the hall, consoling him. But he didn't really seem broken up by this development—the death of his own *father*. Instead, he was moaning about the pressure of funerals, taxes, and settling the estates. Did that strike you as 'off'?"

I had to admit, "It did. But then I figured, everyone has their own way of responding to grief. I think he was just dealing with it by focusing instead on the sheer 'busyness' of unexpected death. You can't think two things at once, and he chose to think about chores—rather than the grim reality."

"Yeah," said Jazz, "you're probably right…"

I asked her, "But…?"

"But as soon as he started talking about wills and trusts—both his father's and Wendy's—it occurred to me that Keith, as Harold's only child, probably stands to gain a *lot* from all this. I mean, that house in Rancho Santa Fe, what's that *alone* worth?"

Her point was well made and had merit. "But," I told her, "I just can't bring myself to think of Keith in that light. He's clearly not hurting financially, and he established his independence from the family years ago. I doubt if he's been lying in wait to add a few zeros to his net worth."

With a soft laugh, she agreed, "Probably not. And hey—I'm starting to think, just *maybe*, Keith might be right for Christopher."

Wryly, I told her, "That thought has crossed my mind."

After we'd ordered and the waiter disappeared, another lull drifted over our table. I said, "I won't be doing much this afternoon."

Reacting to my non sequitur, Jazz eyed me askance. "Oh, yeah? Why not?"

I took a deep breath, then told her what I'd learned at Sunny Junket that morning, concluding, "My world is feeling sorta topsy-turvy."

"Ummm ... look, Dante. While I didn't expect this current case to be *pro bono*, things have been really *good* for me lately. And you've had plenty to do with that. If you want to consider an arrangement that's more 'official,' let's figure it out. So remember: you've got options."

I nodded, feeling not so topsy-turvy after all.

She said, "And as long as you're not doing much this afternoon, maybe you could drive back to Rancho Mirage and drop in at the rental house."

"Exactly what I had in mind."

"Two things," she said. "First, find out what you can about the police search for the letter. And second, if Keith is there, sound him out about his inheritance—discreetly, of course."

I laughed. "There is *no* subtle way to pose such a question."

She shrugged. "Try pillow talk—it's worked before."

Admittedly, I'd resorted to such techniques in gleaning crucial information for prior cases, but I couldn't imagine that Jazz was suggesting I should take that route with the man she wanted to land for her ex-husband.

As if reading my thoughts, she blurted, "Just *kidding*."

Later that afternoon, shortly before four, I drove back to Rancho Mirage and parked the Karmann Ghia, as usual, at the curb in front of the rental house. I noted at once that there were no police vehicles present. Walking through the parking court, I saw that all of the visitors' vehicles were still accounted for— including Harold and Wendy's white Chevy Suburban.

What, I wondered, would become of that? I presumed it was now—or soon would be—Keith's. How would he juggle the logistics of dealing with the giant SUV, along with his smart little Mercedes, more than a hundred miles from home? Pondering this, I became more sympathetic to his fretting over the many loose ends of unexpected death.

When I stepped up to the front door and rang the bell, it took longer than usual for anyone to answer (but I reminded myself that the number of guests staying there had been reduced by two).

Keith opened the door. "Dante! Great to see you. C'mon in." His tone was far more chipper than I would've expected.

Walking with him into the great room, I saw that Rebecca was busy in the kitchen—apparently still in charge of meals. Heather and Näzh were out by the pool, but losing sunlight in the waning afternoon. Lights were on inside the guesthouse, where I assumed Brooke and Tyler were hanging out.

I said to Keith, "I understand there was a forensics team here today."

"I was away most of the day—didn't see them when they arrived, and they'd left by the time I got back."

Rebecca turned to tell me, "They made a *mess*. Finally left around two."

Glancing about, I said, "Things don't look so bad."

"In Harold's *bedroom*—it's a disaster."

"Don't worry about that. I'll send in a crew when Detective Madera okays it."

Derisively, Rebecca told me, "It was a wild-goose chase. Obviously, there was *nothing* to find. Heather's story about a *letter*— what rubbish."

Keith gave me a perplexed shrug. "Honestly," he said, "I don't know *what* to think. On the one hand, I doubt that Dad would get involved in such craziness. But on the other hand, I doubt that Heather would lie about it."

Rebecca slid a heavy casserole into the oven and thumped the door closed—hard. Checking her watch, she strutted across the great room and retreated into her bedroom, closing the door behind her. She didn't quite slam it, but she used enough force to convey her disgust.

Keith blew a silent whistle. "Things have been a bit tense. Can I get you a drink?"

"No, too early for me, thanks. But help yourself."

"I believe I will." He stepped over to the kitchen, and I followed, seating myself on one of the stools at the island as he poured himself a glass of white wine from a bottle in the refrigerator. Joining me, he sat at the next stool, asking, "Busy day?"

"Yes and no." I didn't want to get into the shaky situation at Sunny Junket, so I asked, "How about you?"

With a grin that verged on Cheshire, he informed me, "I spent the day—well, most of it—with Christopher." He lifted his glass, then sipped from it.

"Cheers," I told him. "Was it fun?"

Keith nodded, sipped. "After he dropped Emma off at school this morning, he called me, asking if I'd like to see his office."

"I take it you were duly impressed." I'd been there with Jazz a few times and had found the sprawling facilities in downtown Palm Springs to be a thriving enterprise with multiple attorneys and partners. Christopher himself had not one, but two, secretaries—in addition to the others in a posh reception room. A quaint little one-man shop it was not.

"Was I *impressed*?" asked Keith. "No, I was blown away. He's built quite a practice."

"Well," I said, "he's a great guy. He deserves his success."

Keith leaned to me. "Know what he did?"

Though tempted to take a few guesses, I shook my head.

Keith explained, "He offered the use of his conference room tomorrow. Dad was overdue for an announcement of the terms of Wendy's estate plan—and now, of course, the terms of his own revocable trust should be disclosed as well. I can handle Dad's end of things, and since Wendy had her own lawyer on the coast, I've arranged to have him join us tomorrow."

"Sounds like killing two birds with one stone." I grinned.

Keith nodded. "Yes, so to speak. So we're all going to gather in Christopher's conference room tomorrow morning at ten. Care to join us?"

Of course I did, but I paused. "There's something I really need to take care of tomorrow—but I'll bet Jazz would *love* to sit in."

"Great idea. She belongs there." As an afterthought, he added, "She's still on the case, right? For Dad?"

Highly relieved that Keith had opened this door for me, I told him, "With Harold's death yesterday, Jazz is assuming that her account with him is now closed—unless you'd like to follow through with her."

"Absolutely. Let her know, please, and we can button it down when I see her tomorrow."

"Sounds good—she'll appreciate that." Then I hesitated. "This is awkward, Keith. When Sunny Junket tried running some charges on Harold's account this morning—"

"Yikes," he interrupted, "say no more. Last night, I routinely shut down all of his transactions, till we get things sorted out. Sorry for the hassle. Just switch the rental charges over to me." And he pulled out his phone to text me an account number.

A huge weight had been lifted from my mind, and I was feeling so mellow that I barely heard my name the first time. Then Rebecca said it again, louder. "Mr. O'Donnell?"

Both Keith and I looked up from our conversation to see Rebecca standing at the far end of the great room, just outside her bedroom door. Pinched between her thumb and index finger was the corner of a standard white business-size envelope. Even from across the room, I could see handwriting on it.

Her earlier strident attitude now melted to quiet dismay as she said, "I stand corrected. It seems that Harold did indeed leave us a letter. I found it just now, beneath a few of my things in the top drawer of my dresser."

Keith and I turned to look at each other, stunned. I asked him, "Got a plastic bag?"

He grabbed one from the cabinet beneath the sink and handed it to me as we rushed to Rebecca, who met us in the middle of the room.

She dropped this newly discovered evidence into the bag, which I then turned so we could read the front of the envelope: TO BE OPENED ONLY AFTER MY DEATH.

It was signed by Harold Gibkin and dated October third—the day Wendy had died.

On the back of the envelope, he had added an inky thumbprint to the edge of the sealed flap.

When I phoned Jazz and told her that I now had in hand Harold Gibkin's letter from the grave, she first confirmed with me that it was still sealed, then phoned Arcie Madera with the news. Arcie took the call while driving back from her meeting with the district attorney in Riverside, west of Palm Springs. She could be at Jazz's office within a half hour—plenty of time for me to bring the letter from Rancho Mirage, east of Palm Springs.

I was first to arrive at the office above Huggamug, a few minutes past four thirty. Jazz took the plastic bag from me and perused the front and back of the enclosed envelope. She asked, "No one else at the rental house has touched this, correct?"

I nodded. "Just Rebecca and presumably Harold, as far as I know. I'd bet money, though, that everyone else at the house *knows* about it by now."

Jazz chortled. "But they don't know what's *in* it—ought to make for some lively dinner conversation."

About five minutes later, we heard rapid footsteps climbing the stairs to the office. Walking through the door, Arcie said, "Let's hope this is the big break we've been waiting for—Peter Nadig is getting *very* antsy."

Jazz handed Arcie the plastic bag, telling her, "I have a feeling our hotdog DA can get a few juicy headlines out of this."

Arcie led us back to the conference room and placed the bagged letter on the Parsons table along with her briefcase, which she opened. She removed from it a scalpel, tweezers, and a pair of latex gloves. Jazz switched on the bright overhead lights as Arcie donned her gloves, removed the letter from the plastic bag, and used the scalpel to slit open the envelope. It contained two sheets of folded paper bearing printed text, at the bottom of which Harold Gibkin had left another inked thumbprint, as well as his dated signature.

Arcie placed the pages of the unfolded letter on a clean cloth near the edge of the table, where the three of us then gathered and leaned forward to read it.

To my family and loved ones:

I've always considered myself a man of action and purpose and ideas, but not much of a writer, so leaving these words for you is a challenge. In fact, this might be the biggest challenge of my life.

By the time you read this, I'm guessing you've figured out that Wendy Ames Gibkin, my wife of twelve years, did not die of natural causes last night. Yes, she had various afflictions—food issues, allergies, moods—but they were nothing compared to what was ahead for her.

By the time you read this, you might be aware (maybe not) that Wendy had contracted Flassman syndrome, a god-awful disease that would eventually kill her. She kept this to herself, and I only recently found out about it. Naturally, once I knew, I had to discuss it with her. She seemed relieved that I'd been told but was also pissed that someone "betrayed" her. She wasn't thinking right. Under those circumstances, I understood her confusion and anger. I loved her deeply—and that was my sole motivation for what happened next.

By the time you read this, you probably know that Wendy died from an allergic reaction to honey, which was added to a dessert pudding, called posset, that we all had a hand in making last night during a family reunion in Rancho Mirage.

By the time you read this, you might have suspicions that I was the one who put the honey in the posset. If that's what you think, let me clear the air. Yes, I did it. I killed Wendy. When we first talked about her Flassman disease, she begged me: "Just shoot me, Harold. Just shoot me! I can't face this." Well, I didn't have a gun, and even if I did, I was sure I'd never be able to pull the trigger and watch her die. So I decided on a cleaner method that was just as lethal and sure. I knew that honey would do what needed to be done—it would save Wendy from all the agony ahead.

By the time you read this, I hope that everything has been straightened out with Zola Lorinsky. If she's still around, please give her my apologies. The frame-up was never meant to stick. It was meant to confuse the cops for a while. To make sure of that, I plan to hire Jazz Friendly to clear Zola's name. My heart, believe it or not, is in the right place.

By the time you read this, I hope that Zola has found contentment in her later years with my newly found second cousin, Richard Gibbs. I hope that my son, Keith, has found love in his life and great success in his law practice.

I hope that my kid sister, Heather Ferris, has found the time and forgiveness to soothe the tragic loss of her husband, Jason. I hope that my beloved niece, Brooke Ferris, has been rewarded with the gratitude of the many patients she will have nursed and comforted in her noble calling.

By the time you read this, I hope that the planet will have changed course and kicked the fossil-fuel habit. And last but not least, I do fervently hope that little Koo-Loo, the miserable wretch, has choked on his last damn banana.

I've said my peace. And with that, I wish all of you a loving farewell.

These words were written and signed in
the early hours of the day Wendy died.

Harold Gibkin

"Well," Jazz told me, "we were on the right track. It was Harold after all—assuming this is genuine."

Arcie said, "I should be able to get a forensic evaluation overnight. But I tend to agree: we know who killed Wendy."

I reminded them both, "This also tells us that a single killer wasn't responsible for both murders. Nothing in Harold's letter suggests that his death was a suicide—so there's still a *second* killer staying at that house."

Early Tuesday morning, Jazz phoned to let me know that Arcie's forensics team had determined that the letter was indeed what it purported to be—Harold Gibkin's signed admission that he had killed his wife. In addition to the inked thumbprints, the letter and envelope were found to be virtually covered with fingerprints matching those already on file for Harold. Also, a certified document examiner was called in to compare the handwriting to other known samples from Harold, concluding that a match was "extremely likely."

Keith had invited Jazz and me to that morning's reading of the provisions of both Harold's and Wendy's estate plans, to be held at Christopher Friendly's law offices in Palm Springs. Jazz, as I had predicted to Keith, was eager to attend. I myself had declined the invitation, telling Keith, vaguely, there was something I needed to take care of.

That something, however, wasn't exactly a "need," but an opportunity.

With everyone away at the law offices, the rental house would be vacant for an hour or two, giving me the chance to do some quiet snooping, free of distraction. My job as a concierge and field inspector for Sunny Junket gave me the keys, the passcodes, and the *right* to enter our properties in the best interest of both the owners and the guests. (At least that was my rationale.)

I arrived at the house just before ten that morning, confident that our six surviving guests had left for Palm Springs. Parking at the curb, I noted that my Karmann Ghia was the only car on either side of the street. Strolling through the front courtyard, I saw that all the vehicles were gone—except for Harold and Wendy's white Suburban and the unhitched Trot-n-Tipple horse trailer—exactly as expected.

Following protocol, when I stepped up to the front door, I rang the bell several times—respecting our guests' privacy, but also reassuring myself that the coast was clear. Then I used my passcode to enter.

Inside, I closed the door behind me and called, "It's Dante. Anybody here?" Dead silence.

The nearest bedroom wing contained the suites used by Keith and by Rebecca. By now, of course, I had come to think of Keith as a friend—gay brethren, no less—and I felt no serious suspicion that he had anything to do with his father's death, in spite of his likely inheritance. Even so, I reminded myself, I was there that morning to consider all possibilities, hoping to uncover something that had been previously overlooked, so I went to Keith's bedroom first.

Standing outside his closed door, I felt foolish knocking—I already knew there was no one on the premises, and I realized the knock was a matter of neither protocol nor etiquette. Rather, it was a stalling tactic, a lame denial that I was feeling a voyeuristic thrill at the prospect of invading Keith's personal space.

I opened the door and walked in. I could smell his cologne. It didn't surprise me to find his quarters perfectly neat and presentable. The bed had been made with military precision, which was surely his doing, as daily housekeeping service was not part of our rental contract. Unlike many guests, who live out of a suitcase for as long as possible, he had unpacked and put everything away—closets, dresser, and bathroom were all impeccably well organized. Though tempted, I did not finger through his things, but I did make a quick check of every drawer, which revealed nothing to raise concern—no weapons, secret dossiers, or mysterious potions. Relieved that I had been true to my mission, I quickly left Keith's bedroom and closed the door.

I didn't even bother knocking on the door to Rebecca's suite. In fact, I felt a rush of satisfaction as I turned the knob with purpose and walked right in, hoping to find something that would shed light on what had happened to her late employer, Harold Gibkin, who had also been the object of her affection.

Alas, I was disappointed. Though the rooms did not rise to

the level of Keith's compulsive orderliness, her space was tidy enough—no clothes left about, no jumble of makeup and unguents on the bathroom vanity, no dishes or glasses or evidence of snacks. And her bed was made, but unlike Keith's, you couldn't bounce a quarter on it.

I was highly reluctant to make a thorough search of her things, but I took a few liberties examining her desk. Her employment by Harold included secretarial duties, so I was bold enough to open her laptop. It turned on, but as suspected, I couldn't get past the login. There were a few icons of recent files on the home screen, but none seemed the least bit sinister. I shut down Rebecca's computer and left the room, closing the door behind me.

Crossing the great room, I checked the other bedroom wing and found that, as expected, the doors to both Harold's and Wendy's suites were still blocked off with yellow police tape, which I wasn't even tempted to violate.

So I returned to the great room—more precisely, the kitchen end of this large space—and went through the lower cabinets beneath the island and counters, where pots and pans were stored. Sunny Junket maintained a list of kitchen items required to be supplied by all property owners, and I'd done an inventory the day before the Gibkin-Ferris party checked in, so I knew what should be there. Most of our guests never cooked a meal—they dined out. But the reunion guests had prepared many meals at the house.

I went through every cooking vessel that could have conceivably been used to make a reduced extract of tobacco juice, a process that Arcie had described to us. The pots were clean, of course, since everything would have been washed after using it—especially if it had been used for a deadly purpose. But I searched for any telltale smell or residue from tobacco, finding nothing. I checked the dishwasher, in case it was still loaded with unwashed items, but it was empty. To glean any evidence of murderous intent from that kitchen, it would take a forensics team far more knowledgeable than I was.

After closing all the cabinets, I wandered through the rest of the great room, looking for areas I might search in hopes of finding... *anything*. Although I spotted nothing of significance, I now sensed that I had saved the most promising search for last.

Glancing out to the rear terrace, I focused on the freestanding guesthouse not far from the pool, with its two additional bedroom suites. One had been occupied by Heather Ferris and Näzh Hoyle, the other by Brooke Ferris and Tyler Evans.

Heather's involvement, her *complicity*, with Harold's secret news of Wendy's death had already been established—by her own admission. Then, that involvement was all but dismissed by the investigation because her story about the letter from the grave had proven true.

Even so, Heather's role in all of this still gnawed at me.

I went out to the patio and walked back to the guesthouse. Most visitors, during their stay, were careless about keeping the guesthouse locked, since it seemed relatively secure behind the main house. But when I tried the glass slider that morning, I found it locked tight.

This told me that at least one of the four guests was being uncommonly cautious. But it did not keep me out. I looked up the passcode on my phone, entered it on the keypad by the door, and stepped inside.

The common lounge area, with its small kitchen, was not as tidy as the rooms I'd seen in the main house—it looked more like the accommodations of people on vacation, people who were there to relax and enjoy themselves, without fussing too much with the niceties of housekeeping. A couple of beach robes were draped over a chair near the door, with several pairs of sandals on the floor, at the ready for swimming or sunning. The breakfast bar was littered with toast crumbs and a few almost-empty coffee mugs. The coffeemaker had turned off, with its unwashed glass carafe still containing in inch or two of brew, now cold and stale. While this certainly didn't qualify as a frat-house debacle, I myself wouldn't like returning to it—so I would've cleaned it up before I'd left. (But who am I to judge?)

When I checked Heather's bedroom, where Näzh had also been sleeping, I found it orderly enough, but the bed had merely been tossed together, with no concern at all for its appearance. On one of the nightstands were a few "toys" not meant for my eyes. The closets, less roomy than those in the main house, were stuffed with clothes, leaving no space for Heather's shoes and riding boots—there were a *lot* of them—which were lined up along one wall of the bedroom.

Brooke's bedroom, shared with Tyler, reminded me of dorm life, which, to be fair, was only a few years in their past. The bed appeared not to have been made since the day of their arrival, with its rumpled sheets exposed and the covers puddled on the floor. One quick look in the bathroom, and I was *outta* there.

Returning to the shared lounge area, I noticed through the sliding doors that Max Hazer had arrived for his semiweekly servicing of the pool. While he fussed with setting up the vacuum hose, I decided to do an inventory of the short list of items provided in the guesthouse kitchen, which was not designed for the preparation of meals. While hunkering down and banging around in the cupboards, I could see at once that the few pans had never been used—they were brand new, with adhesive labels still attached.

Closing all the cabinets, I stood. Max had just lit up a cigarette, puffing away as he cleaned the bottom of the pool. I turned to the refrigerator for another look at Näzh's so-called vision board. The Rolls-Royce, the Wall Street bull, the gold bricks, the man in a turban, the architectural rendering—all of these images were still there.

The picture of *me* that had been added when I last set foot in this room—that photo was still in place with the others. And then I noticed that a new photo of another familiar face had been added. There, stuck between the Rolls and the gold bricks, was a picture of Harold Gibkin, now deceased but very much alive in the photo that Näzh had snapped ten days earlier when everyone had arrived at the rental property. Huh?

I stepped outside to ponder this discovery: What possible reason could Näzh have had for including Harold in his collage of wishful thinking? I already knew that *I'd* been added to this rogue's gallery because Näzh had set his sights on me, erotically. But Harold?

"Hey, *Dante*," Max called to me, interrupting my thoughts as he pulled his equipment out of the water.

When I strolled over to him, he asked, "Where *is* everybody— did they go home early?"

"No," I said, "they're all meeting with lawyers this morning, but they'll be back. There's been a bit of trouble since they got here."

"Nothing serious, I hope."

Not wanting to engage with him on the topic of what had happened (he could out-gossip any hairdresser I'd ever known), I tried to close the conversation, telling him, "You're doing a great job, Max. We appreciate all the effort." And I turned to walk back to the house.

He touched my arm. "But *Dante*, I wanna tell you about something." He grinned as I turned to face him.

God, I thought. *Please, not another of his pointless stories.*

He said, "Remember that woman I was telling you about—down the street—with the kimono and the peach yogurt and the trail mix?"

I slowly nodded, wondering how to escape.

"*Well*," he said, "if you thought *that* was weird, just listen to this."

"Don't tell me." I guessed dryly: "She has a sister."

"*Nah.* Well, I dunno, maybe she does have a sister, but that's not what I'm talking about. I'm talking about that lady staying *here*." He jerked his head toward the guesthouse.

"Oh?" I was suddenly more interested.

"I was mindin' my business, just workin' my job, and she comes out of that ... *bungalow* or whatever ... kinda nervous but real polite, and she—"

I interrupted, "When was this, Max?"

"Saturday morning, last time I was here, three days ago. So she comes over to me and says, 'Excuse me, sir, but I couldn't help noticing that you *smoke*.' And I'm like, 'Gosh, sorry, ma'am. If it bothers you, I'll just—' But then she says, 'No, no, no, it doesn't bother me in the least. In fact, I'm a smoker myself, and I *swore* to the others I've quit, but I'm really crawling the walls, and they're away right now, so I wonder—'"

I laughed. "She tried to bum a cigarette off you?"

"That's what *I* thought she was doing, but no. She says, 'Do you possibly have a *pack* you can sell me?' And I'm like, 'How much is it worth to you?'"

I laughed again. "You tried to shake down one of our *guests*? You *didn't*, Max—did you?"

He shrugged. "Dante, a guy's gotta make a living. So then she says, 'Just tell me how much you want.' And off the top of my head, I tell her, 'How about twenty bucks?' I'm figuring, that's twice what I've been paying for them, so if she goes for it, I can buy two packs for myself. And right away, she says, 'Great. Do you have them with you? I've got cash.'"

Astonished, I said to Max, "Christ, it sounds like a drug deal."

"For her, maybe it was. I dunno. So I tell her, 'Actually, I've got three packs in the truck—if you want them all.' And she goes, '*Yes*. I'll meet you back here with the sixty dollars.' So I *run* to that truck, and when I get back with the cigs, she comes outta that little house again and pays me on the spot." Max paused, looking very proud of himself. With a grin, he leaned near, saying, "And you know what else?"

I told him, "Try me."

"Believe it or not, she's now carrying this little teapot, looks like metal, black. The lid's kinda clanging while she fusses around, stuffing the cigs in her pockets. She tells me, 'Thank you so much.' Then she walks off to the big house with everything." Max crossed his arms, asking me, "Is that a great story or what?"

"Not bad, Max. But just so I'm clear: Can you describe the woman?"

"*Sure*," he said. And he confirmed everything I needed to know.

Moments later, while leaving the rental house, I called to tell Jazz what I'd learned. She said on the phone, "I'll fill Arcie in. Let's gather the suspects. Tonight."

I waited till afternoon, then called Keith to set things up for that evening, but I didn't tell him what I now knew. Instead, I explained, "Jazz and I would like to come over and reveal the contents of Harold's letter from the grave. I assume everyone staying at the house will find this of interest."

"*That's* an understatement," he assured me. "We've spoken of little else since returning from Christopher's office this morning."

"Ah, yes. The reading of the wills."

"Revocable trusts," he corrected me, "not wills."

"Whatever. How'd it go? Any surprises?"

He said, "It was all fairly dry and predictable. Dad left most of his assets to me, with token remembrances to Heather and Brooke. Wendy left enough for Koo-Loo's care and well-being, with the rest going to her brother, Cecil Ames—if we can locate him."

"So," I asked, "what time should Jazz and I drop by?"

He suggested, "How about six? It's been a trying day for everyone, so we thought we'd all go out for dinner tonight. Better to deal with Dad's letter first. You and Jazz can join us for a cocktail hour at the house."

"Sounds good." I was tempted to add that if he was planning to make dinner reservations, they would need a table for five people, not six. But I wasn't ready to broach that—not yet.

Jazz drove me from Palm Springs in her menacing black SUV, arriving in Rancho Mirage at six o'clock. As we parked on the street, the sun was just setting, signaling the end of not only that particular day, but also the nine-day ordeal that had brought two murders—and false accusations against two dear friends. Fortunately, there was no need to include Zola Lorinsky or Richard Gibbs in this evening's cocktail showdown. We'd known since late yesterday that Zola hadn't killed Wendy, and we now knew with certainty that Richard hadn't killed Harold.

Walking through the parking court, I carried a slim folio of paperwork. At my side, Jazz wore a discreet shoulder holster under her mannish black blazer—I assumed she anticipated no need for the gun, but it was meant to be noticed. We stepped up to the front door, and I rang the bell.

Keith—now the "man of the house"—admitted us, martini in hand.

When we entered the great room, everyone was assembled and expecting us, clustered near the fireplace. Heather and Brooke held glasses of white wine. Näzh had red wine. Tyler held a tall glass of something like Coke. And Rebecca, like Keith, had a martini. No one, apparently, had a taste for Old Nine-Tails.

Rebecca set a toothpick aside—she had presumably eaten the olive. Rising from her chair, she asked Jazz and me, "Can I get you something to drink?"

"No, thanks," said Jazz. "I'm fine."

I told Rebecca, "Maybe later. Nothing now, thanks. This is a working visit." Through the rear wall of glass, I saw the lights switch on in the swimming pool.

Jazz told everyone, "I think you already know why Dante and I asked to meet with you tonight. Yesterday, the letter left by Harold was found—the letter pertaining to Wendy's death, with instructions that it shouldn't be opened till after his own death. When he wrote it and sealed it, I'm sure he had no idea that it would be opened just a few days later."

Heather asked, "Can you tell us what was in it? I've been *consumed* with curiosity since the day he told me about it—the day he wrote it."

"I've consulted with Detective Madera," said Jazz, "and she'll keep the original—it's *evidence*. And forensic investigation has already determined that the letter is most likely genuine. Harold wrote it and signed it. Because he addressed it to 'my family and loved ones,' Arcie agrees that its contents should be shared with all of you. So Dante has a set of photocopies to hand out."

I unzipped my folio, took out the stack of copied letters, and distributed them to the six surviving guests, who each reached to take one.

The room went quiet as they began to read, but the silence was soon broken as they began to react to Harold's missive—shock and horror that he had killed his wife, sighs of empathy when he explained his reasons for doing it, and finally, with his farewell wishes to Keith, Heather, and Brooke, sobs of grief for their loss of him.

When everyone had set the letter aside and looked up again, Jazz said, "The truth isn't always easy, but it ends the confusion— and it's far better than being left to wonder."

Heather wiped a tear. With a sniffle, she said, "At least we know he meant well."

Jazz reminded her, "He killed his *wife*. Granted, she begged him to do it, but in the moments before she died, she changed her mind. When she realized she'd been poisoned by the posset, she frantically tried to find her Epi-Pen, which Harold had snatched away. To my way of thinking, this letter doesn't *absolve* him—far from it."

"Regardless," said Keith, who also had been crying, "he can't be held accountable now."

"Right," I said. "Someone else has already settled the score."

Brooke glanced around the room, telling everyone, "I was *so* afraid of this. When I first talked to Uncle Harold about Wendy's condition, I thought he already knew about it. If I'd just kept my mouth shut, none of this would've happened. I'm so sorry..." And she wept.

Tyler wrapped an arm around her shoulder and hugged her. "You didn't know, baby. You didn't know. And you sure as hell didn't kill Wendy. *Harold* did."

"And who killed *him*?" Heads turned as Rebecca continued, "I worked for Harold for *seven* years. We had a bond you'll never understand. And now, *he's* gone. My life is a shambles, and nothing is being done to bring Harold's killer to justice."

"Trust me," said Jazz. "*Plenty* is being done."

Rebecca gave her an incredulous, scornful look. "You don't even know how he *died*. Sure, there must have been something in his whiskey. But what? And who did it? Bottom line: you just don't know."

Jazz and I glanced at each other. She gave me a subtle nod.

"Actually," I said, "we *do* know how Harold was killed. We also know who killed him—and that person is in this room."

Näzh said, "You've certainly captured our attention, Dante. But aren't you being a tad dramatic?" He sounded amused.

I cautioned him, "I wouldn't be so glib if I were you. Can you explain why Harold's picture has been added to your vision board on the door of the refrigerator in the guesthouse?"

That wiped the grin off his face. He stammered, "That was just a *tribute*. I was manifesting *healing* for Harold. He'd lost his *wife*. He was our host here—and Heather's brother."

I pointed out, "*Heather* didn't care that Harold had lost his wife. Wendy was responsible for the drug death of Heather's husband. She hated Wendy."

Näzh said, "That was *way* before my time."

Heather reminded me, "Wendy's murder is now *solved*. Harold admits to it in his letter. So why drag *me* into this? I had nothing to do with Wendy's death."

Jazz told her, "We're no longer talking about Wendy."

Nodding, I added, "We're talking about *Harold's* death."

"He was my big *brother*," said Heather. "I loved him. Why would I poison him? I wouldn't even know how to do it."

"Well," I suggested, "you *could* do it with a highly concentrated extract of nicotine, added to Harold's bottle of Old Nine-Tails."

She looked at me as if I were out of my mind. "I'm not a *chemist*. I'm not a *doctor*. How would I know that?"

I explained, "You, like anyone, *could* learn about it on the internet and could even find instructions for making a home brew. You could crumble loose tobacco into water, boil it, and reduce it to a deadly 'nicotine tea,' so to speak. You could use a little kettle made of black iron."

Jazz added, "And in fact, Harold died of nicotine poisoning."

Heather and Näzh stared at each other in stunned dismay.

Looking betrayed, Näzh said, "I *wondered* where the teapot went."

Heather threw both arms in the air, shouting, "I *didn't* do it!"

A breathless silence fell upon the room. The sky beyond the windows had faded to twilight. Jazz lifted her phone, sent a text, and stepped to the door. When she opened it a few moments later, Detective Madera entered, as planned. They joined the rest of us near the fireplace.

I told Heather, "I'm sorry for the confusion. I never said you did it; I said you *could* do it. But in fact, I knew that you *didn't* kill Harold because"—I turned—"Rebecca Jiang did it."

Rebecca calmly drank the last of her martini and set down the glass. Its base clacked as it touched the marble top of the cocktail table. The rim of the glass bore the pink imprint of her lipstick. She told me, "You can't be serious."

I said, "You've been something of an enigma from the start, Rebecca. I know that your relationship with Harold was complicated, and I think that your affections for him were one-sided, but we've hashed that out before, and you seem to enjoy your delusions. Frankly, I don't even *care* about your soap opera of a life. But I do know that you killed Harold."

"You *fucker*—you don't know a damn thing."

"I know what Max Hazer told me."

Several people, including Rebecca, asked, "*Who?*"

I said, "The pool guy."

With a sarcastic snort, Rebecca said, "That weirdo? How could you believe anything you heard from *him*?"

"Normally," I conceded, "when Max starts talking, I tune out. Today, though, he told me about a crazy lady with a teapot who paid him sixty bucks for three packs of cigarettes when he was here on Saturday morning."

Rebecca stiffened as her eyes met mine.

I said to the others in the room, "Max told me about this because *he* thought it was hilarious—but the seeming nonsense of the details made perfect sense to *me*, leaving no doubt that his story was true. And the corker? When I asked him to describe the woman with the teapot, he said she was Asian."

Rebecca's shoulders slumped. Everyone else, convinced of her now obvious guilt, stared at her coldly. We waited.

At last she said, "Saturday morning, early, I went shopping for groceries—Harold was planning another big dinner, which of course *I* was expected to take care of. When I got back with everything, he was drinking already, and he went through the bags asking where the cigarettes were. He insisted he'd told me to get some, and I knew he didn't, but anyway, he blew up. I mean, we've had the *occasional* disagreement before, but *nothing* like this. It tuned into a full-blown screaming match, and a *lot* of things were said, hurtful things. I would've been mortified if anyone had heard us, but the others were away that morning. And here's the ironic part: Even though I was angrier than I'd ever felt in my entire life, I also realized, finally, that I would've been better off hearing these hurtful things from Harold long ago. Back then, I might've dealt with the situation a bit more... *sanely*."

She paused, shaking her head, as if letting this sink in.

I said, "Then what?"

"Harold went back to his bedroom to drink. I needed to clear my mind and get out of the house, so I went over to the guest-house, where it was quiet—where I could calm down. I happened to notice the teapot, thinking nothing of it. A few minutes later, I noticed the pool cleaner arrive, smoking, so I went out to ask if I could buy a pack of cigarettes from him—to tide Harold over till I was able to go shopping again. But then the pool guy offered me *three* packs, and I remembered the teapot and the uncapped gift bottle of Old Nine-Tails. It was a truly inspired moment." She flipped her hands, telling us, "Next morning, Harold started drinking from the gift bottle. And that... was that."

Indignant, Näzh said, "You *stole* my teapot?"

She rolled her eyes. "I *meant* to give it back, okay? But after it steeped overnight, I started to fret about residue and, you know, *evidence*. So early Sunday morning, I wrapped up the pot in a grocery bag, went out for a walk, and stuffed it into a neighbor's trash—which was picked up yesterday. So it's gone. Sorry."

While Näzh stomped about the room, fuming over his lost teapot, Jazz leaned to me, whispering, "Harold's letter didn't even *mention* Rebecca."

"Neither did his estate plan. Too bad she couldn't see what was so plain to everyone else."

Arcie stepped over and recited Rebecca's rights... then hauled her away... never to be seen again.

EPILOGUE
ZOLA'S BACK

CHAPTER
FIFTEEN

Six months later, in mid-April, the desert's social season was in full swing. Within a month or two, all the snowbirds would flee to their cooler summer roosts, but now, the warming weeks of Eastertide packed the calendar with final flings and fond farewells—at least until fall.

It was exactly the right time of year for a big open house celebrating Zola's official return to the local design scene. And there was no better place to stage the event than the main house at Richard Gibbs's estate in Palm Springs, where Zola had taken up permanent residence. The location was pertinent to her reignited decorating career because of the recent completion of her total redesign and renovation of the house's interior—a nearly yearlong project that now served as her ultimate calling card.

The invitation to this gala, a housewarming of sorts, was simply headlined: ZOLA'S BACK! Invitees included not only prospective design clients and trade publications, but also friends, numbering well over a hundred. With very few exceptions (weddings, intensive care, and a stint at Betty Ford), everyone replied that they would attend the doings, and then, on a perfect Sunday afternoon, they descended upon Richard's estate, where a team of valets made cars disappear while a convoy of caterers kept the canapes coming and the liquor flowing.

Isandro and I attended, of course, and we didn't have far to go—down the stairs of the coach house and across the pool terrace, which was crowded with revelers. As they ogled the ten-foot Inca warrior's astonishing endowment, a string quartet played a jazzy mashup of Bach suites and preludes. Perched on the fronds of a fan palm, a surly raven surveyed the action with skeptical, beady eyes.

When we passed through the French doors and entered Richard and Zola's kitchen (yes, they were now considered a couple), I spotted Jazz coming in from the front of the house. She was with Blade Wade and her daughter, Emma, who held Blade's hand. Blade had recently converted a little-used office and powder room at his loft into a cozy bedroom suite—meant for Emma—and then persuaded Jazz to move in with him. She had since allowed the lease on her apartment to lapse, and now, whenever Emma stayed with her mom, they both slept at "Jazz and Blade's place." If Emma had any questions or concerns about this arrangement, she never voiced them. In fact, she seemed thrilled to have such ready access to Blade's studio, where her prodigious experiments as a very young painter continued to thrive.

Emma skipped ahead of them and ran to the arms of her father, Christopher, who had already arrived with Keith Gibkin. The two lawyers had been seeing a *lot* of each other, and now, whenever Keith came to the desert for the weekend, he was staying at Christopher's house, sharing the same bedroom with him, even when Emma was there. She apparently found this arrangement as unremarkable as the sleeping logistics at her other home with Jazz and Blade. In fact, according to Mrs. Cubbins at Gilded Palms School, Emma had recently bragged to one of her kindergarten classmates that she had "three daddies."

Keith, Christopher, and Emma now stepped away from the

crowd and were joined by Jazz and Blade. When Jazz spotted Isandro and me, she waved us over with a broad smile.

Standing together at the quiet end of the living room—while most of the guests were clumped near the kitchen or out by the pool—we exchanged greetings and hugs and a few kisses. Recent months had marked a juncture in all of our lives, snatching happiness from the jaws of tragedy at the ill-fated reunion of the Gibbs-Gibkin clan.

Our wistful reminiscing must have been found boring by Emma, who shuffled and fidgeted while looking about. Blade hunkered down and told her, "Every party has cake. Wanna see if we can find some?"

Emma nodded eagerly. Blade gave the rest of us a wink and a wave as he walked off with the little girl.

I said to Jazz, "She seems to approve of all the changes."

With a soft laugh, Jazz noted, "She's young. She's flexible. Every day's a new adventure."

Christopher turned to Isandro and me. "Speaking of 'new adventures,' Keith and I have a little announcement."

Isandro and I glanced at each other, bug-eyed. Were they getting *married*?

No—that wasn't the announcement—but I had to wonder if it might be the next step.

Christopher explained, "You might remember that the last partner I brought into the law firm didn't work out so well. *That* situation sorta shook my faith in my own judgment, and I've been reluctant to fill that vacant office—till now."

Keith told us, "Christopher wants me to join his firm. My one-man practice has lost its appeal over the last few years, and I feel ready to move on to something bigger, right here. So I've decided: I'm going to work for Christopher."

"Uh-uh-uh." Christopher reminded him, "You're not working *for* me. We're working together—as partners. And why not? We're already *living* together."

"*Are* you?" I asked. I'd known they were spending plenty of time together, frequently overnight, but I hadn't been sure of the exact nature of their relationship, which now seemed to have overtones of commitment.

They shared a glance, then nodded. "Yes," said Keith, "if you'll pardon the legalese, we're cohabiting. I've been moving things into Christopher's house here, and we've had getaways together at my condo on the coast. I'll keep that—we've started calling it our beach house."

Christopher added, "Not a bad thing to have, when you're living in the desert."

Jazz asked Keith, "What about the big house in Rancho Santa Fe? Your father's house."

"I'm getting rid of that. I grew up there, but the memories turned sour after the mass suicide next door. Then Wendy. Then the damn *monkey*."

With mock concern, Isandro asked, "Whatever will become of poor little Koo-Loo?"

"'Poor'?" said Keith. "That stinker is loaded. We were finally able to locate Wendy's brother, Cecil, who was of course delighted to learn of his windfall inheritance. Under the circumstances, he readily agreed to take responsibility for Koo-Loo—but he has *no* idea what he's getting into." Keith didn't even try to suppress a snide laugh.

Christopher leaned near to ask him, "Have they heard about your dad's patents?"

Keith scanned our wondering faces. "Guess not." He explained, "Dad's unfinished development work with AtmosPhuel included several patents for technology and processes that might not be as far-fetched as we assumed. He wasn't the only one out there persuing the dream of generating electricity out of thin air—and now his competitors have approached me with an interest in acquiring those patent rights. Stay tuned."

"*Nice*," I said. "And what about the Ferris branch of the family? The Trot-n-Tipple crowd."

"Brooke and Tyler are fine," said Keith. "They're both happy in their jobs and happy with each other, and I'm guessing that—maybe a year from now—they'll decide to get away from the vineyard and strike out on their own. Together."

Warily, Jazz asked, "What about Heather and Näzh?"

Keith hesitated. "Get this: I've just learned that Heather, at fifty-two, is pregnant—presumably with Swami's demon seed. I have no idea if she plans to carry it to term, but I'm sure Näzh is busy updating his vision board with expanded plans for his crazy 'institute.'"

Jazz said, "Heather's no fool. She knows what's going on."

"I agree," said Keith. "And whatever she decides to do—that's *her* choice."

Christopher hugged Keith to his side. "On a happier note, I see dancing on the patio." The string quartet had taken a break, replaced by a deejay, who had livened things up.

Keith laughed. "If you're asking, I'm dancing." And they left.

Isandro told me, "Think I'll check out the buffet." And he left.

"Well," said Jazz with a shrug, "it's 'just us.'"

"Not really." With a smile, I reminded her, "You've got Blade in your life. And Emma. Not to mention her other two daddies."

Jazz nodded. "It amazes me, but things are pretty damn good. And how about you and Isandro—feeling settled? Happy?"

"We are," I admitted. "I thought it would never work out—now I hope it never ends."

"Mm-hmm. Still," she said, "you've got that...*job* situation."

"Oh. That."

"Yes, *that*. But don't forget: if you want to make *our* working situation more 'official,' we can figure something out. Up in my office, I've got that empty reception room with an empty desk. And the place could *still* use some dolling up, which is your domain. Plus, I've actually started turning *down* a few clients. Business is brisk—and getting better. I could use more help, Dante."

Pondering this, I thought aloud, "Things have gone from bad to worse at Sunny Junket. The new boss is a pill. And with summer ahead, the few rentals we've got are bound to dry up." I told Jazz, "Maybe it *does* make sense for you and me to sit down and have a conversation."

She grinned. "Tomorrow? Monday morning is a great time for a fresh start. My office at ten?"

I nodded. "Thanks, Jazz."

We noticed that the crowd in the house had thinned, and people were heading out from the kitchen to the pool. The music had stopped, as if something was about to happen. So Jazz and I joined the exodus.

Out on the terrace, everyone had gathered in a loose semicircle around a small platform, about a foot high, that had been used by the quartet as a low stage. Zola was now standing on it with Richard, who held a microphone. As the crowd settled in, Jazz drifted over to Blade and Emma, and I moved to join Isandro, who'd caught my eye and winked.

"Hello, everyone," said Richard, tapping the mike. "Welcome. Hope you like the house, the music, the food, and this gorgeous day in paradise. But the one and only undisputed star of this gathering is none other than *La Decorina* herself. I give you: Zola Lorinsky!"

Richard stepped back and Zola stepped forward with the microphone. People hooted, whistled, and clapped (as best they could with drinks in their hands), while the deejay played a canned fanfare.

Zola shushed the crowd. "I'm too old for this," she croaked with a grin that debunked her claim. *Never* too old, this priestess of pizazz was resplendent in her sequins, her thirty-inch sun hat, and her eighty years of spunk. She continued, "Richard tells me I'm due for a comeback. And he puts his money where his mouth is, so it seems I'm back in business…"

She *knew* how to play an audience. Her off-the-cuff shtick, littered with racy innuendos, had us laughing and recalling her heyday and loving every word as she announced that she was taking on new clients.

"… I happily accept cash, credit cards, or indecent proposals …"

Photographers crouched, inching closer for better angles.

Isandro and I were standing at the back of the crowd, watching. He leaned to tell me, "Zola needed this—a new beginning."

"I've been needing one, too, kiddo."

He turned, alarmed. "What do you mean, *coração*?"

I kissed his nose. "I'm thinking of going to work for Jazz."

He gave me a skeptical look. "Does *she* know about this?"

"She *asked* me, goofus."

"My God, Dante—I *wondered* when this would happen."

"You approve, then?"

He placed both hands on my cheeks and kissed my lips. "Of course I approve. We need to celebrate."

"Zola shouldn't take *too* much longer. Then we can dance."

He pulled me close and gave me a discreet, friendly grope, a nonverbal but precise statement of his intentions. Through a purr, he said into my ear, "Let's save that dance for another time. Right now, wouldn't you prefer something more... 'private'?"

There was no graceful way to sneak out—Zola was on a roll, strangling the mike with a death grip—so we simply skirted the edge of the crowd, made our way around Mr. Big, and traipsed over to the coach house, where we began climbing the outdoor stairs to the loft we called home.

Nearing the top, we were in plain view of most of the crowd, but they were watching Zola, who had her back to us. Isandro opened the door and was stepping inside as I paused to look over the railing.

From the mass of faces, Jazz glanced up, locking eyes with me.

I blew her a kiss.

She flashed me a sly, knowing smile.

Michael Craft is the author of twenty novels, four of which were finalists for Lambda Literary Awards. The first installment of his Dante & Jazz series, *Desert Getaway*, was a 2023 MWA Edgars nominee for the Lilian Jackson Braun Award. The second installment, *Desert Deadline*, was a Gold Winner of the IBPA Benjamin Franklin Award, as was his 2019 mystery, *ChoirMaster*. In addition, his prizewinning short fiction has appeared in British as well as American literary journals.

Craft grew up in Illinois and spent his middle years in Wisconsin, the setting for many of his books. He now lives in Rancho Mirage, California, near Palm Springs, which provided the setting for his current Dante & Jazz mysteries.

In 2017, Michael Craft's professional papers were acquired by the Special Collections Department of the Rivera Library at the University of California, Riverside. This comprehensive archive is now cataloged and made available for both scholarly research and public enjoyment.

Visit his website at www.michaelcraft.com.

ACKNOWLEDGMENTS

This book, *Desert Reunion*, is my twentieth novel, a milestone in my journey as a writer, which began in 1980. Back then, becoming a novelist was merely an aspiration—by no means a done deal. More than twelve years of drafts, submissions, and rejections would pass before my first novel, a slim little literary paperback titled *Rehearsing*, was accepted for publication, appearing in early 1993. It's been a long haul.

Without you, my readers, this venture would have ended long ago. Your ongoing enthusiasm has provided the validation that drove me forward with each successive book, and I sincerely thank you for always wanting more.

While writing *Desert Reunion*, I relied on David Sirek, Tom Schmitt, and attorney David Grey for their generous assistance with various plot details. Barbara McReal and Larry Warnock served as early readers of the manuscript, lending countless suggestions for improvement. And I am highly indebted to Jim Thomsen, whose incisive editing and thoughtful prompting have been invaluable in polishing the text.

Hugs to fellow gay novelists Michael Thomas Ford, Sidney Karger, and Rob Osler, who graciously contributed early endorsements of this book.

As always, Mitchell Waters, my literary agent for more than twenty-five years, has been tireless in guiding me through the often obscure byways of the publishing world.

And finally, my husband, Leon Pascucci, has remained a steady font of patience, support, and good cheer.

Heartfelt thanks to all.

— *Michael Craft, 2024*

ABOUT THE TYPE

The text of this book was set in Garamond Premier Pro, a 2005 interpretation and expansion of Adobe Garamond, which was designed in 1989 by Robert Slimbach as a digital revival of Claude Garamond's original array of metal typefaces dating from the mid-1500s in France. Garamond is a serif typeface classified as "old style," meaning that its strokes and serifs have a slightly more organic, handwritten feeling than transitional or modern serifs.

Known as the most conspicuous example of French Renaissance typography and one of the key font families worldwide, Garamond can be easily recognized for its elegant forms and excellent readability. Its smooth curves and simple serifs convey a classic and easygoing beauty, well suited for long blocks of text. Among print designers, Garamond is often favored as a timeless choice for text that is authoritative, highly legible, and slightly dressy.